One Dead Judge

Preston Pairo

Walker and Company
New York

First published in the United States of America in 1993
by Walker Publishing Company, Inc.

Published simultaneously in Canada by Thomas Allen & Son
Canada, Limited, Markham, Ontario

Library of Congress Cataloging-in-Publication Data
Pairo, Preston.
One dead judge / Preston Pairo.
p.   cm.
"A Dallas Henry mystery."
ISBN 0-8027-1250-9
I. Title.
PS3563.A312905   1993
813'.54—dc20   92-31441
CIP

Printed in the United States of America

2 4 6 8 10 9 7 5 3 1

To my parents, and Moira,
steady beacons of encouragement

Author's Note

Thanks to Harry Giardina for providing technical information on excavation and construction around the beach, and my apologies for any instances where I didn't keep it straight.

Also, many thanks to those editors, agents, and publishers who have helped me over the years. In order of appearance: V. K. McCarty, who got me started; John Robert Bensink, who still keeps me going; Nick Ellison, Hy Stierman, and Sandy Richardson for my first book; Philip Spitzer for being brave enough to agent a terminally mid-list writer; Marc Lichter and Barry Janoff for all the work; Janet Hutchings for getting me on point, and Michael Seidman for keeping me there.

Son, strangers you can trust.
It's friends who know your weak spots.

1

"**H**EY, BOSS. WAKE UP. Boss. Hey!" Herbie Gonner's breath carried the smell of fried onions from a midnight steak sub.

Dallas Henry's nose flinched.

"Boss. Hey, let's go. Wake up."

Dallas grumbled. His own breath counterattacked Herbie's with potent remains of Beck's beer and tequila shooters.

The bikini contest girl snoozing beside Dallas pulled a pillow over her head.

"Boss . . ."

No response. Dallas refused to leave his dream.

The bikini girl, head covered by a pillow but otherwise undressed, groaned a muffled "Go away."

The sound of a female voice brought Dallas to life. He blinked at Herbie, who waved.

"Heya, boss."

"Susan?"

"Not hardly."

Dallas sensed a presence beside him. His hand searched and found a naked thigh. "Susan?" So hopeful.

His overnight guest jerked the pillow off her head. Fire jade eyes stared out beneath askew bangs of blond hair. "Susan?" She was clearly insulted. "It's *Kelly*."

"Oh, yeah . . ."

Even in dim light, she looked incredible. But still not Susan. None of them were.

Kelly tore through a sizable pile of clothing on the second bed in Dallas's motel room—the accumulation of an active summer season. And it was barely July.

Dallas asked what she was doing.

"Making room for Susan."

"Susan?" Dallas acted surprised. "What are you talking about, Susan?"

"You called me Susan."

"No, I didn't. Come on." Dallas would have reached for her, but he was too tired. And it was barely July. "I would never have called you Susan."

"Yeah, you did," Herbie confirmed.

"Who said that?"

The blond said, "He did," about the same time Herbie said, "I did."

Herbie sat on Dallas's listing three-legged sofa.

"Herbie, help me out here. Tell her I didn't call her Susan."

"You called her Susan, boss."

Dallas punched a flat pillow. "Dammit, Herbie."

Shorts pulled on, Kelly rummaged for a top.

Dallas rolled toward her. "I didn't *mean* to call you Susan. It was a dream."

"Sure."

"A really, really *bad* dream."

"Nice try." Kelly slipped on a shirt Dallas last washed around Easter. "Thanks for the drinks . . . I think." She slammed the door on her way out.

Jalousie glass panes rattled.

Face down, Dallas hung over the side of the bed and sighed. "She was a pro. You can't win back the pros with bad lines." He sighed again. "I gotta get in shape. My mind's going to mush."

And it was barely July.

"Boss," Herbie replied, "get some pants on. Judge Crenshaw's on the phone. He says someone's trying to kill him."

Pulled mostly upright, Dallas stood a notch or two above six feet. Not quite as tall as when prowling The Marlin Club five hours ago. At age thirty-four, his hair was too long, face unshaven, suntan so deep it would take months of cloudy skies for the brown to fade. His general physique was that of a volleyball player who consumed too many doughnuts, pancakes, and rum.

"No one," Dallas assured Herbie, "is trying to kill Judge Crenshaw. He's retired. People *used* to want to kill him all the time. If his decisions from the bench didn't get you, his practical jokes would. Like the time he sent a beer truck to Alan Kramer's office to deliver a hundred cases of Natty Boh."

"That's a practical joke?"

"Mothers Against Drunk Drivers were considering Alan for their general counsel. Crenshaw made sure the beer arrived while the MADD folks were in Alan's office. . . . Alan got plenty *mad*, but didn't get the job."

2

"Nice guy." Firmly holding Dallas's shirtsleeve, Herbie pulled his employer through the small office that linked Dallas's room to the knotty pine confines of the motel lobby.

Outside, the neon Ocean Tides sign glowed garish pink and blue. The NO before VACANCY was turned off, as always. No one could remember the last time the Ocean Tides had been full. Odds of finding thirty-three folks brave enough to fill the place were remote.

Behind the front desk, a phone system yet to catch semimodern times showed one blinking light. Retired Judge Crenshaw on hold.

"Did you tell him I was out of town?"

Per the unwritten Ocean Tides handbook, that was the first thing to say when the caller asked for Dallas.

Herbie handed Dallas the phone and punched the button for line one.

"Dial tone," Dallas said. He held the receiver to Herbie's ear for verification. "He hung up. Crenshaw always was an impatient bastard."

"Maybe they got him."

"Who?"

"Whoever's trying to kill him."

"*No one* is trying to kill Raymond Crenshaw. It's a practical joke. When he retired and moved down here, he said he was going to pull one of his gags on me. This is it, okay? So forget it." Dallas pointed outside. "Now go find that blond girl—what was her name?"

"Kelly."

"Kelly—right. Go get her, tell her this was all your fault."

"*You* called her Susan." Herbie took the phone from Dallas and hit *69, the AT&T code that dialed back the last caller—for a fee.

"That seventy-five cents is coming out of your paycheck," Dallas griped. "Phone company bandits charging for a computer to do a one millionth of a nanosecond operation."

"He's not answering," Herbie said, concerned. "I think you better go over there."

"No way in hell." Dallas crossed his arms over the front of a Hawaiian print shirt and shook his head.

Herbie, skinny but determined, said, "You didn't hear his voice, boss. I'm telling you, it didn't sound like any joke. This guy was scared."

"Uh-uh. You don't know Crenshaw. He's a great actor. He fooled everyone into thinking he knew the law for years. It's a prank."

3

"Okay . . ." Herbie put down the phone. " . . . but I sure wouldn't want it on my conscience."

"What's that supposed to mean?"

"Nothing." Herbie sat in a swivel chair, put his bare feet on the counter next to the registration book, and went back to last month's *Scientific American*.

"You think somebody's trying to kill Crenshaw and I could stop it by going over there?"

Herbie turned a dog-eared page.

"You think the family of some guy Crenshaw put in jail is out to knife him? Someone he ruled against has a grudge?"

Herbie wriggled his toes and whistled.

Dallas sighed angrily. "Where're my damned car keys?"

"Check your pocket?"

▽

2

"I DON'T BELIEVE I'M doing this." Dallas shoved his ailing 280Z into third gear and wound it out, crossing the draw span of the Route 50 bridge.

His two-seat sports car was more rust and less silver paint by the minute. A minor accident over the winter, sliding over frozen roads and *under* a tractor trailer, had peeled off the roof like opening a can of Cat Chow. The windshield was replaced, but the rest of the Datsun was so rusty it had been impossible to attach a new top.

Dallas had a woman who manufactured boat sails fashion him a quasi-convertible top. It looked like hell—as though a painting crew had dropped a tarpaulin on him—was a sieving bugger in the rain, and flapped deafeningly at speeds above forty-five, but Dallas was damned if he was giving up this car. Even if ninety-five percent of its value was a new stereo and Pirelli racing tires.

Leaving Ocean City—an over-condominiumized atoll of golden island in a setting of dark green ocean—Dallas took a left and wound along a single-lane road into West Ocean City.

A onetime hideout for fishing crews and those who couldn't afford or stand the busy resort island, West OC was fast becoming a retirement haven. Amidst marsh and woods, new developments and golf courses sprang up on land once thought uninhabitable.

Bay Shores was one of the few neighborhoods with lots larger than an acre. The forest had been minimally sacrificed, which added privacy and seclusion. The roads were narrow, winding, and without street lamps.

Coming around one sharp bend a little too zestfully, Dallas's headlights froze a doe in the middle of the lane. He hit the brakes, laid a little Pirelli rubber.

The doe, wide-eyed and innocent, didn't flinch until he tapped the horn. Then she scuttled into the woods.

Dallas considered the delay insignificant. He knew damned well no one was looking to kill Judge Crenshaw. It was a joke and Dallas was going to have to take it. Ha-ha, Judge, that's a good one.

Crenshaw lived on two and a half acres, a site heavily sequestered by a pleasing blend of established evergreens.

The place was dark save an insect repellent bulb in the pole lamp; it cast a soft yellow glow across the small home's log facade. A macadam driveway made a single curve around a stand of feathery Norfolk pines to an open carport.

At the head of the driveway, Dallas pulled up behind the judge's mammoth old Chrysler. A four-wheeled boat. Dependable transportation used during Crenshaw's final years on the bench when, demoted to fill-in duties at district courts across the state, the judge logged more miles than a back-roads Bible salesman.

Dallas cut the 280's engine. A parade of moths flew jerky circles around his headlights until he switched them off.

"Judge . . . ?" Wary of Crenshaw setting some juvenile trap.

He closed his car door and its thud echoed softly against the pines. Singing frogs in summer symphony chirped from nearby inlets. The scent of fallen pine needles, despite summer temperatures, reminded Dallas of Christmas.

"Judge?" Dallas's sneakered feet reached the front walk. "Okay, Judge. I'm here. You got me. This's real funny. A great practical joke."

Dallas walked straight into a spiderweb stitched between the pole lamp and downspout. "Dammit." He spit fuzzy web from his mouth, pulled it from his face and arms, hoping the critter responsible for ambushing him wasn't poisonous. "Judge, where the hell are you? I gave up a good erotic dream for this crap."

What was it about spiderwebs once they got on you, you could never get them off? Dallas was still brushing his arms as he went up two log steps to the front porch. Enough was enough.

He banged on the door. "Judge! Let's go. The fun's over. In fact, it never started."

An owl swooped silently across the yard, wings spread, a specter seemingly the size of a Greyhound bus. Dallas jumped.

With staring yellow eyes, the owl investigated who was making all this noise, then rose to a sturdy branch with a powerful swipe of wings and continued her vigil from an unseen perch.

"Damn I hate nature!" Feeling foolish for being startled, Dallas kicked the front door. "Judge! I'm telling you . . ."

The door opened. Its hinges creaked.

"Swell." Dallas peered inside; it was dark except for squares of moonlight showing through windowpanes. "Just like the damned horror movies." Louder then: "Is that what this is supposed to be? Huh? *Spooky Goes to the Beach*? You got a sheet over you and come jumping out going *boo*, I'm gonna kick your ass I don't care how old you are you simple son of a bitch!"

Dallas threw the door all the way open, half hoping Judge Crenshaw was hiding behind it. Let the door edge hit him in the nose. But the door swung open all the way back to the wall, rapping it. If Crenshaw was there, he'd lost a helluva lot of weight, was down to the size of a strand of linguini.

Dallas crossed the threshold into the living room. Furnishings, visible only as shadows, were arranged in tidy fashion. A potbellied stove used for winter heating was rigged to a brick chimney.

Dallas announced, "If there's any money in here, I'm taking it." Crenshaw was a notorious cheapskate. He wouldn't spend fifty cents for a practical joke. The beer delivery he'd sent to the would-be MADD attorney had been COD.

Outside through the woods came the distant sound of squealing tires. Kids racing cars over winding roads in the middle of the night. They mapped out courses and did timed runs, sometimes ran head-to-head. When his 280 had been in better shape, Dallas had joined them. In recent years, his participation had been limited to cop lookout for other drivers. Had this not been the beach, he supposed he could have been considered contributing to the delinquency of minors. But only to a really narrow-minded judge. Speaking of which . . .

"Come on, Judge. Enough is enough."

Dallas started toward the stairs to the left of the fireplace, but decided against it. He'd be halfway up there and Crenshaw would do something like toss a ham down the steps, a big Silver Label he'd have painted a face on to make Dallas think a head was coming at him.

"Okay, that's it. I'm going home. Enough playtime. See ya." He tiptoed toward the kitchen and peeked behind the swinging door, thinking, I'm gonna get you, you old fogey. "Going home now, Judge. Bye. Maybe see you at the convention this week."

This was Dallas's least favorite hot-weather time of year: the state bar association was in town for their annual meeting. Dallas had been giving away supercheap rooms at the Ocean Tides to keep from getting stuck with any lawyers checking in.

"See ya, Judge." Dallas threw his voice toward the front door and slipped into the kitchen. He'd wait the old bastard out. Catch him at his own game. Not there two minutes when he heard someone walking around outside. Coming around front.

"Dallas?" It sounded like Crenshaw. "Dallas, where are you?" A little edgy.

No, Dallas told himself, don't fall for it. You've got the upper hand. Hang in there and hammer the crazy coot.

"Dallas?" Crenshaw whispered, nearing the opened front door.

"Heh-heh-heh," Dallas laughed under his breath. He inched open the refrigerator, urging quietly, "Gimme something good."

A head of lettuce—great. Ketchup—good. He scanned the countertop: a knife—perfect. And leaning in a corner: a broom—tahdah!

"Dallas, where are you?" A slight quiver in his voice.

Dallas poked the broom handle into the head of lettuce. Jabbed the knife in and poured ketchup over the lettuce's "wound." Could barely control himself as he grabbed the straw end of the broom and waved the stabbed lettuce head through the swinging kitchen door. Went, "Wooooooohhh. Wooooohhhh." Like a tortured ghost.

Crenshaw fired the shotgun twice, blowing apart lettuce like a buckshot Cuisinart. Splinters of broom handle went flying.

Dallas dove for the floor. "What the hell are you doing!"

Crenshaw kicked open the kitchen door and put his double-barrel Remington a foot from where Dallas covered his head. "You idiot!" he shouted, seeing who it was.

"Me!" Dallas rolled faceup into the gun and grabbed it from the judge's grasp. "You could've killed me."

"No shit! Because someone's trying to kill me!" At age sixty-six, Crenshaw remained a fierce man. His squinting eyes were forced half shut by puffy cheeks and a bulbous drinker's nose. His stomach stretched a black T-shirt; his jeans were zipped, but unsnapped, held up by a cheap strap belt.

"No one's trying to kill you."

"The hell they aren't. Why do you think I called you?"

"Because I'm the sucker du jour." Dallas didn't need to yell given the judge's proximity, but being shot at had a rattling effect on him.

"What're you talking about?"

"Give it up. It's another one of your jokes. That's why you called."

Crenshaw stared at him. "No," he said firmly. "I called because I knew you were the only one who'd come."

That was likely true. Who else would be a good enough sport to let an old retired goofball judge make a fool of him in the middle of the night?

Or *was* Crenshaw serious this time? For once in his life? Not like when he'd been asked to watch a friend's house while the guy was on vacation and listed the place for sale with a real estate broker and sold it within five days.

Tonight, Crenshaw displayed a sustained sincerity and concern that went beyond your normal practical joke. But stunts like this were supposed to be believable, weren't they? That's what made them work best.

"Please," Crenshaw insisted, "sit with me a couple minutes. Hear me out."

Since better judgment was not part of his bench repertoire, Dallas agreed.

Crenshaw talked nonstop for ten minutes. Pacing the living room, back and forth, hands jabbing in the air. Derailed trains of thought. Repeating himself frequently. Details were obtuse at best, but the bottom line was that someone had been creeping around his house, looking to get at him.

Finally, Dallas asked the obvious. "*Who* would want to kill you?"

"I can't tell you."

"What? Why not?"

"Because . . ." Crenshaw deliberated a few seconds, then snapped, "Don't ask so many questions."

"That was two questions."

"It seems like a hundred. You never did ask good questions. You always rambled around in my courtroom."

"The hell I did. You were too impatient to listen. Like now."

"I'm not impatient, I'm scared."

"Then call the police."

"Stop asking so goddamned many questions."

"That wasn't a question."

"Yeah it was."

"You're nuts." Dallas figured Crenshaw had broken his orbit with reality. Maybe a lifetime of doing people dirty was coming back from his subconscious to haunt him in the early twilight of retirement.

Dallas tried to remember if Crenshaw had any family. He'd been divorced forever. Was too belligerent for anyone new to put up with. Dallas thought there was a son, but wasn't sure. Come morning— not that many hours away—he'd check. Crenshaw wasn't acting right. Maybe Alzheimer's—God forbid.

Crenshaw got down on his hands and knees and reached under the sofa—what the hell was he doing now? Dallas wondered. The judge came out with a cardboard box and handed it to Dallas. A five-by-five-by-five square wrapped like a mummy in shipping tape.

Instructions handwritten on the top: *Do not open unless I end up dead*.

Dallas shook the box. Something small and weighty pushed against packing material. Dallas grinned. He got it. "This is it, isn't it? *This* is the joke. . . . Nice performance, you old fart." He cuffed Crenshaw's sturdy shoulders with his open palm.

"I don't know what you're talking about."

"This. This box. It's a joke, right? What, I open it and dye explodes all over me? Toy snakes spring out? A note saying ha-ha, I got you?"

"This isn't a gag."

"I see the gleam in your eye." Dallas had to hand it to him, this was a stellar performance. "You really had me going. Someone's trying to kill you. . . . Yeah, right." Dallas laughed. "Here, look, I'll open it now." He searched for an end of tape to pull. "So you can see me get it. You deserve that, if not an Academy Award."

Crenshaw's small hand grabbed Dallas's wrist. His fingers were cold and clammy—probably licked them when Dallas wasn't looking. "No. *If* I get killed. Then you open it."

Dallas saw Crenshaw wasn't going to give up. "Okay, Judge." Not taking him at all seriously. "When you die, I'll open it."

As though having been offered a bond of faith, Crenshaw nodded. "Good." Shotgun in hand, he led Dallas to the door. "Be careful driving home."

Dallas waved good-bye with the box. "You could've sent me a truckload of beer, you know. I'd've even paid for it."

Crenshaw closed the door.

Dallas tossed the box into the 280's hatchback. Crenshaw would have a new story to tell the boys at the bar convention. How he got Dallas good. Dallas didn't mind. Everybody needed a hobby.

Dallas headed home and was just about to the downtown bridge when a *slap-flap slap-flap slap-flap* sound—above and beyond that of his car's makeshift canvas top—made him close his eyes. "Dammit!" He smelled burning rubber.

His new Pirelli tires. He pulled onto the shoulder, got out. He had two flats. Both rear tires. "Very funny, Judge. Very funny." At least it wasn't a long walk home.

▽

3

DALLAS WAS GENTLY PRODDED awake as hot sunshine spilled across his face.

"It's ten after one."

Even seen by blurry eyes, Susan Vette in a strapless white sundress was exquisite. Her slender arms and legs were olive-toned by sun and Italian heritage. Black hair curled around her beautiful face like soft feathers. She possessed sensuous brown eyes and Dallas's all-time favorite smile: bright teeth, slightly imperfect, with canines coming to a subtle point in what Dallas considered carnivorous allure.

"You're all dressed up," Dallas said to his Ocean Tides day manager, wishing, as always, she'd jump into bed with him.

"I went to the breakfast meeting at the bar convention."

Dallas groaned. Through blissful sleep he'd forgotten: the lawyers—his mostly former but sometimes still peers—were in town. "How horrible was it?"

"Decent, actually." Susan did a little tidying up while Dallas worked on becoming conscious.

Amazing how much clutter and debris—bodyboards, swim fins, wet suits, empty liquor bottles, pizza boxes, and dirty laundry—could pile up around two beds, a sofa, and kitchenette.

Susan said, "There was a speaker on the new workman's comp rules."

"Ugh." Dallas pulled the covers over his head.

"And a workshop on cross-examination of Breathalyzer operators."

"Double ugh."

"And then," she added humbly, "I gave my talk on environmental law."

Dallas flapped the sheet down to his waist. "I said I was going to come to that, didn't I?"

"It's okay. I had a full house."

"In that dress . . . I bet you did."

Susan was still keyed up from her performance. Dallas knew she missed lawyering and would one day go back to it, finally recovered

11

from the trauma that had her on the sidelines the past few years. Dallas would lose her then—miss her bad.

Susan was inching back into law practice as it was. Over the winter, she'd gone down to Richmond as co-counsel in a federal case: representing a private landowner against a multinational medical waste disposal firm whose dumping practices turned his private wildlife refuge into a semitoxic hell.

The jury awarded him five million bucks. That suit was the subject of Susan's bar association speech: that attorneys shouldn't be intimidated by big corporations, especially concerning environmental issues.

She never told Dallas what her cut of the fee had been for that headline-nabbing case, but she'd returned to the beach driving a shiny new Mercedes convertible.

In contrast, Dallas had spent part of January defending a local record store owner charged with obscenity for selling cassette tapes and CDs with questionable lyrics.

At trial, when Assistant State's Attorney Brent Bannister had played the music, a stone-faced, *American Gothic* jury gasped in such shock they nearly sucked the enamel off their teeth.

There would be no lip-sync-service played to whatever First Amendment/free speech song and dance Dallas might care to serve up. That music was vile to the bone.

At the end of all the evidence and arguments, when the judge excused the jury to deliberate, the foreman stood and said he thought he could save a heck of a lot of time by finding the record seller guilty on the spot.

Eleven simultaneous nods set a Guinness record for the fastest verdict in history. *Geeel-tee.* Hang 'em high.

The record shop owner packed up and left town after paying Dallas's fee in trade: an Onkyo rack stereo system that now occupied a corner of his Ocean Tides room, the new Alpine rig for the Z, and a couple hundred CDs.

It was the CDs Susan neatened while Dallas got out of bed, sheet wrapped around him, looking for something to wear. She found one title interesting. *"The Best of Sergio Mendes?"*

"Yeah. I been having sixties yearnings."

"You were just a kid in the sixties. You were no hippie."

"I'm a nostalgic hippie—thank you very much." Dallas bowed out of his sheet and quickly grabbed a pair of shorts to slip on.

Susan offered an if-you-say-so shrug.

"What's going on with my car?"

"I sent Jas out to pick it up on the rollback this morning. Ash and Jim are likely patching the tires as we speak."

"Ash and Jim," Dallas corrected, "are likely getting *arrested* as we speak." Dallas put on flip-flops. "That old fart Crenshaw. I want you to sue him for me."

"Sue him yourself."

"What? And have an idiot for a client?" Dallas did a rim shot with his palms on the counter. "Bah-bum-bum. I'm practicing my lawyer jokes." He grabbed a wrinkled Sideout T-shirt from the clothing melee on the spare bed. "You hear about the lawyer who fell into shark-infested waters? Know why the sharks didn't bite him?"

"Professional courtesy." Susan had heard it a hundred times.

"Right." Dallas headed for the door. "I'm off to the convention." He was two steps into the motel office before he did a one-eighty turn back to his room. "Borrow your car?"

"The old one."

"Come on, the Rabbit? How 'bout the Benz?"

"No way." Susan shook her head.

Dallas scowled, then brightened with a counteroffer. "I won't be mad if you move a little to the left. Let some light show through your dress from behind."

Susan took a flirtatious half-step toward sunlight beaming through opened curtains, but stopped short of being caught in revealing light. She pouted a sexy "Uh-uh" and flashed brown eyes. The harmless game they played that always remained a game.

Dallas frowned. "I'm having a lousy day."

"Lucky for you it's already half over. VW keys are behind the front desk."

For a few years running, the Sheraton had been playing home court to the Maryland State Bar Association's annual shindig. It was a business risk weighing extra revenue against the fact those persons filling a third of your rooms would just as soon sue you as shake your hand.

The hotel hired extra security and maintenance for the weeklong assault to make sure the elevators were in perfect working order lest someone get stuck, feel woozy from claustrophobia, and sue. It was also necessary to quickly wipe up puddles of water tracked in from the swimming pool so no one would slip, fall, and scream "whiplash!"

Dallas parked Susan's VW near the highway and walked to the hotel under hot sunshine.

This was the high-rise end of the island—concrete, metal, glass and glitz. A hundred blocks from the old wood buildings of what the locals referred to as downtown.

Dallas didn't dare take a look at the ocean; he might get really depressed at the prospect of missing good waves to be shut inside conference rooms packed with lawyers.

In the lobby, a bulletin board easel greeted WELCOME MSBA, not mentioning anything directly about a bunch of lawyers being there lest they tempt a letter bomber, arsonist, or spree killer (any of whom would likely have been in jail had it not been for a lawyer).

Someone, however, obviously knew what MSBA stood for, because taped inside the elevator was a quote from Shakespeare, which may or may not have been exactly accurate—Dallas wouldn't know, he never read stuff like that. The line was: *First thing we do, let's kill all the lawyers.* A ballpoint pen had scratched over *kill*, substituting *maim*, which had been x-ed over in felt tip and changed to *go to bed with*.

Dallas hated this already.

The conference-level foyer, featuring new carpeting under sparkly chandeliers, was empty. The schedule listed only one activity at present, but it was a sure hit: "Higher Profits for Fewer Hours."

Dallas strolled to the Breakers Room. It was unusually quiet in there. Very odd for a couple hundred lawyers to clam up for too long.

Dallas eased open the door to a shocking sight.

Rows of round tables were arranged before a raised podium and projection screen. Every seat was taken. And every lawyer's head was bowed in silence.

Dallas grinned. "Neat, they've all been poisoned."

A few harsh *shush*es told him otherwise.

A hand touched his forearm. "Hi, Dallas."

He turned toward the whispered greeting. "Tobey, hey, how are you?"

Tobey Brehm, long hair pinned in a Victorian Gibson, stood to the side of the entrance.

"You and George fly down?"

She motioned for him to lower his voice as a few more indignant *shush*es were spat from bowed heads. "We just got in an hour ago. George had some last-minute business."

"Maybe this week won't be a bust after all. Let's all get together, okay?"

Tobey nodded.

Hands in his pockets, Dallas bent an elbow toward the silenced group. "What the hell's going on here, anyway?"

"A minute of meditation."

"Beseeching God for more billable hours now, are we?"

"No. It's Judge Crenshaw."

Dallas suppressed a laugh. "That's great. Only Crenshaw could get a bunch of lawyers to pray."

Tobey nodded somberly. "That happens when you die."

4

IT WAS TOUGH TO get a straight answer from a bunch of lawyers, because a lawyer who doesn't know an answer makes one up.

Everyone Dallas spoke to claimed to know how Judge Crenshaw died, but no two stories jived.

Jim Beam, a negligence lawyer in the midst of a medical malpractice case he hoped would make him rich, attributed Crenshaw's death to myocardial infarction, using one of the official medical terms he'd been brushing up on to impress his jury.

Alex Hendrick said Crenshaw choked on a chicken bone in the same Ocean City restaurant that gave his wife ptomaine poisoning via rancid blue cheese dressing night before last. (Hendrick had already dictated a demand letter to the restaurant on microcassette and FedExed it back to his office for typing.)

Mimi Jennings claimed Crenshaw slipped on a loose riser of his basement steps and pitched ass over tin cups onto his neck. "Snapped it," Mimi said, cracking her knuckles, "just like that." Mimi was tough. Unfortunately, her geology was weak, otherwise she'd have known Ocean City's water table made it impossible to construct homes with basements. You couldn't dig that deep without striking primordial ooze.

Dallas had his own version of events. "It's a hoax. The old fart's no deader than I am. He's orchestrated one mass practical joke to con the entire convention and you rubes are letting him get away with it."

Mimi Jennings said, "Crenshaw's viewing's tonight at eight. Funeral tomorrow morning."

Dallas smiled. "Suckers . . ."

"You won't believe this." Dallas tossed Susan her car keys and told her about Judge Crenshaw's "death."

Susan hadn't heard anything about it that morning.

Dallas rolled his eyes, going along with the gag. "I guess nobody found his body until after you left. What a con artist." He sidled up beside Susan, whiffed the magnificent allure of her perfume, and had a damned hard time keeping his hands to himself.

He checked the guest register, which the Ocean Tides still kept on paper. There were no "futuristic" computers—much to Herbie's chagrin. "We full up yet?"

"Half."

"Half?" Dallas had been recruiting beach idlers, kids, lifeguards—anyone without a place to sleep, offering rooms for ten bucks a night, one-tenth the rack rate. "Sus, this weekend the bar convention really gets going. A couple hundred *more* lawyers are coming into town. We've gotta fill up by Thursday. No lawyers. I don't care if we gotta *give* the damned rooms away." Dallas grabbed a pink message slip from his mail slot, annoyed that someone would call him. "What's this?"

"Jason stopped by."

"Yeah?"

"I told you I sent him off with the rollback to tow your car?"

"Yeah?"

"He can't find it."

Dallas closed his eyes and slumped against the desk. "Did you tell him it's by the Route Fifty bridge?"

"Yes." Susan crossed her arms. She'd won a five-million-dollar lawsuit and he was checking her efficiency at giving simple directions?

"Where is he?"

"Up in his room with Wendy."

Dallas headed for the door.

"Knock quietly," Susan warned. "They're very tired. That's why they spend all their time in bed."

"Yeah, yeah."

"Second," Jas called from inside.

Dallas heard him hop out of bed, hitting the floor like a human spring. Jas was very active. Through opaque panes of jalousie glass, Dallas saw him hop into a pair of shorts. He did a lot of hopping.

Jas opened the door. "Hey!" Smiling, always happy to see you. Twenty years old. Tall and slender, with short-cut, blond, bedroom-mussed hair, water blue eyes, and white teeth. Girls would still call Jason cute when he was fifty.

Wendy wrapped a sheet around her and waved from bed. "You always catch us like this," she said, no less cheerful than Jas.

" 'Cause you're always like this."

Behind Wendy, curtains were opened across the sliding-glass door. A view of green-blue ocean glistened with flecks of bright sunshine.

17

Dallas had moved them into this third-floor unit as soon as Towson State's final exams were over and crammed knowledge floated free of young brains like used dishwater. Finding either Wendy or Jas outside their room for anything more than a beer run was a rarer event than spotting endangered waterfowl.

Two rooms down, a door was kicked open. C.J., another freebie college hermit guest, staggered out. His arms strained lugging a huge plastic tub of brackish water that looked to be a failed attempt at homemade beer. Ah, the resourcefulness of underage drinkers.

C.J. dumped the tub over the balcony. A torrent of thick liquid did a slick ballet down two stories to the tar and chip lot and landed with a wet slap. Eyes bleary with hangover, C.J. told Dallas, "Don't ask."

Dallas waved. "That's always been my motto."

C.J. schlunked back into his room. The door slammed behind him.

Jas shrugged a shoulder in C.J.'s direction and laughed. "Sheesh."

"Jas, where's my car?"

"Oh, shit, yeah." He became serious quickly. "I don't know. I thought you got it."

"It had two flat tires, what was I gonna do with it? Wheelbarrow it home?" Jason was considering whether some bizarre circumstances might make that work when Dallas said, "You *did* go down there and look for it?" This was none-too-subtle interrogation, wanting Jas to state exactly where he'd gone this morning with the rollback—*if* he'd even gone.

Jason repeated Susan's directions exactly. He'd driven the rollback to the correct place all right.

"And my car wasn't there? The two-eighty? Rust on silver? Drop-cloth top?"

"Wasn't there."

Dallas couldn't believe it. Who would steal that car? The Alpine stereo system, maybe, but not the car, especially not with two flats. Some overzealous summer cop must have towed him for being illegally parked. Which was going to cost Dallas seventy-five bucks to get it out of the impound lot—again.

Wendy, draped-toga sexy in white sheet, came up behind Jason, wrapped her arms around his thin frame, and rubbed his belly. Jas shuddered with pleasure.

Wendy had on her glasses, cute studious frames that were half intellectual, half hippie throwback. Her thick black hair looked a mile long. "Lose your car?" she asked Dallas, not finding that implausible.

"So it seems."

She was pretty. Smart and practical. Jas needed her, especially *if* they ever decided to leave this room.

Jas said, "I'd help you look for it, but, you know I'm feeling pretty tired." He hugged Wendy. "I think we're going to catch some z's." He laughed. "No pun intended."

The jalousie door was politely closed in Dallas's face. From inside came the distinct thump-thump-thump of Jas hopping somewhere. And Wendy laughing.

And why not? There were better things to do at the beach than look for a car that had been impounded. To hell with the 280; Dallas could always bum a ride, and who knew what he'd be missing if he went looking for it now. Great waves. Hotter sun. Darker tans. Smaller bikinis. Or a 375-pound police chief named Rupert Dawson . . .

Rupert Dawson turned his unmarked cruiser into the motel lot. Good shock absorbers prevented the Crown Vic from bottoming out over a high driveway apron.

Dawson squeezed out of his vehicle, his motions overstated and slow. He was in his mid-fifties and two hundred pounds overweight; those proportions when the heat index was in the high nineties did not make for a sprightly attitude or gait.

The chief was a serious, small-town man who'd risen through the ranks to head the resort's police force, trying to rein in what, in season, was a small metropolis.

Although the mayor would have preferred otherwise, Dawson never hid his disgust with big-city tourists and their downtown morals. That he coped was about the most generous way to describe his style of law enforcement.

Dallas's usual reaction when Dawson came around was to run. Because Dawson didn't make social calls; his presence meant something Dallas had done was about to catch up with him.

"Hey, Rup."

Dawson turned his head toward this cheerful greeting, then away, then back again—what would have been a double take had his massive skull not taken so long doing two quarter turns on a meaty neck.

Dawson's eyes were shadowed by the fleshy overhang of his forehead. His skull, hatless as always, sported a to-the-skin whiffle unintentionally in keeping with the current surfer rage.

Dallas said, "You know, I think one of your summer rent-a-bozos had my car towed last night."

Sweat filled the soft furrows of Dawson's face. "That's what I'm here to talk about."

Dallas didn't like the chief's tone. It wasn't exactly accusatory, but official purpose lurked like a mugger in a dark alley.

Susan same to the side door and leaned halfway out. "Hi, Mr. Dawson."

"Hello, sweetheart." Susan was one of the only people who made Dawson smile. "That's a pretty dress."

Susan asked what Dallas had done this time.

"Maybe, seeing as you've been his lawyer in the past, you want to come over and listen."

Susan showed concern.

"It's about his car," Dawson said.

"Great. Where is—?"

Susan held out her hand to silence Dallas. "What about the car?"

"We found it over in West Ocean City." Dawson paused to see if this would elicit information.

Susan said, "And . . . ?"

Dawson wedged his hands inside his armpits to hold his arms crossed. "Car'd been involved in a crime."

"What?"

"Shut up, Dallas," Susan warned. To Dawson, she offered another "And . . . ?"

"Got a pretty big dent in the hood."

"Dammit," Dallas swore.

Susan's brown eyes hardened and cast Dallas the same caution she'd already spoken twice.

"The way it looks now," Dawson said, "someone used the car to run over Judge Crenshaw."

"Oh, please," Dallas groaned. "Not you, too. This is the biggest practical joke"—Dallas considered Dawson—"I've ever heard of"—Dawson wasn't smiling—"in all my life." Dallas's posture, normally a little lax, slumped further. "Damn. He's really dead, isn't he?"

"Sus, it's okay. Trust me. You stay here."

In the Ocean Tides lobby, she considered him gravely.

"Don't worry about it. I didn't do anything. Certainly didn't run over the old fart, that's for sure. I'll go down to the station, talk it over with Rup, try to figure out what happened. Be back in a couple hours. Work on filling those empty rooms, will you?"

"What do you always tell your clients?"

"I know, *I know*. Never talk to the police. It can only make things worse. But this's different. I didn't do anything."

"That's the point. Innocent people don't talk. Guilty people do because they're trying to get out of something."

"I just want my car back. Besides which, Crenshaw told me someone was trying to kill him. I've got to fill Rup in on that."

"It's a mistake."

"Don't worry about it."

Two hours later Dallas called and asked Susan to check how much they had in petty cash. He needed bail money.

$\triangledown$

5

THE EVIDENCE WAS BARELY circumstantial, but Assistant State's Attorney Brent Bannister didn't care.

Last winter, defending his record store client, Dallas had given a newspaper interview and called Bannister a neo-Nazi. Bannister had taken gross offense. Paybacks were hell.

"What we've got," Bannister outlined officiously, "are two shotgun blast holes in the wall. Coupled with your free and voluntary admission you broke into Crenshaw's house."

"The door was open, you boob."

"That's no defense to breaking and entering," Bannister snapped.

"I was invited."

"Invited and then shot at? That's what you're telling me? An out*ra*geous lie. At three in the morning, Crenshaw calls *you* because someone's trying to kill him?" Bannister phonied up a laugh, so amused with himself.

Dallas fought the urge to remove one of his flip-flops and smack the assistant state's attorney with it.

Inside the cramped, grungy walls of the court commissioner's office, Brent Bannister rested his scuffed wingtip shoes on the seat of a cane chair. Smirking, he rolled a No. 2 pencil between his fleshy palms.

Bannister had a late-middle-age mentality in a twenty-nine-year-old body. His hair was dark and trimmed closely to small stick-out ears. His face was bland as hominy, matching his personality. Outfitted à la wash-and-wear JC Penney from stem to stern, Bannister wore khaki trousers half a size cramped for his round bureaucrat's behind and fleshy gut.

"Also," Bannister continued, tapping the pencil eraser on his newly opened case file, "there are impressions in the hood of your car that fit striking a human body. And"—Bannister pointed his pencil at Dallas, enjoying this—"you have no alibi witness."

"It was four in the morning, you moron. I walked home."

"That's almost a mile. Why didn't you take a bus?"

"I don't ride the bus since the town imported those diesel stinking pieces of mass transit crap from Baltimore City. I liked the old green-and-white tin cans on wheels lots better."

"I'll be sure to pass that on to the budget committee," Bannister noted sarcastically, then added, "Still, you could have called one of those little college or high school misdemeanants you're always showing up with in court. Or hitchhiked."

Dallas sat forward, elbow on the commissioner's desk. "What about motive? Why would I have wanted to kill Judge Crenshaw?"

"The charge is vehicular homicide—for the time being. That doesn't require a motive. It could have been accidental." Bannister had more sour in him than a lemon orchard.

Dallas slumped back and stared up at the dirty ceiling where the same cheap fans had been twirling since the late fifties when this office was built. He was angry. A judge who cried wolf, that's what this had been. An old story reinvented. A man who loved practical jokes looking like he was setting up his biggest coup ever, only it was no gag. Crenshaw was dead and Bannister was using the tragedy for infantile revenge, no more interested in finding out who really ran over Crenshaw than smearing himself with honey and living in the forest with bears.

"Brent, remember when I called you a neo-Nazi?"

Bannister bristled like an anal retentive porcupine. His mother had seen that article.

"I take it back. You're no neo-Nazi. You're just an ass. And there's nothing neo-anything about that."

"I'm sure," Bannister said, gathering his papers, "the commissioner will take that comment into consideration when he sets bail."

"Fifty thousand dollars?" Susan stared at Dallas through the holding cell bars.

Dallas was one of the dozen detainees in the big tank, and the oldest of the group by at least ten years. But it was his kind of crowd: kids arrested for underage drinking, disorderly conduct, making too much noise, sleeping on the beach, general obnoxiousness. Being around them gave Dallas a chance to cool off.

The twenty-by-twenty cell-block had a single exposed toilet nicknamed Ugly Marge—no one knew why Marge, only that the feminine name was because the can got hugged by more drunks than Ocean City's loosest women.

"I only need to post ten percent."

"Well, you can forget about petty cash. The motel doesn't have that much in the bank. If you'd charge for the rooms instead of giving them away, we might have a couple grand."

"Out of the question until all the lawyers leave town."

Susan had changed from her sundress into a designer lawyer suit. Proper blouse with below-knee skirt and Valentino blazer, cream with blue pinstripes. Crisp lines. Stunning enough for Dallas's cell buddies to finally awaken from drunken stupors—at five-thirty—to take notice.

Dallas stuck his arms through the bars and made like he was going to grab Susan and lock her in a wild embrace. "This could be kind of kinky, huh?"

Susan smacked his hand and stepped back. She opened her leather briefcase and withdrew a wallet-sized checkbook. "I'll *lend* you the five grand."

"Thanks." He did appreciate it.

"I'll be back with your papers to cut you loose." Susan started down the hall.

Dallas called after her. "Ask them to hurry it along, will you? I'd like to get a couple of waves before dark."

A kid behind Dallas—rawboned, sunburned, and failing horribly at growing a goatee—attempted to stick his head through the bars to watch Susan walk away. "Jeez, man, she looks like that and has money, too?"

"Amazing, isn't it?"

"Radically awesome."

"So much for the waves." Dallas sighed. Stepping from the Dorchester Street precinct into balmy night, he took a deep breath of salty sea air.

The first stars of evening glowed faintly, tiny pin dots spread across a canvas of hazy purple sky and patchy clouds.

It was a quarter past eight. Commissioner Hammerman, following orders from ASA Bannister no doubt, had dragged his feet on Dallas's release.

"I'm starved." Dallas hadn't eaten all day.

"I'm a little hungry myself." Susan slung her blazer over her shoulder. Strolling the sidewalk, her briefcase tapped her legs. Professional warrior finished for the day.

"Let's get some crabs." Dallas was chipper for a man accused of running someone over. "Take them to Judge Crenshaw's house and have a feast."

"Sure," she replied sarcastically.

"I'm serious."

Susan loosened the collar of her blouse.

Dallas said, "More, more."

She smiled and directed him to her new Benz.

Traffic was heavy on Ocean Highway with tourists heading for the boardwalk's rides, video games, caramel popcorn, french fries, and T-shirt shops.

Dallas and Susan jogged across the street at a break in traffic. Kids in a jeep hooted at Susan. She waved. One of the guys. Harmless summer.

"Can I drive?" Dallas asked.

"No."

Susan unlocked her door. The passenger side lock, on a vacuum system, opened automatically. Dallas got in. The white two-seater only had three thousand miles on it. Leather so freshly tanned Dallas expected it to moo.

Susan turned over the engine. "Judge Crenshaw's house, huh?"

"I doubt he'll mind."

$\triangledown$

6

"GOD, THEY SMELL GOOD." Susan inhaled the lush aroma of spicy steamed crabs.

Dallas held the shopping bag on the floorboards between his feet. When heat off the crabs clouded the windshield, Susan turned on the defogger.

"Next left," Dallas said. They were off Route 611, winding through tall pines. "Careful around this bend. There was a deer in the middle of the road last night."

Susan, who generally drove five to ten miles over the limit, slowed cautiously. "Do you think he was murdered?" she asked, thinking more about Crenshaw the closer they got to his house.

"He seemed pretty convinced someone was after him. In an irrational way. But how do you murder someone with a car?"

"I read the coroner's report and Sam Paul didn't turn up anything contrary to the judge being run over."

"I don't know, Crenshaw wasn't *that* old, and he still had his reflexes." Dallas thought about how deftly the judge had fired that shotgun. "He'd have heard a car coming in time to get out of the way."

"So . . ." Susan made another turn where Dallas indicated. ". . .this is going to be it, then? Our case for the year?"

"What would summer be without one?" He pointed just ahead. "Here."

Susan followed the driveway around the Norfolk pine. The house lights were out. Crenshaw's *U.S.S. Chrysler* was at the head of the driveway as it had been the night before.

Knowing the man who'd lived here was dead made the secluded site seem even more so. Dallas tried not to let it get to him. If he started thinking about all that life, death, and hereafter stuff, he'd be awake all night.

Carrying the crabs, he started for the front door, hand in front of his face in case his spider friend had spun a new web. He picked the morning and evening newspapers from Crenshaw's stoop.

The door was unlocked. Flicking a wall switch, Dallas turned on the driveway light for Susan to find her way. He turned on inside lights as well.

The house smelled cleanly of pine. Scent from the trees outside carried in through screened windows. The open floor plan left the sectioning of a living and dining room to the arrangement of furniture. The decor was Montgomery Ward circa 1975, probably sold by a fellow in a polyester suit and white plastic shoes. Perfect for a widower or divorcée, it was the sort of junk a woman would set fire to when Goodwill refused to take it. Plain, simple, and broken-in.

A matched sofa, love seat, and easy chair in nubby brown-orange plaid. Indestructible wood coffee table. Moth-eaten scatter rug over scarred dark hardwood. Curtains and a few wall hangings straight out of the bland department.

A fancy picnic table and two matching benches in high-gloss pine served as the dining room.

From the sense of order, it didn't seem the police had undertaken a very thorough search inside the house, just enough to observe and collect the obvious: the knife Dallas had "played with" last night; shreds of "shotgunned" lettuce now dried to the floor; and mean holes Crenshaw had blasted in drywall.

Oddities notwithstanding, the responding officers apparently didn't think Crenshaw's being discovered along the road, fifty yards from his driveway and the apparent victim of a hit-and-run, warranted calling in homicide—leave that to Brent Bannister, thinking he had a way to make Dallas's life miserable.

Dallas spread newspaper over the picnic table and dumped out steaming crabs. "Ahhhh."

True jumbos. Bigger than Dallas's hand from shell tip to tip. Meaty claws doubling their width. Glossy red, sweaty, and coated with hot spice.

Susan passed through swinging kitchen doors in search of drinks. "Tanqueray, my fave."

Dallas sat on one bench and grabbed a hot crab. This was hardly disrespectful, eating in a dead man's house. You could get a real feel for a person mashing crabs in their place. It was beyond a meal; it was an experience. A summer ritual that could go on well into the night. Pulling off crab legs. Banging claws with a mallet. Digging succulent backfin with a knife or fingers. Dab it in a pile of Old Bay seasoning and let your lips catch fire.

Dallas cracked a claw and pulled out a clean tooth of moist meat, offering it as a toast. First gesturing upward, then down, to cover all bases. "Here's to you, Judge."

* * *

"I'm stuffed." Dallas plopped onto the worn sofa and put his feet on the coffee table, full of crabs and a little drunk. He'd never had gin and tonic with crabs before. It was a nice combination. Add to that spending time alone with Susan and it didn't get much better.

Dallas looked over his shoulder at stairs leading to the second floor. "Wonder what's up there?"

Susan, still picking a final crab or two, said, "I'm not going to bed with you, Dallas. I haven't had *that* much gin." But she had. Over the past two hours, her laughter had come more easily and grown louder. Her elbows, perched on the picnic table, took the strain off her spine as she slouched forward.

Dallas, for once, hadn't been making a pass. "Crenshaw must keep his papers around here somewhere. Doesn't look like down here."

First-floor furnishings didn't include a desk, shelves, cabinets, or other amenities where one might do banking business or letter writing. Judge Crenshaw would have had a place like that. Most judges who took any pride in their work did; and Crenshaw, contrary to the opinion of many lawyers, had considered himself an excellent jurist.

Somewhere, there'd be a cache of personal papers, law books, newspaper clippings of cases he'd tried before appointment to the bench and decided once seated. Perhaps such a collection would also contain a hint as to who Crenshaw thought wanted to kill him—and may have succeeded.

Dallas boosted himself out of the chair and headed up the stairs.

"You're going to be disappointed," Susan warned, meaning she wasn't going up there with him.

"Not unless I don't find what I'm looking for."

"If you have to look for it," Susan said with innuendo, "that really *would* be disappointing."

"Funny, Sus."

With half a mouthful of crabmeat, she called, "Maybe put together a search party."

Dallas, at the top of the steps, took off his shorts and threw them down the stairs. "Found it!"

Susan responded with a ribald shriek.

In boxer shorts, flip-flops, and T-shirt, Dallas felt along the wall until he located a light switch.

Exposed beams followed the roof angle, creating a loft effect. Like downstairs, it was primarily one room. Only a bath and closet had doors.

The double canopy bed—sans canopy—was no doubt a veteran from Crenshaw's married years. The sheets were pulled down as though Crenshaw had jumped out of bed and never gotten back. The chest of drawers was shut, as was an old hope chest at the foot of the bed.

In a corner was an antique rolltop desk. The drawers and top were locked. What Dallas needed was something to bust it open. Which is what he was looking for when Susan threw his shorts at him and turned off the light.

Words a little slurred, she warned, "Put those on. Someone's sneaking around out back."

$\triangledown$

7

T HE TROUBLE WITH FALLEN pine needles was they acted as a cushion, silencing footsteps. In Crenshaw's darkened bedroom, Dallas stood by the rear window and tried to make sense of muffled sounds outside, mostly the indistinct rustling of branches on a windless night.

"Do you think they saw you?" Dallas whispered to Susan, assuming it was a person out there.

"I don't know. I heard a noise coming from the kitchen first. Someone turning the knob of the side door."

"Did *you* see them?"

"No. I didn't want to chance it. How could I explain being here?"

"What about the lights?"

"What?"

"You turn them off?"

"No."

"They're gonna see the crabs."

It was quiet for a few moments. Then . . .

Sobering up fast, Susan said, "Hear that?"

Dallas nodded.

Directly below them, the window screen was being jiggled. Someone was trying to get in.

Susan said, "You wouldn't happen to have a gun, would you?"

"Sure . . . back at the motel."

The screen shook harder, then stopped.

"Are they in?" Susan whispered.

"I don't know." Dallas hoped not. He looked around for the judge's shotgun, but couldn't find it. The hell with this. He didn't like hiding. He started taking off his clothes.

"Dallas!"

"Never underestimate the surprise involved in showing up naked. Freaks 'em out every time." Dallas was down to his underwear. "When I say go, you scream, okay?"

Susan backed up half a step.

He shed his boxers. "And watch what you're looking at, lady."

"Sorry."

Bare-assed, Dallas tiptoed to the top of the stairs. "Now," he whispered.

Susan screamed.

Dallas charged down the steps, yelled, "*Banzai!*"

As he reached the first floor, the screen snapped shut at the dining room window. Whoever—whatever—was outside scrambled to get away.

There wasn't a back door, so Dallas ran out the front, hollering like a kamikaze. He sprinted to the back of the house, the soles of his feet callous enough to take it, but his eyes couldn't acclimate fast enough to the dark. Ducking a pine branch at the last minute, his bare back was raked by prickly needles.

Footsteps ran ahead of him—heavy, solid steps. Unable to see much of anything for darkness, Dallas pursued by sound alone, sweeping his arms in front of him to deflect pine branches, like swimming the breaststroke on land. Whoever he was chasing, they weren't that fast, but knew their way in the dark.

Dallas's chest ached. He was in miserable shape; worrying how much longer he could keep up the chase when his ankle caught on something. He was airborne. Did a skinny-dipping belly-flop onto woodsy turf. *Ooooof!* What little breath remained in his lungs was knocked out by contact with hard ground.

Oh, God, I'm dying, is what he'd have said had he been able to inhale. He crawled on all fours, fighting for oxygen, and found what had sent him to the ground: a piece of rope drawn between two trees. A tripwire. It looked like Judge Crenshaw had booby-trapped his woods.

"Now this side." Dallas rolled over in Judge Crenshaw's bathtub. Faceup, he smiled at Susan.

"Ah-hem." She cleared her throat and handed him the washcloth and soap she'd used to scrub his back clean of sticky pine sap. "I think this exceeds my medicinal purposes here." Susan shook water off her hands and reached for a towel, a pretty nurse with her sleeves rolled up.

Dallas splashed her, living out cheap Daytona Beach fantasies of seeing her in a soaking-wet top.

Susan escaped the bathroom relatively unscathed, though not unwet.

"Well, this is no fun alone," Dallas moped. He checked the slight brush burn raised on his ankle by the trip line, then got out and mostly dried off.

He joined Susan in Crenshaw's bedroom where she was placing the judge's personal files into cardboard R-Kive boxes she'd found preassembled and stacked in a corner.

"Anything good?" Dallas asked, looking over her shoulder with dripping wet hair.

"Case files. It looks like the judge had gone back to practicing law. He'd actually gotten clients."

"Well, he's been keeping it damned quiet."

"I hadn't heard anything about it." Susan handed Dallas one of two packed boxes. "I'll come into the motel tomorrow morning and we can start going through these."

"Susan!" Dallas feigned shock. "Are you actually suggesting we remove these files?"

"What can I say. You're a corrupting influence."

"I like the sound of that."

Lugging both R-Kive boxes, Dallas managed a good-bye gesture— half cock of head and shoulders—to Susan as she pulled out of the Ocean Tides lot.

Susan was heading home for yet another night that would leave Dallas wondering—and regretting—what she was doing without him; thoughts he had so often they were almost reflexive. Oh, well . . .

Dallas kicked the glass lobby door. "Herbie! Lemme in."

Herbie Gonner, frazzled blond hair and brains night manager, meandered to the door and opened it. He wore a Pittsburgh Penguins T-shirt and cutoffs. "I don't do paperwork," he said, eyeing Dallas's parcels.

Huffing and puffing, Dallas made his way to the counter and dropped the boxes like concrete blocks. He frowned seeing his mail slot jammed full of pink message slips. "What the hell's all this?"

"That," Herbie said, resuming his reclined position on an operator's chair behind the front desk, "is why the phone's off the hook."

It was, too; its curled electronic umbilical cord ran from the phone console to a drawer where Herbie had stuffed the handset.

"Most every one of them," Herbie said as Dallas rifled through his messages, "are congratulations for your killing Judge Crenshaw. Although they said twenty years ago would have been better timing. I pointed out you weren't old enough to drive back then, but they said at least you'd've been charged as a juvenile."

There must have been thirty calls.

Herbie said, "I think one call was an appellate judge, but he was mumbling like a kidnapper—had a handkerchief over the phone."

"Did you point out I didn't run Crenshaw over?"

Herbie shrugged. "They're talking about giving you an award at the bar conference. I didn't want to spoil it."

"Thanks." Dallas balled all the messages up.

"Ah-ah," Herbie cautioned. "They're not all candygrams. You also got a buzz from Victoria Callere—accent on the *re*."

"Who's that?"

"She said, tell you Victoria Secrets called."

Dallas went numb, the result of blending disbelief, shock, hope, and pain without a license to dispense prescriptions. "Vicky Sterrett?"

"She said Victoria Callere."

Dallas uncrumpled the messages, searching a little too eagerly for a name from his past. "I can't find her."

"Try Coconut Malerie's."

Dallas froze. "She's in town?"

"Yup."

Dallas broke his stare and headed for the door, stopped two steps into the parking lot, and came back. "I need your car."

"Forget it." Herbie was very possessive of his '69 VW Beetle.

"Herbie, come on." Dallas wiggled his fingers impatiently. "My car's impounded."

"Take Susan's Rabbit."

"She's got the keys."

Herbie twisted a long strand of blond hair, nothing better to do. "I'll drive you for ten bucks."

"Do it for nothing and take the rest of the night off."

"Deal." Herbie chose from a variety of closed signs kept handy for these impromptu walkouts and hung it on the door—BACK SOON. Very vague.

In the Beetle, engine rattle-whining, Herbie drove Dallas northward.

Coconut Malerie's: a classy suite hotel overlooking the water. The stars and moon brightening Assawoman Bay. Dallas and Vicky Sterrett—Victoria Secrets—on a private balcony.

Dallas tried to restrain his imagination. Impossible.

Herbie shifted to the fast lane. The windows were cranked down. With one hand on the wheel, he banded his hair back in a ponytail to keep it from blowing out of control.

"You drive too fast," Dallas said.

"I'm not wasting my youth in traffic."

Dallas couldn't argue with that. Maybe he'd try it as a defense in court.

"By the way," Herbie said over the engine and wind, "Victoria said this has something to do with Judge Crenshaw's will."

"Crenshaw's will?"

"Yeah. I think you're in it."

8

"**H**E'S LEFT YOU FIFTY thousand dollars."

"What?" Now Dallas was really stunned.

"Conditioned on your finding out who killed him. *If* someone killed him." Victoria Callere, née Vicky Sterrett, aka Victoria Secrets, wore a splashy paisley dress with a wide white belt like she'd walked off the pages of *Vogue*. Short hemline. Mid-length sleeves rolled above her elbows. Long sandy hair swept to one side, as though photographers kept a fan blowing toward her for the perfect picture.

In the living room of Vicky's suite, Dallas leaned against a heavy armoire, unsure which made him dizzier, the prospects of fifty grand or seeing her again.

"Drink?" Vicky asked.

A freshly uncapped bottle of Bombay Sapphire gin stood tall on the high-gloss coffee table alongside a silver pitcher of ice and two martini glasses.

What was it about beautiful women and gin? Dallas wondered. "Three," he replied.

"I beg your pardon?"

"I'll have three drinks. I like to order in advance in case the bar closes."

Her long eyebrows rose suggestively. "I'm open all night."

She didn't used to be like this—a flirt, or even glamorous. Dallas met her another life ago: law school days. She'd been a mousy, please-don't-notice-me first-year student. Dallas had found her innocence and softness appealing.

Vicky wasn't like the other brassclaw female law students looking to bash their way into what was then a male-dominated field. She'd seemed out of place, and the contrast drew Dallas to her like a moth seduced by flame.

After a month of talking, another month of maybe, she'd finally agreed to go out with him. First was a very safe breakfast after Israel Siff's crack-of-dawn UCC class, followed by a somewhat less safe lunch after Weston's Torts the following week, then dinner after a make-up night session of Bourne's Federal Procedure.

Vicky invited Dallas to her apartment after dinner, ostensibly to review property cases Professor Gilligan was giving her hell for not knowing. Dallas had no reason to suspect or expect otherwise. Not until he saw she was living in a thousand-dollar-a-month condo in a rehabbed city high rise. Especially not when she changed into a nightgown as pale and thin as moonlight.

In terms of offer and acceptance, Vicky Sterrett was a full-blown fraud, though Dallas had been far from protesting her charade. This seemingly demure girl had a closet full of killer lingerie, dangerous weapons in the battle of the sexes. There was some sincerity to her public shyness, but she was like a baby falcon working on her wings. The foundation for confidence was there, she just had to work out the kinks—so to speak.

She and Dallas didn't leave her apartment for three days. He'd nicknamed her Victoria Secrets, not only because of the source of her lingerie, but because her full name was Victoria, and she had good secrets.

They saw one another constantly. Dallas moved in with her. Found he could barely think of anything else. Law school, generally no more than a cold-weather diversion from sleep anyway, seemed immeasurably unimportant. And then, one day, without warning, it was over.

Now Dallas sipped Sapphire gin from a long-stemmed glass and tried to remember you couldn't go back. "Crenshaw put a provision in his will to have me find out who killed him?"

Vicky read from pages bound in a blue will folder imprinted with her firm's name. "In the event that my Personal Representative shall find the circumstances of my death in any manner suspicious, I request that my dear friend, Dallas Henry, of Ocean City, Maryland, investigate the cause of my death. Should he successfully undertake this request and, to the sole satisfaction of my Personal Representative, determine the cause of my death, whether ultimately found to be by suspicious or innocent means, I direct my Personal Representative to pay as an expense of my estate, a service fee to Dallas Henry in the amount of fifty thousand and zero one-hundredths dollars."

Unbelievable.

Dallas sat in a polished Queen Anne chair and rested his hands on his knees. He stared at the imprints Vicky's bare feet had pressed into thick carpeting. He wanted to see the will for himself.

Vicky offered the document. Leaning over, the unbuttoned front of her dress parted briefly. She still wore expensive underwear.

Dallas stole a glance in that direction, then considered Crenshaw's Last Will and Testament. "You're on this pretty quick."

"I was in town for the convention."

"And had the will with you?"

"I'm not psychic." Vicky returned to the striped sofa. "When I heard the news at lunch, I had it messengered from my office. I looked for you at the viewing tonight. You missed it."

"I was otherwise detained."

"The learned Brent Bannister, I heard. If you'd have been there, maybe you could have saved me from Harvey."

Dallas saw that the will had been initialed on every page and signed on the last. Notarized. Two witnesses. "Who's Harvey?"

"Crenshaw's son."

"Really."

"He's the one making sure the judge gets buried within forty-eight hours of his death. He says that's what his father wanted."

"Uh-huh . . ." Dallas wasn't paying attention to much besides the will. "The judge just signed this last week?"

"Nick of time."

"In your office?"

"Mmm." Vicky poured herself a fresh gin.

"Your *D.C.* office?"

Another "Mmm."

"You didn't find this odd? A guy thinking his death might be suspicious?"

"I just represent them, Dallas, I'm not their mother. Besides, Crenshaw was odd."

"Yeah, but this is beyond odd, bordering on paranoid. Did he give you any details? I saw him last night and he wouldn't say dirt. Which makes me think he was hearing voices in the middle of the night and was afraid to admit it."

"Footsteps."

"How's that?'

"He was hearing footsteps. A person or persons creeping around outside his house. Even getting inside."

Dallas considered relating his experience of a few hours ago, but decided to hold off for now. "Weird," was all he said.

"Yes," Vicky replied, sipping gin, "he was."

Dallas leafed through the will again in case something new jumped out at him. It wasn't that long, just a few pages beyond what most firms churned out for seventy-five dollars.

"Keep that copy if you like. . . . For your investigation."

"You assume I'm interested?"

"For fifty thousand dollars?" As though he'd be crazy not to be. "All you have to do is, like the will says, 'satisfy' the personal representative. That's me, and you've never had any trouble in the satisfying department before."

Dallas ran a hand through his tangled hair. "Is that an invitation?"

"Oh, I don't know." Vicky cast a seemingly absent gaze toward the bedroom door. "Don't let it scare you."

"I'm not scared of tonight. It's tomorrow that scares me."

Vicky looked away.

Dallas folded the will back to its precreased form. "Why'd Crenshaw go to you for this—I mean besides your brilliance?"

"With his reputation, I suspect he figured no Maryland lawyer would talk to him." Her attitude became a bit rigid. Dallas had struck a nerve with his comment about being afraid of tomorrow.

He regretting having said it, but pressed on. That part of their past had hung between them for so long, dealing with it would likely be more awkward than trying to forget it. "So Crenshaw goes to Capitol Hill's finest, Victoria Secrets. Defender of congressmen, diplomats, and multinational corporations."

Vicky never tired of that categorization; she'd worked hard to get it.

"When did you change your name, by the way?"

"I married the French ambassador to China last year."

"Exotic."

"Very."

"How long did it last?"

"Three months."

"New record." Dallas polished off his drink. "It's a joke." He smiled when her eyes, reflecting gin, took on some ice. Dallas set his empty glass on the coffee table. "Okay, Vicky, I'll look into it." He lightly slapped the will across her thighs, an area to which her skirt seemed allergic given the scant contact it made with her legs.

When he turned to leave, she grasped his forearm. "You don't have to go."

A dozen comments came to mind, some bitter, others pathetic, a few what-the-hell horny. Dallas ended up shaking his head, said, "Yeah . . . I do."

"You're sure?" Vicky stood, hip cocked, dress in random disarray as though scattered by a sea breeze. She started slowly for the bedroom, each step a warmer degree of seduction. "Sure . . . ?"

Her back to Dallas, she began unbuttoning the remainder of her dress; crossed the bedroom threshold and stepped behind the wall. She was hidden from direct view, but her shadow cast clear imagery; the dress was coming off.

Dallas let himself out and walked home. Called himself an idiot a few hundred times before someone stopped to give him a lift.

This was the beach. Why had he left? Victoria Secrets. He wondered if anyone else had ever not said yes to her. Why get tangled up in the past's invisible strings? *It was the beach, dammit!* There was only today, screw tomorrow. What lasts anyway? If it feels good do it, that worn cliché.

Tonight, however, even in spite of the gin—maybe *because* of it—Dallas couldn't muster those carefree ways. Vicky triggered too much of the past. Fleeting years and lost opportunities. All that he had hoped would be, yet never was.

Dallas remained a little lost in sentimental haze when the kind stranger driving a Ford Tempo dropped him back at the Ocean Tides.

In the parking lot, about to enter the squalor he called home, Dallas didn't notice a man sitting in a bronze Jaguar: window rolled down, drinking from a bottle of something potent.

The man, visible only in shadows, took a slug from his liter bottle, then spat a very angry, "Hey! Hey you!" Obviously drunk.

Dallas ignored him until the bottle came sailing across the parking lot. Exploding against macadam, bits of glass and amber liquid stung Dallas's heels.

Dallas spun around hard. "Get out of that car and I'll make shark bait of your ass."

The drunk, his door half-open, foot about to touch the ground, stopped.

Seeing the guy wore tasseled loafers lessened Dallas's concern. He'd never met anyone in tassels who was much of a fighter. Which was good, because neither was Dallas. He just talked a good fight and got lucky sometimes.

"Ioughtakillyou," the drunk bellowed, words running together. But he stayed in the Jaguar.

The ignition point—that moment when rage overcomes logic and starts throwing punches—had passed. Most likely, this was going to be an argument, not a fight.

"Killyou 'n' buryyoufor dead." The drunk tried to put spaces between his words like wedging apart cubes of Jell-O with his tongue. "Talkin' craziness tomyfather."

"Get the hell out of here." Dallas estimated the time it would take to unlock his door and get inside, not wanting to turn his back in case the drunk had another bottle.

"It'smine youasshole andI'm gonnaseeyou don'get nothing."

"Fine." Whatever he was talking about.

"Youset'im up'nthenkilled'em!" Was he sobbing now? "Sonofa-bitch!" No, just angry-drunk. Preparing to drive out of the lot.

"Hey, wait a minute." Dallas started toward the car.

The drunk shifted into reverse, peeled backwards, and smashed into a street lamp. The trunk of the Jaguar was crushed painfully. Glass shattered. The driver's head snapped back. "Shit! Lookitwhatyoumademedo!" His door swung open.

Dallas jogged toward him. "You're gonna kill yourself."

"Get away fromme!" the drunk yelled. "Get away!" He stomped the gas. The Jag spun a wild turn and bounced out onto the street. The opened driver's door struck the rear of a Dodge van and was slammed shut. The Jaguar kept going, ignoring the Dodge's horns of protest.

Watching the drunk weave up the highway, Dallas braced for the impact he thought sure to come. But there were only blaring horns and angry screams that faded like a train heading off across the prairie.

Beneath the streetlight, where broken chunks of taillight sparkled like cheap rubies, Dallas picked up the license plate that had fallen off the Jag. Pennsylvania vanity tag: ISUE4U. An out-of-state lawyer who thought Dallas had killed his father.

Maybe if Dallas had asked Vicky a few questions about Judge Crenshaw's son, this meeting wouldn't have been so awkward.

$\triangledown$

9

DALLAS PUT THE KNIFE between his teeth like a pirate in a B-movie and climbed the metal ladder with one free hand. He threw open the access hatch and pulled himself onto the Ocean Tides' roof, a flat expanse of paved tar overlooking the boardwalk, beach, and rolling Atlantic Ocean.

To the distant north were the twinkling gold lights of condo row. Not so far south were the thrill rides of boomtown.

Besides the serrated knife, Dallas had a third full bottle of Cuervo Gold tequila; a baggie of limes; and a scrunched box of Morton kosher salt, grains of spice the size of tenth-carat diamonds.

This was his private domain. Trespassers allowed by invitation only. His beach chairs, sun-worn through many summers, were strapped to exhaust vents to survive bad weather. Dallas unchained one, snapped it open, and sat down.

The roof surface, covered by ocean mist, was cool and damp to his bare feet. Dallas usually reserved his melancholy times for sunset, but since today's dusk had been spent in jail, he'd settle for a morose moonrise.

This, Dallas thought to himself, opening the tequila, is why he never got married. Among other reasons, but mainly this. Too moody. Too wrapped up in things you can't do anything about. Thinking about Victoria Secrets when he should be going through Judge Crenshaw's files, figuring out if he was murdered or not. Collect that fifty grand.

Ah, screw it for tonight. If you couldn't make a million, why bother? He'd just get used to the money and want more. Besides, he did well in quasi-poverty.

Dallas stretched his legs and considered his cocktail wares. He could never remember whether you did it lime-salt-tequila or salt-tequila-lime, or whatever. Unable to decide, he performed the routine at random to surprise himself.

It was a great night on the roof. Watching tourists stroll the boardwalk and kids playing volleyball on the beach under the motel lights.

The four high school girls he was letting stay gratis on the second floor were right out of striker heaven. The three Ls and an M: Laurie, Laura, Lisa, and Meghan.

They played volleyball real cutesy until four would-be studs came along to challenge and/or try to pick them up. Then they'd get serious and pound the hell out of those helpless guys. Smash that jungle green Mikasa ball over the net like a giant firefly blasted from a cannon.

Dallas let the pleasure of watching youth distract him, and thought, enjoy it while you can, kids, it gets complicated in a hurry. Boy does it ever.

How many nights had he sat here and grappled with the passage of time? Listening to old music. Thinking back on a youth so feverishly experienced and so quickly gone. A race that seemed to have ended just as he'd caught his stride.

Even accepting some of his memories were improved by charitable recall, it had been fantastic. God, but he wished he could go back and gulp deeply of years lost to the mist if just long enough to taste it on his tongue like salty air.

Ah . . . a fool's idle dream. Like trying to jump into the stars.

Dallas swigged tequila and threw a lime over his shoulder.

A little voice said, "You almost hit me with that."

Dallas turned and saw a kid coming up through the roof hatch. "Hey, don't come out here."

"Why not?" She stepped onto the flat roof clutching a brown paper bag. Ten, maybe eleven. Blond hair, cuter than cute.

Dallas started toward her. Just what he needed, a little kid taking a nosedive off his motel with a pack of lawyers running loose through town. There'd be a line around the block to sue him. "You might fall."

"So might you." Careful to stay near the center of the roof, she went up on her toes and peered over the edge. "It's not that far."

"Far enough to kill you."

"I won't fall." Confident, indestructible, ten—good grief. "Are you Mr. Dallas?"

"Just Dallas—yeah." He hated being called mister anything. "Who are you?"

"I'm Jill. Those are my sisters." She pointed to the volleyball players. "Those two: Laurie and Meghan." Her voice was clear and bright as a pealing bell. "I'm chaperoning them."

"Ah." Dallas suddenly felt guilty about the bottle of tequila.

Depravity beheld by the eyes of innocence. He tried to slide it behind his beach chair with his foot.

"Drinking's not good for you, you know."

Dallas took a deep breath. "What's in the bag?" Changing the subject.

"Hermit crabs. Wanna see?"

"Uhh . . ." Not sure until she looked at him with eager eyes. ". . . sure."

She knelt down, knees of her white jeans getting dirty on the tar roof. Laying the paper bag carefully on its side, she gently prodded out the crabs. There were half a dozen in all; teeny, tiny crustaceans with one sizable claw living in discarded conch shells, trading up as they grew like humans moving into bigger trailers.

Jill said, "We could have races . . ."

Dallas shrugged, okay.

". . . for money."

"Sure. Hope you brought your checkbook." He knelt down, but should have drawn a correlation between Jill and her volleyball sisters; a good hustle ran in their genes.

They raced crabs till midnight—Dallas lost ten bucks—then talked past two. Jill finally drifted off to sleep in a beach chair and Dallas carried her down to her sisters' room. Suddenly, nothing seemed so bad.

"You can't possibly be here to wake me up." Dallas's face was stuffed into his pillow. He had no idea what time it was, but had a feeling he didn't want to know.

Susan said, "We're going to be late."

"I prefer being late."

Susan smacked his butt. "Get up."

Dallas groaned and eventually managed to roll over. His memories of last night were especially clear for a change. Which was nice thinking about little Jill, rotten contemplating Victoria Secrets and Judge Crenshaw's son.

Susan opened Dallas's fridge and searched long and hard for something she could make him believe was breakfast. The orange juice was only mildly sour. She poured a glass. "What're these?" Asking about the pants soaking in the kitchen sink.

Dallas staggered beside her. "You know how to get tar outta white denim?" In his boxer shorts, he sunk his wrists into sudsy water and took another shot at cleaning the knees of Jill's jeans.

"I scrubbed my ass off about two hours last night. The damned tar won't budge."

"Lighter fluid," Susan said. Seeing how small the white pants were, she asked, "How hot's that water anyway?" Thinking he'd shrunk them miserably.

"They're not mine. The volleyballers' little sister came down to stay with them for a while."

"Did she bring a note from her parents?"

"I don't know. I got enough problems."

"And an entire day ahead of you to deal with them for a change." Susan, looking proper in a short black dress, sat on Dallas's bed. "I did some checking around on Crenshaw last night. He had gone back into practice. He started taking clients about six months ago. Nothing has gone to trial yet, which is probably why word hadn't gotten around." Susan adjusted the red carnation in her lapel. "Supposedly he's got office arrangements you'd like."

"Oh, yeah?" Dallas doubted that. The only good office was a closed office.

"In the clubhouse at Hurricane Bay."

"You're kidding. Specializing in what, golf law?"

"Rumor is he picked up a five percent ownership stake as part of the deal."

Dallas dredged the white jeans through soapy water. "What's a golf club need with a staff lawyer? Unless he can threaten balls to go in the hole."

"I'm trying to find out." Susan looked at a CD poking out from beneath the sheets: Pink Floyd's *Dark Side of the Moon*. "So how was your night?"

"Downhill once you left."

"Sweet."

"I lost ten bucks at the hermit crab races"—Dallas tried S.O.S. on the jeans—"and got a call from Vicky Sterrett."

Susan tensed.

"She's in town for the convention and—coincidentally—to be PR of Crenshaw's will." Dallas could hear Susan grinding her teeth from fifteen feet away.

"So," Susan asked with sweet and sour spite, "how is the blond bitch?"

"I suspect, profitable."

"Does she want to see you?"

"She does and she did." Dallas recounted last night up to and including Vicky's come-on.

"And did you?" Susan asked, referring to the come-on.

Dallas would have given a day of good waves if only Susan sounded jealous. But that wasn't it. Susan didn't like Vicky Sterrett. Victoria Secrets represented something different to Susan than she did to Dallas.

Dallas said, "Maybe next time."

"Well, you better get some ironclad condoms." Agitated, Susan checked her gold Rolex. "And you better get dressed."

Dallas wondered what it was about Vicky Sterrett that made people lose their beachhead ways and start acting like they were back in the city. As though Vicky hauled all that was stressful, competitive, and bad about life across the Bay Bridge with her.

For Susan, however, Dallas knew Vicky was a symbol of what could've been. *If* Susan had grabbed higher-profile clients. *If* Susan had hired herself a good publicity firm. *If* only Susan hadn't taken that last divorce case; on the opposite side of a crazed, homicidal husband who'd planted a bomb under her Corvette and blown it sky-high, meaning to take Susan with it. A close call she was having a hard time getting over.

Nothing nasty ever happened to Vicky Sterrett. Vicky's life was charmed and unscarred. Still, Susan was convinced if Vicky's car had been bombed, Vicky would have stuck it out, toughed her way through it. Not caved in and gone running for cover at the beach.

Susan didn't think she was tough enough. And she wanted to be so badly. She *had* been, too. A damned successful trial lawyer. God, why had that guy tried to kill her? Everything would have been different.

Yeah, Dallas had told her more than once—different, all right— she could be dead. All the years of study and work and for what? A pretty tombstone?

"You're tough," Dallas said, riding shotgun in Susan's Benz to Crenshaw's funeral. "You're plenty tough."

Susan didn't say anything. She kept her eyes on the road and, after a few seconds, nodded. Not necessarily in agreement, but as thanks.

10

Portable photo floods were set up outside Saint Paul's-By-The-Sea, their false white light washing out morning shadows that streaked the cedar church. A small enclave of beach-attired onlookers craned their necks to get a glimpse of what was going on.

At first, Dallas thought Crenshaw's death had attracted a network-affiliate news crew all the way from Baltimore or D.C.; then he saw differently.

Mack Trial, Esq., public access TV show host, law practice franchisor, and TV advertising attorney extraordinaire, was taping a new commercial against the background of the Episcopal church and, apparently, Crenshaw's funeral.

Mack Trial, born Leonard Sawgrass thirty-five years ago, was having his cheeks patted with pancake powder by a makeup girl in tight bike shorts. Seated in a canvas director's chair, mindful of creases in his fifteen-hundred-dollar suit, Trial reviewed his three-page script.

"Probably," Dallas commented to Susan, "the first thing he's read in years." Walking up the block, they considered contrasting sights before them.

A church built within one block of the boardwalk and ocean. A breezy summer day and a funeral. Approximately one hundred mourners in black suits and ties crossing the same curbs as families toting umbrellas, blankets, and surf rafts to the beach. But worst of all: a line of lawyers filing into the church.

"If God's awake yet this morning," Dallas said, "he's gonna hit this place with a lightning bolt."

Susan brushed a strand of dark hair from her eyes. She was watching the church's red door, bracing—Dallas suspected from her mood—for an encounter with Vicky Sterrett. So far, though, so good.

Meanwhile, Mack Trial—or "Mock" Trial, as he was referred to by his fellow attorneys—drew most of the attention, as was his habit. He was, after all, on TV. A cause célèbre, albeit a tacky one.

Nowhere did distaste for Trial run more potently than among

those trotting up wood steps to Crenshaw's funeral. From the silk-stocking corporate lawyers to the plaid-jacketed ambulance chasers, Trial earned high marks of scorn—and hidden envy—as a man of feeble abilities who'd managed to parlay a barely competent four-year stint as a lower-court prosecutor into a megamillion-dollar storefront legal machine. Churning out harassing slap suits, legitimate medical malpractice claims, and DWI defenses as mechanically as a 7-Eleven microwaved burritos and lobbed them over the counter as lunchtime hot-to-go.

In six quick years, Trial had built a mammoth practice with billboard and TV advertising that cost more than the gross national product of many Third World nations. He also had a catchy slogan: *It Feels Great To Litigate.*

This morning, his production crew included two cameramen, one of whom filmed attorneys parading into Saint Paul's while Trial rehearsed his lines: "Some lawyers would line up around the block to be as successful as I am." Smirk. "When you and I know they don't have a prayer. Don't gamble with your legal rights. Don't treat your case like a pair of dice and let just anyone roll for you—because they might *roll* over. Call me. Mack Trial. I've got thirty offices statewide."

Dallas raised his hands and clapped. "Author! Author!"

The young woman doing Trial's makeup propped her hands on thin hips and glared at Dallas.

Trial, oblivious to Dallas's mocking, bounced out of his chair with a performer's energy, paper bib still tucked in his collar to keep base makeup from staining his shirt. "Back in a minute, babe," he assured his makeup honey. He strode toward Dallas and Susan with the long strides a media consultant advised would make him seem taller. It was an awkward gait, like he was superstitiously trying to avoid cracks in the sidewalk. "Hey, stranger, how you doing?"

Susan, smiling politely, whispered to Dallas, "You know this yutz?"

Trial extended a thin hand to Susan. "Trial. Mack Trial." A cadence like Sean Connery used to say, Bond, James Bond. Trial always introduced himself by name—an act of false modesty, as though Susan hadn't watched any TV in the last six years.

"Vette," Susan replied, "Susan Vette."

"You an item with this old horn dog?" Trial asked, jabbing his elbow into Dallas's side. "Or did he just get lucky walking down the block?"

47

Susan got her hand back and stepped around Trial. "See you inside," she told Dallas.

"Brrrr." Trial feigned a chilled shudder, then turned to watch Susan. "Too bad. Nice rump."

Nearly a foot taller than Trial, Dallas looked over the back of the TV lawyer's head; a pattern of hair implants dotted what would have otherwise been a glossy dome. Dallas wished he had a felt tip so he could play connect the dots.

"So," Trial said, turning back around, "what's new with you? Got some big cases?"

"What's that?" Dallas hadn't heard the question, distracted by Trial's hair. He wasn't sure, but it looked like Trial's surgeon had woven the implants in a pattern like the constellation Orion.

Seeing Dallas's interest in his head, Trial self-consciously patted his landscaped scalp while, across the side street, Trial's production assistant grew concerned. "Ready, Mr. Trial. We're losing the light."

Dallas looked north between low buildings and considered the sky. Sure enough, a line of gray clouds was tumbling in from the north. Behind them, the horizon was stormy black.

Trial smacked Dallas's stomach with the back of his hand. "We'll catch up later."

His two cameramen were eyeing the changing sky. The light man was fidgety, taking meter readings and shaking his head.

Wind picked up and smelled of rain. Heavy and sweet. A distant boom of thunder shook the ground. Tourists heading toward the beach made an abrupt about-face.

"Looks like God woke up," Dallas said to himself. Some hypocrisy you could overlook, but a church full of lawyers . . . no way.

The weather turned apocalyptic in a hurry. God obviously didn't want to give them damned lawyers no time to escape. The breeze, which had been southerly all morning, was suddenly turning back on itself as a nasty front rolled in from the north.

The sun was smothered in an instant. Trial's crew worked frantically to stow expensive equipment.

Low, black clouds overtook gray underlings, rolling in like buffalo spitting lightning. Meeting the southerly breeze head-on, dark clouds began to swirl slowly as though forming demonic cotton candy.

Across the dune line a block away, lifeguards whistled swimmers out of the ocean.

The first raindrops were heavy, landing feet apart like liquid baseballs bursting against the sidewalk.

Thunder boomed and rattled the asphalt. Lightning sizzled loudly as it struck the ocean. Close.

Dallas hustled up the church steps two at a time. Better get Susan out of there before God improved his aim.

Mack Trial ripped off his makeup bib and screamed at the storm. "This's costing me money!"

Rain let loose like a cork had been pulled from the sky. More thunder. Another lightning strike—*Zzzzzttt*.

Within seconds, the deluge turned flat streets into shallow streams. The entire south end of the island seemed to be taking on water like a rickety rowboat. In rough weather, Ocean City offered little resistance to the elements. Little more than a tenuous plain of sand between two bodies of water, she didn't offer any angle for drainage.

In less than two minutes, Mack Trial was up to his Italian loafers in water, but held his ground as though facing down an opponent in a divorce settlement.

Someone screamed at him, "Get inside, you jerk!"

And then, someone else, slightly more belligerent, took a shot at Trial. A booming report from a handgun was quickly followed by a second. Right beside Trial, a car windshield cracked. A second near hit chunked a piece of cedar off the church.

Trial flopped into a gutter of storm water, lying low.

Screams were smothered by the rain.

Dallas ducked inside the church door and tried to see where the shots had come from.

Vacationers by the dozen scurried wildly for cover from rain and gunfire. One man, however, ran a beeline of purposeful retreat across the street. Visible only in silhouette, he sprinted into an alley, pistol at his side.

Dallas took off after him. The sound of his own feet splashing through puddles was blanketed by a loud thunder boom. Within ten seconds he was soaked.

The gunman's escape route was a wide alley between a series of old wood-sided apartment houses. Dallas reached the north end of the block as the shooter cleared the south side and turned right.

Dallas got a quick glimpse of him: white guy, five ten to six feet. Compact, strong looking. A hundred and eighty pounds. Wearing long pants, maybe jeans; a long-sleeve shirt, no collar. Good runner, a smooth athletic stride.

Lightning's hard light shot across the sky; its reflection lifted details from the alley's gray shadows.

Dallas hurdled a trash can lid, breathing hard. Two chases in two days—sheesh—the most exercise he'd had all year. By the time he covered the length of the block, his "chasee" was long gone. Disappeared amidst countless apartment houses and cottages, lines of cars stuck in traffic, and people escaping the rain inside doorways and under awnings.

Dallas bent at the waist and grabbed the front of wet pants for support. He hoped none of his vital organs exploded.

"Hey," a cheerful voice called from above. "You're getting rained on."

Dallas looked to the second floor of a weather-beaten apartment. On a screened covered porch, three college girls drank raspberry tea in their underwear.

"You see a guy . . ." he gasped, ". . . run by here with a gun?"

"No," the tall one answered, unconcerned.

"Want some tea?" the stocky brunette asked.

Dallas staggered back toward Saint Paul's-By-The-Sea sipping sweetened steaming tea from a plastic cup. He slicked back his hair and wiped rain from his eyes. The shirt and slacks Susan had picked out for him to wear now resembled the latest in drowned-rat fashions.

For about two seconds he considered taking up jogging or bike riding to get in shape, then realized being unfit had probably just saved his life. What would he have done if he'd caught that guy? It was pretty stupid to chase a man who had a gun without one yourself. Lucky for him he'd run out of breath when he had.

By the time Dallas reached the end of the alley, a police cruiser, lights twirling, had arrived and blocked off Third Street. A patrolman outfitted in a yellow rain slicker with POLICE stenciled across the back leaned inside his vehicle to pick up the radio mike.

Mack Trial was still in the gutter. On all fours. Waving away a second cop who offered assistance.

The officer backed off, clearly puzzled.

"Get it right this time!" Trial shouted to his camerman. "No excuses about bad light." Directions given, Trial lowered himself back into the puddle for a retake.

This, Dallas thought, is what made Trial a successful attorney. Not a good one, but successful. Profitable.

Five minutes ago, Trial was trying to become one with the curb, dodging bullets. Now, he was yelling for his cameraman to get this on tape.

Dallas could see the headlines now: PROMINENT TV ATTORNEY ESCAPES CERTAIN DEATH. Only Trial could turn near disaster into free publicity.

A third patrolman gathered witnesses beneath the deck of the church's residence house. Out of the subsiding rain, he took their statements. Currently, he was interviewing a young woman wrapped in a wet beach towel.

She flung her bare arm toward the alley, indicating from where the shots had been fired. She said, "Over there is where—" Suddenly, her arm went rigid like the tail of a hunting dog cut loose on the hunt. "That's him!" she screamed, seeing Dallas.

The cop dropped his pad and pencil, drew his magnum, and came running.

Dallas moaned. "Here we go again." He took a final drink of tea, tossed aside the cup, and raised his arms.

11

In dramatic "Geraldo" fashion—Hey, Mom, look at me, look at me!—Mack Trial flung himself across the hood of Rupert Dawson's Crown Victoria like a beached perch. He pounded the windshield with his fist. "You're arresting an innocent man! I demand you release him immediately!"

Over Trial's shoulder, the TV lawyer's cameraman filmed this bold "rescue" mission.

The summer squall was fading as quickly as it had approached. Still, a faint enough drizzle remained for Chief Dawson to switch on his windshield wipers. In the process, he nicked Trial's pinkie as his fist beat the glass.

Trial overreacted, grabbing his hand like he'd been cut in a knife fight. His feet were already off the ground, waist leaning against the fender, so with his arms raised, he became balanced precariously like the scales of justice lady with hair plugs.

"Get off the car, asshole," Dawson ordered, his voice mean enough to carry over the sedan's huge engine.

Seated beside the chief, Dallas held up his wrists to show he wasn't cuffed. "I'm not under arrest."

The cameraman zoomed in tight on Trial's grimace.

Dawson shifted the big sedan out of gear. "You should've run over *this* guy instead of Crenshaw." He hit the siren and gunned the engine.

Trial, thinking he was about to get launched, scrambled off the hood and retreated to the sidewalk.

Dawson jammed the Crown Vic into reverse and tried backing onto Baltimore Avenue, but it remained bumper-to-bumper. As badly as Ocean City drained, it handled traffic even worse. When the rain had looked to make the day a total beach washout, everyone had packed up the surf mats and sunscreen and loaded into the family van-a-bus. They were ten blocks into a journey to the video arcades, malls, or movies when the sun began to peek out from behind thinning clouds. Now they wanted to get back to the beach, bad.

"Will you look at this," Dawson complained. "Twenty minutes of rain and this town goes to hell." He leaned a heavy elbow out the window. "I liked it better when there was nothing but sand dunes from Twenty-third Street out."

Dallas nodded. Even though he wasn't old enough to remember that, he liked the idea.

"Too many people. Too many crazies." Dawson turned on the defroster when the windows began to fog. He was in a worse mood than usual. Within thirty-six hours, a retired judge had been run over and a flamboyant pain-in-the-ass attorney had been shot at. Both stories would hit OC's weekly papers with a tabloid splash. For a resort town that hadn't yet caught up with metropolitan trends in crime, this was large news.

Dawson dreaded negative press. Very bad for tourism. The mayor would be riding him like a fifty-cent merry-go-round.

"So far," Dawson complained, "we got ten different versions of this shoot. One old man claims it was Lee Harvey Oswald firing from the bell tower of City Hall."

Dallas shook his head. "That's nuts. I saw the guy: it was Elvis, plain as day."

Chins resting on his sternum, Dawson rolled his stalk-haired head toward Dallas. His eyes were alligator serious. "How good a look *did* you get at him?"

Dallas recounted his unsuccessful chase, adding, "Too bad you and skinny weren't on the scene." Referring to Dawson's fleet-footed partner of twenty-five years ago who would chase and catch suspects, then hold on for dear life until Dawson caught up to pound the bad guys silly.

"Old days . . ." Dawson experienced a brief fond memory, then began mentally cataloging local ne'er-do-wells who fit Dallas's vague description; doing this while watching the scene outside Saint Paul's.

Mack Trial was getting a quick drying off and pinkie bandaging from his makeup girl. Determined to salvage production costs, he'd ordered the lighting boys to set up again.

Dawson asked, "Judge Crenshaw and this here goofball Trial have any past history together?"

"You're thinking whoever took a shot at Trial also did Crenshaw?"

"A thought."

"Well, Trial was a prosecutor in Crenshaw's jurisdiction for a couple of years. I'm sure they had some contact."

"Wonder how long it's gonna take me to get cooperation out of the boys up in the city to check into that."

"You want me to ask around?" Dallas offered, knowing damned well the chief was hinting at that.

"You do," the chief bartered, "and I'll talk to Bannister and get him to drop the case against you."

"Nah, I want to mess with that weasel a little bit first. Make him eat those charges."

"You get him mad it just gets you in trouble."

"It's fun."

Dawson grunted.

"I would like my car back, though."

"I'll arrange it."

"Thanks. I'd still like to know how someone drove it with two flat tires."

Dawson didn't comment about that, but rarely involved himself too much with Dallas's excuses, many of which history had shown to be concocted.

Dallas shaded his eyes as the sun burned through the final layer of clouds and threw its heat across Dawson's car like an overzealous prosecutor. The rain was gone, leaving behind thick humidity like hot exhaust. The remainder of the day was going to be a glue-boiler.

Mack Trial's film crew tested their lights; one flood bulb exploded in a shower of sparks like a cheap firework. Trial cussed and stamped his feet like a grumpy kid who needed a nap.

"Goddamn," Dawson said, observing the spectacle. "I *do* wish I could arrest people for stupidity and bad taste."

"And you think the jails're full now."

"Goddamn. *Goddamn.*"

The red door opened to Saint Paul's and the lawyer mourners, at long last rid of Judge Crenshaw, paraded out into what was now a full return to sunshine.

Mack Trial, aware fellow members of the bar would love to see him struggling, hurried to the production company van and hid inside.

Susan was one of the last to exit the church. At the top step, she assumed a natural pose two-grand-a-day models worked years to achieve. Her fingers gracefully touched the iron handrail. One hip cocked slightly. Sun highlighted the wave of her dark hair.

"What she sees in you," Dawson said for at least the millionth time since Susan had been in Ocean City, "I'll never know."

Dallas opened the door. "That's the trouble. She doesn't see anything in me." He got out and waved.

"Where've you been?" she called, slightly annoyed.

Dallas assumed, given the noise and fury of the storm, that gunshots hadn't been heard inside the church. He crossed the side street, stepping over the snaked wires of Mack Trial's lights.

Susan said, "You're soaked."

"Yeah, how about that. How was the ceremony?"

"Father Barton was in fine form. He'd like to see you."

"Nothing about confessions, I hope."

"Episcopalians don't confess." Susan led Dallas into the church. The woodwork and stained glass reminded him of older places of worship, nothing like the modern monstrosities of clear glass, metal, and avant-garde statuary.

Dallas wiped his feet on a runner behind the final row of pews. "Place cleared out in a hurry."

"The free mimosa brunch at the Sheraton only lasts until eleven."

Father Barton, a practical, handsome priest now surviving clergy infighting for his fourth decade of service, met Dallas and Susan halfway to the pulpit. He had big hands and a firm grip, none of that lily-of-the-valley wilted-finger stuff. " 'Lo, Dallas." Barton's voice echoed off high-beamed ceilings.

In spite of the father's gregarious nature, Dallas whispered his reply. Since he only made it to church for funerals, Dallas very closely related spirituality with death. As such, the whole religious icon decor thing spooked him a little.

"I have a problem," Barton said loudly enough to stir resting spirits.

"What's that?"

Barton turned in place with the precision the military drilled into him forty-three years ago. His vestments pivoted around his hips. On a hand-carved half-column set stage right of the pulpit, a bronze urn rested on a gilded purple cloth. Father Barton grabbed the urn with both hands, a strong yet graceful motion, and held it toward Dallas as though presenting a knight with a sword. "I don't know what to do with this."

"What is it?"

"Judge Crenshaw—in slightly modified form." Father Barton smiled at Dallas's puzzlement. "His ashes."

"Ohhh." Dallas didn't like this one bit. Very creepy.

"His son never told me the burial arrangements."

"Oh, yeah . . . ?" Dallas looked around. Where was that liquor-bottle-throwing Pennsylvania lawyer anyway?

Susan said, "He missed the funeral."

"Kids are so ungrateful."

Herbie put down the college physics text he'd bought at a flea market for fifty cents. Long-hair intelligentsia brushing up on a little terminal velocity. "That's not what I think it is." He considered the urn Dallas carried into the Ocean Tides lobby.

"Little souvenir from the funeral," Dallas whispered.

"We're not keeping it in here."

"My sentiments exactly." Dallas set the urn on the counter like it might go off. "I'll give you ten bucks to take it home."

"Uh-uh. I'm not taking responsibility for someone's eternity."

"Twenty."

"Forget it."

"All right, then . . ." Dallas looked toward the room log. "How we doing occupancywise?"

"Nine rooms open."

"Give Judge Crenshaw something with a view."

"Are we using his real name or will the judge be having a little afterlife tryst he'll want to keep quiet?"

"Who knows. Register him under Mr. Ash. But do it later. Right now I need a ride to get my car out of jail."

12

"**H**EY, DALLAS, GOOD TO see you again. You, too, Herb." Carney Reuwer unlocked the chain gate and rolled it open.

Carney was a stub of a man, short arms, legs, and fingers; a body built for climbing in, under, and around cars. He favored hats Dallas had last seen cocked rakishly on Goober's head while pumping gas into Sheriff Taylor's Mayberry PD squad car.

In his prime, Carney had been a car thief and a real estate salesman to varying degrees of success. As the result of a guilty plea ten years ago, he'd been sentenced to two hundred hours of community service, which he'd logged minding the Ocean City impound lot. He took to the job so well, the city hired him full-time, even kept him when he later served two years on work release for time-share fraud.

Carney lived on the scorched-earth lot in a tin-can trailer. It was a quiet, meditative life fit for a poet. His naps in a hammock slung between oak trees were interrupted only now and then by tow trucks bringing in illegally parked cars.

For company, Carney kept a junkyard German shepherd, Edsel. Edsel had a mean bark, but was a real sweetheart, and would have been fun to pet were it not his habit to roll in used motor oil.

"Keeps the mosquitoes off him, though," Carney proclaimed, perhaps speaking from experience. Carney stayed in such constant contact with engine oils his skin seemed tattooed by it.

Edsel loped over to Dallas. His fur was matted and congealed like a reggae singer gone swimming in a tar pit. Panting energetically despite the heat, his wagging tail flicked beads of 10W-30.

Dallas said, "You should hang a No Smoking sign around this pup. Someone drops a match near him, he's going to explode."

Carney directed Dallas and Herbie to where Dallas's 280 rested comfortably in the shade of a stand of pines. "Recognized her as soon as she come in. Said, uh-oh, Dallas done got hisself towed again."

Dallas wasn't an especially conscientious parker. There were too many restrictions where you could or couldn't leave your car these days. To Dallas's way of thinking, if it was okay to park there when he was a kid, he continued to do it. Forget that a twenty-story condo now stood on the lot and you needed a permit.

"I already done cleaned off fingerprint powder the cops left on the inside. Didn't wash the outside, though. Afraid if I knock off some of that rust she might fall apart on me. Fixed your ignition, though. Joyriders didn't beat it too bad."

"I appreciate it. Send the bill to the motel, all right?"

"That's okay. I wadn't doin' nothing else." Carney circled a leftover rain puddle and bent over by the rear tires. Both were as flat as Dallas had last seen them. "Somebody done you good." Nose almost on the dirt, Carney fixed plier tips against the right rear tire and tugged.

With effort, he removed a dark silver nail about four inches long, a quarter inch in diameter, with grooves along its side. Bent like the letter L, it was sticky with an amorphous jelly ball of goo around its head.

Carney tossed it to Dallas's feet and rapped the left tire. "You got a twin over here."

Dallas examined what had punctured his tire.

"Masonry nail," Herbie said.

Carney crawled to the other side of the 280. Flat on his back, he banged Dallas's tail pipe. "Muffler's almost shot."

"Uh-huh." When it started dragging down Ocean Highway, Dallas would replace it.

Carney put the pliers to the second flat and inched out from under Dallas's car with an exact match of the first nail, L shape and all.

Herbie rubbed one of the masonry nails between his fingers, examining the gluey substance stuck to it. "Answers that."

"What?"

"How someone drove your car on two flats."

"Fix-A-Flat," Carney said, leaning against the 280's trunk. "Once you left the car, somebody came along, popped aerosol gunk in your tires. Gives 'em enough air and a temporary patch job. They could've gotten fifteen minutes, half hour out of it."

"Tricky setup," Herbie said. Kneeling by one flattened tire, he set a nail on the dirt, point side up, and wedged it against tread. "You bend the nail, lay it here, maybe get the tip to penetrate a little rubber to hold it in place. The bottom half of the nail's braced against the ground, so when the car backs up—*thhupp!*—in it goes." Herbie stood. "Although it probably wouldn't work on dirt like this." He scraped his tennis shoe over pale earth. "Too soft.

The nail would get driven into the ground." Herbie twirled long hair around his finger. "What's Crenshaw's driveway made of?"

"Macadam."

"That would do it."

"So it was a practical joke after all. The judge gives me two flats, then grabs my car, pumps in Fix-A-Flat, and joyrides it."

"Kinda funny," Herbie said. "Shows some thought."

"So then how does he get run over by the car *he's* driving?"

Carney strolled to the front of the 280 and peered along the impacted lines of the hood. "Car didn't hit no judge," he said.

"According to Brent Bannister it did."

Carney made a face. "That tightassed sissy. His father *prosercuted* me ten years ago. He weren't no good, either." Carney had something pinched between his fingers.

Herbie said, "I'll be damned."

Stuck in Carney's oily fingertips were short strands of coarse hair. "Deer fur," Carney said. "This car didn't hit no judge less'n he'd grown antlers."

Ash and Jim arrived at Carney's lot half an hour later. The young entrepreneur owners of Worcester County's only no-name-brand gas station, they bounced two wheels (rims and tires) off their will-it-make-it-another-mile tow truck.

"They don't match," Dallas said of the wheels.

Burning cigarette stuck between his lips, six six, size sixteen work boots, Jim said, "They're free."

"I like 'em fine."

Ash, a born supervisor, watched while Jim started jacking the 280.

"But why," Dallas asked, "do I have the feeling there's two three-wheeled Datsuns somewhere within five miles of here?"

"That's gratitude," Ash snapped indignantly. Pushing back a shock of red-brown hair, he wiped sweat from his forehead. A former municipal bus driver, Ashley had an entire apartment wallpapered with traffic citations and court notices. From firsthand experience, he was so knowledgeable of district court procedure, especially appeals, that Dallas often referred clients to him. Crashly may have been a bad driver, but he was a damned fine paralegal. Probably could whip Mack Trial in court.

Jim had the right flat off already, so good at jacking cars and switching tires, he could do it in the dark—which was how he usually operated. "You want these patched?"

"Yeah, just don't steal the rubber off someone else's car."

"Gratitude," Ash snapped again, holding on to the tow hook, watching Jim work. "By the way"—Ash removed a crisp laminated business card from his shirt pocket—"we're in a new business." He turned the card over in his hand like a magician, presenting it to Dallas print side up. "Limo drivers."

"Hot Seat Drivers, a division of Door Dings, Incorporated."

"Our motto is: 'You pick the car, we'll pick you up in it.' "

Carney Reuwer looked on like a proud father at graduation day. "Taught 'em the tools of my former trade. Slim Jim and Hot Wire, I call 'em."

Dallas handed back the card. "You boys might want to consider bringing on a bail bondsman as a partner."

"No," Ash said, "we'll call you. You're free."

Dallas had just pulled onto Route 50, heading back to OC, when he jerked the 280 onto the shoulder and hit the brakes. Old bottles of suntan oil and a busted flip-flop shifted violently across the open hatchback.

Dallas got out and opened the canvas cover that used to be his trunk. He rooted around like a pig working overtime in a truffle field. Busted umbrella, dog-eared paperbacks, cassette tapes stuck with sand, Popeye's chicken napkins, Hawaiian Tropic Royal Tanning Gel, golf tees, a crushed cup from the Dairy Queen, condom wrapper, more golf tees, more condom wrappers. Hell. No box. No box that Judge Crenshaw had given him, a container to be opened in the event of the judge's death.

13

T HE OCEAN TIDES LOBBY was empty, or so Dallas thought until Jill hopped up behind the front desk, laid her arms across the counter, and said, "Can I help—? Oh, it's you. Hi." Smiling wave.

For a second, Dallas thought Susan had gone blond and shrunk; but this was the little girl who'd hustled him out of ten bucks last night racing hermit crabs. Dallas found her smile uplifting. "What're you doing here?"

"Aunt Susan said I'm in charge."

"*Aunt* Susan?"

"Yeah," Jill sang. "That's what she said I could call her." She hefted the registration ledger onto the counter. No easy task. "I'm doing good, too. Want to see? We're almost booked." She pointed out four rooms she'd rented, adding proudly: "And none of them are lawyers. Susan said, *you* said, no lawyers."

"Nice job." Jill had even given the new guests cash receipts for their deposits, a bookkeeping exercise Dallas frequently overlooked. "Are we paying you for this?"

"I don't know." She shrugged cheerily.

"Well, we'll talk about it." Dallas started toward his office and motel room home beyond. The storm had probably kicked up some good waves. He could get in some rides, hang out on the beach—

"Aunt Susan said you should go up to the war room and see her."

"Don't tell her I'm here, okay? Our secret." Dallas was halfway through the office when Jill picked up the phone.

"Aunt Susan. Hi. It's Jill. He's back."

Had yet again, Dallas returned to the lobby. "Why did you do that?"

"We women have to stick together."

Room 100 was normally referred to around the Ocean Tides as a wreck room. This was where all the busted TVs, sofas, and window air conditioners were stored until Herbie got around to fixing them (making the place look a wreck, even by Ocean Tides' standards). It only became a war room for that one case that seemed to crop up every summer.

The view was first-floor mediocre: tourists strolling the board-walk interrupted sight of the beach and ocean beyond. The window air conditioner, and three others like it stacked against the wall, didn't work.

Susan had the sliding-glass door open, but that was more wishful thinking than anything else. Nothing short of snow would cool the room off today.

"Get your car back?"

"Most of it."

"How's that?"

Dallas told her about his tires being sabotaged and Judge Crenshaw's box being missing. "I went back and asked Carney if he'd seen it. He said no."

"Are you sure you left it in the car?"

"I think so."

"A man gives you a box to be opened in the event of his death and you're not sure what you did with it?"

"Sus, I thought it was a gag. A box of springy snakes that was going to erupt when I opened it."

"Maybe whoever gave you the flats took the box."

"*Crenshaw* gave me the flats."

"Gave you the flats, stole your car, took back the box, then threw himself in front of a speeding car. *That* is an extremely good practical joke."

"How about gave me the flats, stole my car, took the box, and got hit by a car walking home."

"So how did *his* car end up in his driveway?"

"What?"

"You're saying Crenshaw followed you from his house to steal your car once the tires went flat. . . . How did he follow you? If he took his own car, he'd have to leave it to drive yours."

"There's only one road from Crenshaw's to here. He could've come behind me on foot knowing the car would be left somewhere along the way."

"Too far to walk and too speculative. The tires might not have gone flat. You might have driven it home regardless. Or stayed and waited for help." Susan shook her head. "I don't think Crenshaw was playing a joke on you, Dallas. I don't know what happened, but I don't think it was a joke."

"Wouldn't it be great, though, if God had a bizarre sense of humor. Sees Crenshaw faking he's afraid of being killed and then—*zam!*" Dallas clapped his hands loudly. "Runaway car. One dead judge."

"Until you get a sign of biblical proportions, I think I'll keep sorting through *these* boxes"—referring to the R-Kive containers—"for a hint what was in the one you lost."

Susan was two hours into Judge Crenshaw's files and had them spread across tandem double beds and a kitchenette table in preparation for inventory. It looked a lot like work to Dallas.

Work was what Dallas always had good intentions of getting around to, if only there was time. . . . Right now he was more interested in how Susan had dressed to survive the heat: sleeves of her white T-shirt rolled up like a sexy gang member.

Dallas flopped down on one of the beds, messing up files.

"Hey, be careful." Susan tugged a folder from under his butt. "I'm onto something here."

Dallas reached for her. "I want to go swimming. You want to go swimming? Let's go swimming."

Susan concentrated on business, disciplined like that. "Did Judge Crenshaw mention anything to you about Jumbi Berrell?"

Dallas sighed. He wanted to bodyboard in the ocean.

"Jumbi Berrell?" Susan asked again.

"Sounds like a Cajun restaurant."

"I take that as a no." Susan sat on the sofa and opened a file across her lap. "Jumbi Berrell's doing twenty years for attempted murder. The attempted murder of Judge Crenshaw."

Dallas stared at the ceiling. "When was this?"

"Nine years ago."

"Hmmm. So let's see . . ." Dallas gently guided his brain into gear. ". . . nine years . . . he'd be up for parole—"

"He *has* been up for parole—twice already. Each time Crenshaw wrote letters to the parole board urging them not to grant it. And each time they kept Berrell in."

"So Jumbo's still in because of Crenshaw's say-so?"

"*Jumbi.*" Susan tossed Dallas the manila folder; it landed on his stomach. "Check it out. Almost a crime of passion."

Dallas found a ten-year-old statement of charges. *State of Maryland* v. *Jumbi T. Berrell*. "Jumbi's his real name, huh?"

"Looks that way."

Dallas read the statement aloud: " 'On or about July nine, at one-fifteen P.M., the subject, Jumbi T. Berrell, did enter the Baltimore County District Courthouse. Berrell approached Officer Walling and asked Walling where Judge Crenshaw's courtroom was.

" 'Walling smelled the odor of an alcoholic beverage about Berrell's breath and asked the subject if he had been drinking. At this time, the subject became belligerent and asked Walling where he got off asking if he'd been drinking. Whereupon, Walling grasped the subject's arm in an attempt to detain him. The subject struck Walling in the throat and gained access to Courtroom One at which point he did draw a weapon: a Beretta nine-millimeter handgun. Berrell fired one round of said weapon into the ceiling.' "

Dallas turned the page. " 'At this point, the subject became irate and demanded to see Judge Crenshaw. He swore and used profanity, calling the judge a pervert, queer, asshole, bastard and mother-f. Judge Crenshaw entered the courtroom from the rear hall and ordered the subject to put down his weapon. The subject responded by firing his weapon at Judge Crenshaw two times. Both shots lodged in the wall behind the judge.' "

Dallas tossed down the report, having read ahead. "And then, blah, blah, blah, the responding officers seized and arrested the subject. So," he asked Susan, "what were Jumbi Berrell's shorts all in a knot about?"

"A week earlier, Crenshaw heard an *ex parte* petition filed by Berrell's wife. She said Berrell was a threat to her and their daughters. Crenshaw signed an order temporarily restraining Berrell from the family home or from having contact with his wife or two girls. But while Berrell's barred from the apartment, the wife packs up and goes splitsville with her boyfriend—some weight lifter she met at Holiday Spas. She took the two girls and ended up in hiding in Phoenix. Berrell went to the police, but they wouldn't help him locate his wife or take a kidnapping report because he was on record—wrongfully, he claimed—as being abusive."

"Turns out he was, though, huh?"

"Berrell blamed Crenshaw for causing him to lose his family. When he went to trial for Crenshaw's attempted murder, he had character witnesses testify he was a mild, hardworking man."

"They all say that." Dallas rolled onto his side. "Jumbo have any priors?"

"The report doesn't say. Jum*bi* said he was extremely remorseful. That pressure had driven him over the edge. And that he hadn't intended to kill Crenshaw, he just wanted to get his attention."

"He should have tried writing."

"Judge Reiner gave Berrell twenty years."

"Steep. Berrell probably had Mack Trial defending him."

"No," Susan said, "but close. Trial was the prosecutor."

"Probably the last case he won. Small world, though, huh?"

"Jumbi's coming up again for parole. In three weeks." Susan

withdrew a typed page from Crenshaw's files. "Here's the letter the judge was working on to send the parole board. It doesn't look like he mailed it."

Dallas scanned the letter. A rough draft; terse, mean, angry, vindictive—pure Raymond Crenshaw.

"And there's something else." Susan fanned her face with a folder and pointed to a stack of Crenshaw's files. "I haven't gone through them in detail, but Crenshaw has been contacting a lot of people about clients Trial represented in private practice—represented *and* botched. I can't tell for sure, but it looked like Crenshaw was about to unleash a one-man war against TV's favorite lawyer."

The phone rang.

Susan answered. "Hello . . . Hi, honey." Covering the mouthpiece, she told Dallas: "It's Jill."

"Tell her she's hired and you and Herbie are fired."

Susan appeared concerned, not about Dallas's comment, but what Jill was saying. "No, it's not a real person like Betty Crocker or Mrs. Butterworth. . . . I'll tell him. Thanks for the call." Susan hung up.

"Who's not a real person like Betty Crocker?"

"Victoria Secrets." Susan tried not to scowl. "Vicky Sterrett wants to see you. Supposedly it's urgent."

14

Lɪғᴇ sɪᴛᴜᴀᴛɪᴏɴs ᴡᴇʀᴇ ᴀʟᴡᴀʏs urgent with Vicky Sterrett since she'd evolved from mild-mannered law student and closet seductress to high-profile litigator. The formidable sea change, by definition, required her every act and gesture to be of extreme importance.

Vicky was addicted to the rush of power and influence; her fix was to handle cases like violent twisters upon which she rode tail with a taming whip.

Dallas would try to hold on.

Crossing tidal wetlands by the arched footbridge connecting Vicky's suite hotel to its sister restaurant on the bay, Dallas began to anticipate his ex-lover's presence. God, but she could mesmerize—even more dangerously than Susan.

Dallas wanted to admire, love, worship, tend to, caress, and hold Susan forever. Vicky's ability to bewitch called up urges in him that were much more feral—temporary, hedonistic, and, ultimately, lamentable, because while the electricity of her touch was formidable, the anticipation that she would inevitably run off—again—made it such a shallow deceit.

Knowing all this—and knowing the sight of her would make him forget everything *but* the sight of her—Dallas drew a deep breath of hot afternoon and walked inside Fager's Island restaurant.

When originally built, Fager's was considered a bold venture—starting a business on the then mostly ignored "still water" coast of the island. Its success spawned a blitz of waterfront eateries offering tourists tropical deck drinks and brilliant sunsets.

As a kid, Dallas had spent lots of time on the bay trapping minnows and frogs, so growing up to slurp rum drinks in bars built where minnows once swam seemed a logical, if not somewhat poisoned, progression.

Fager's was stylish, though no longer unique in its decor of glass, dark woods, and hanging plants. Linen tablecloths and napkins were favored in the dining room, while the bar offered a more casual ambience.

Vicky was in the bar, easy enough to find with heads turned her way like compasses seeking north. She sat alone at a polished table, washed in sunlight filtered through an etched window.

With one foot propped sexily on the brass rail of the chair beside her, Vicky wore a double-breasted suit, gray with taupe ticking, and not a damned thing beneath it. The suit's soft lines lay against her body like a long, liquid embrace.

"Dallas." She proclaimed his name dramatically, as though long separated—much longer than since last night. Standing, she pulled his arms around her, pressed forward, and kissed him lavishly on the lips.

A dozen guys at the bar seethed with envy. Vicky's spell had been tossed out like a fisherman's net and record catches were jumping in.

"I hope you don't mind meeting here." Vicky released him and sat down, tossing all that wavy blond hair over her shoulders. "I had to get out of the hotel for a while. I was going a little stir-crazy."

Dallas resisted the chair closest to her; best keep the table between them so he could face the bay and eye the horizon like a wary pilot; keep level with it lest he crash and burn. "So, what's up?" He tried desperately to maintain a casual posture, half slouched in his tennis shirt, shorts, and sockless deck shoes.

"A couple things . . ." Vicky paused when a waiter approached.

Having been told she was waiting for a "dear friend," the waiter had lain back like an assassin. He now took up position just off Vicky's shoulder, trying none too covertly to look down the front of her blazer.

Vicky asked Dallas if he'd eaten.

"No."

"I'll pay. Order what you like."

Dallas didn't need the menu. He told the waiter he'd have the gigolo platter, then said he was kidding when the stiff-shirted man appeared stunned. "Make it a cheeseburger, rare, lots of onions—the red ones if you've got them—and mustard—the yellow kind, not that brown fancy stuff. And a rum on ice."

Vicky commented, "I like a man who drinks in the middle of the afternoon. It shows a certain something."

"Yeah, that I've got nothing to do the rest of the day."

Vicky ordered salmon with some kind of sauce Dallas couldn't spell on a bet, and a bottle of wine of similar grandiose christening.

Their order taken, the waiter roamed off toward the kitchen.

"Do you remember when we were in law school," Vicky said, "that little place on Charles Street we used to go to for breakfast?

You ate piles of pancakes and helped me with torts cases."

Dallas didn't want to remember, but he did.

"God," she exclaimed, "but that was fun. It seemed so complicated, but it was all so easy, wasn't it?"

What happened to you? Dallas wanted to ask. Why did you have to change? But he'd been asking that question—hypothetically—to most people he'd ever felt close to all his life. Eventually, they *all* changed and moved on, and the warmth they'd once generated in him flickered only in memory.

"How goes Crenshaw's will?" Dallas asked, diverting Vicky's reminiscing because it was too early in the day to get maudlin; sunset was hours off.

Although Vicky was intent on lingering in the past, she allowed Dallas to change the subject. "It's interesting. I never thought when Crenshaw walked into my office he'd end up putting all these balls in play."

"Such as?"

"In the past twelve hours, I've gotten two calls from his clients. One mysterious. One angry. And then there's his son, who is not exactly ecstatic about this new will. It seems Harvey—"

"The son?"

"Yes. Harvey was PR under his father's second-most-recent will and was—shall we say—pissed off at being replaced. He also wasn't real keen on your being paid to investigate his father's death."

"So I gathered. He was waiting for me last night when I got back from your place—threw a bottle at me."

"He's harmless. A spoiled, frustrated little boy. Never enough of a man to step out of his father's shadow and make a name for himself. That's why he went to Pennsylvania to practice. He's bounced around three or four firms since he left Legal Aid in Wilkes-Barre. He just can't quite make it." Casting aspersions from the mountaintop, Vicky made not being able to succeed as a lawyer sound like a weakness.

Dallas asked, "How tall is he? Crenshaw's son?"

"About six foot, give or take."

"Fat? Thin?"

"Medium, I suppose. I thought you said you met him."

"He was in his car. Never got out. But earlier this morning? At Crenshaw's funeral? Someone about that size took a shot at Mack Trial."

"You're kidding." Vicky laughed. "Lenny Sawgrass got shot at? That's priceless. It was probably a disgruntled client. I've heard there're some malpractice cases floating around against him. He's supposed to be at war with his insurance carrier trying to get them to settle. And Lenny—pardon me, *Mack Trial*—is up to his ass in loans he's having trouble keeping even on."

"Trial's in financial trouble?"

"Overextended *I* hear." Vicky was more than happy to rumorize. "He didn't open thirty offices in six years without some backing. And all that advertising? My God, he's looking at a few million a year in overhead before he takes home a dime. And lots of his offices are a joke. He's got them staffed with kids just out of law school and has paralegals working personal injury cases from interview to settlement. People are signing away on permanent injuries without ever having a lawyer so much as eyeball their case. It's scary, but, you know, Trial's on TV. People believe TV."

Across the restaurant, the waiter and wine steward were arguing about who was going to have the privilege of delivering Vicky's wine. The waiter, set on a fistfight if that's what it took, prevailed and, having broken a slight sweat, returned tableside and offered the bottle of wine for Vicky's perusal.

Vicky said the wine was fine.

The waiter popped open the bottle and poured while considering the gaped front of her blazer.

At least, Dallas thought, the prewine ritual was avoided: all that sniffing of corks, swirling a quarter inch of wine in a glass, holding it up to the light, swishing it around one's mouth like a shot of Scope, then nodding, *oh, very good, very good, sir.* It was sour grape juice, for God's sake. Something a medieval French marketing whiz dreamed up to bolster Louis the Second-or-something's overseas trade.

When the waiter finally withdrew, Dallas said, "So who were Crenshaw's clients who called you?"

"I assume you know Pete Marjani?"

"Not to speak to. We travel in slightly different economic circles."

Marjani was the owner-developer of Hurricane Bay Country Club and its residential properties. A onetime brick mason turned land pirate.

"Marjani called to tell me the stock deal is off with the judge. Because the judge didn't finish the case he was working on for him."

"I heard Crenshaw had office space in the Hurricane Bay clubhouse. It seemed like an odd arrangement."

"Especially since Crenshaw didn't play golf."

"So what was he doing there?"

"I asked Marjani the same thing." Vicky shook her head, sipping wine. "He wouldn't answer. Only that Crenshaw's estate wasn't getting five percent of the club and Marjani wanted his letter of intent vacated."

"What'd you say?"

"That I'd look into it, but if Crenshaw's entitled to five percent you can bet your ass I'm getting it for the estate."

"Not just because your PR commission's based on the estate's value," Dallas said, in a tone suggesting, *certainly not*.

"I'm having the firm fly over a CPA to take a look at Hurricane Bay's books. They'll give me an idea what five percent would run."

"Good luck. A Hurricane Bay stockholder came to me a couple years ago wanting to file suit because Marjani welshed on a promise to pay dividends while the corporation bought him a new Sedan DeVille."

"Pete Marjani," Vicky assured, "is no match for the team of investigators and litigators I can have swoop in here from D.C. with *one* phone call. I'll have him praying so hard he won't realize he broke his kneecaps kneeling down." Vicky's eyes lit up like she'd just done a line of pure coke. The addiction and the fix.

Nasty habit, Dallas thought. Mercenary and soulless.

Dallas's rum—nearly forgotten—finally made it to the table, delivered at a pace as though it had inched itself across the floor to the quiet thump of taped reggae music playing out on the deck.

Vicky thanked the waiter and asked if he would check on their food. The guy dashed—goddamned sprinted—to the kitchen, making Dallas wonder why waiters, salesmen, *any* guy acted like that around a pretty woman. Like she'd be so impressed by his service she'd throw herself across the table and moan, "Take me, I'm yours." Why *did* guys do stuff like that? Why did *he* do stuff like that?

Dallas drank his rum. "Who was your second client call—after Marjani?"

"A woman named Pamela Meyers. She was the mysterious one. She asked if I knew about the matter—the 'matter,' not the 'case'—Judge Crenshaw had been working on for her. When I said I hadn't had time to review the judge's open cases yet, she thanked me very politely and hung up."

"That was it?"

"That was it."

"Huh." Dallas figured if Vicky was going to get into the judge's pending case files, he should probably confess having them. Although as much as it seemed like they were on the same side, he couldn't overcome the sense Vicky was just on her own side. A team of one.

She was beautiful, though—the way she looked at him now: holding her wineglass close to her lips for a long pause; the liquor's rich hue reflecting across her cheeks as she seemed lost in diverting thought.

"Can I ask you something?" she asked, her tone reminding him of the Vulnerable Vicky he hadn't heard from in years. "Something about back in law school?"

"Sure."

Vicky set down her glass and met his eyes. "Why did you leave me?"

15

"**W**HY DID I LEAVE YOU?" Dallas couldn't have heard Vicky's question correctly—but he had, hadn't he? "Why did *I* leave *you*?"

"You don't have to answer if you don't want to."

"Vicky, I didn't leave. *You* left me."

"What?" She was clearly accused. "Dallas, I came back from a weekend visiting my parents and you were gone. After that, it was nothing more than polite smiles from you. So I figured, okay, it's something I've—"

Dallas, who had been shaking his head, waved a hand in protest. She had it all wrong. "Vicky, you spent the weekend with Jack Whiting. The day you left—*supposedly* to see your parents—I decided to hook Con Law and walk back to the apartment to see you off. I was at the corner . . . I can still picture it—this crisp autumn afternoon, long shadows across the street, smelling baklava cooking in that Greek restaurant down the block—I'm standing there when you came out of the building, weekend bag over your shoulder, wearing a white sweater and blue jeans. Your hair was tied back. You were smiling. I was about to call out to you when you snuggled into Jack Whiting's car with him."

"Jack Whiting?" As though she had no idea who that was.

"Come on, Vicky. . . ."

"Dallas, I never had anything going with Jack Whiting. Did you ever see me with him after that?"

"No, but we weren't exactly public knowledge either. Hardly anyone knew we were living together. I went along with it because you were—you *seemed*—so shy. Later, I figured you probably had Jack keeping your relationship with him a secret so you could see us both without the other ever finding out."

Vicky stared at him right meanly for a few seconds, then, abruptly, slapped his cheek and walked out the door.

Dallas, face stinging, told the waiter he'd take his cheeseburger to go.

Dallas slid open the bathroom window and crawled into his motel home. It was an often-used route, designed to avoid any management responsibilities waiting to ambush him in the lobby.

He didn't want to think right now. About Vicky Sterrett, Judge Crenshaw, Mack Trial, or anybody. He wanted to ride the waves and that's what he was going to do.

He changed into Sideout Pro Team shorts, grabbed his Morey bodyboard and Churchill fins, and pitched back out the bathroom window.

The sidewalk was warm from an afternoon of full sun, all evidence of the earlier rain dried by the heat. Dallas liked the feel of tiny pebbles and grains of sand against his bare soles, a sign of callous feet that meant summer was well under way.

He crossed the boardwalk and followed a fenced path through the planted sea grass of a man-reconstructed duneline, a multimillion-dollar anti-beach-erosion boondoggle sure to be demolished by winter's first good nor'easter.

The beach was clearing for the day and the ocean was glorious. Beads of white water whisked off curving breakers like bits of frothy meringue whipped off a sugary pie.

Bodyboard under his arm, ankle straps of swim fins dangling from his fingertips, Dallas experienced the euphoria of being here. A sensation that time failed to fade.

Back in law school, not long after he and Vicky had split, he'd considered heading out to Columbus, Ohio, and Capital Law School. He even had the applications filled out when Harry Walsh, an Eastern Shore native and classmate at U of B, said, "Ohio. Man, you know how far that is from an ocean?" Dallas didn't transfer.

Now, diving into the ocean, bodyboard leashed to his wrist, he swam toward the breakpoint. Two kids were out "in the line," their colorful swimsuits standing out against the sea like ornaments.

They were good. Very adept at reading the swells and getting into them early. Hard boards slicing along the tube, picking up speed to draw up the curl. They hit the lip to initiate a mean launch out of and above the wave; airborne, they did a three-sixty turn and crash-landed into white water.

Finishing off the ride, the pair, no older than seventeen, bodies lean and raw as distance runners', clasped hands in celebration. "Whoooaa!" "Yes!" They turned and hollered across the waves, "You get that?"

Out farther than Dallas, a girl with a yellow Nikonos III camera strung around her neck kicked up in a swell to pass over a cresting wave. She raised her arms, displaying eight fingers.

The riders celebrated their "score" with another handclasp and headed back to the break line with more energy than Dallas would spend in an entire season.

With the late-day sun warm across his back, Dallas paddled over to them. "You guys are good."

The blond of the duo lay flat on his board, wiping salt water from his eyes.

The darker of the pair—South Seas heritage in there somewhere—said, "Thanks, man. Thanks a lot." Polite, but not really friendly. Sometimes the kids were like that: suspicious of anyone over twenty; who is this old fart?

Dallas said, "You guys are new around here. You'd've been noticed before."

"Yeah," was all the darker one said.

Sixty yards across the water, their "girlfriend" watched with concern. It was hard to determine her age at that distance, but from the lean shape of her body and string bikini she wore, she was likely no older than the boys.

Whatever the deal was, Dallas was clearly making them uncomfortable. "Well," he said. "Enjoy it. We don't get many waves like these."

A nice swell was building off to the north. Dallas paddled fiercely and caught its edge. As the wave's clean power drew him along her line, he pitched the Morey at a slashing forty-five degrees across her face. A plain, simple ride, nothing fancy—exhilarating nonetheless.

He rode all the way to shore as was his habit—a very unpro move. Getting to his feet, dripping tepid ocean water, he looked down the beach.

The two bodyboarders had come in on a wave behind him. Their photographer bodysurfed a small swell after that. Joining the boys on the beach, she led them across the sand. When they were halfway to the boardwalk, she looked back at Dallas like he might be following them.

"What'd I do?" he asked himself out loud.

He was still wondering about them half an hour and a dozen rides later when Susan and Jill came to the water's edge, hollering something he couldn't hear over the waves.

He caught a mediocre ride in, and as the smooth underside of his board skimmed the shore, Jill splashed toward him in shallow water, wearing her white jeans with the tar-stained knees. Susan was close behind.

"What's up?"

Jill squatted down. "Jumbi Berrell," she said urgently, although not sure why.

Dallas looked at Susan.

She said, "He's out of jail. Never came back from a work-release assignment four days ago."

16

"SYSTEM'S SO SCREWED UP it was a day and a half before anyone took action. Some 'grace period' concept. Let AWOL prisoners think better of it and come back on their own." Chief Rupert Dawson registered these unsolicited complaints in Judge Crenshaw's cabin while producing a mug shot that offered Dallas and Susan their first look at Jumbi Berrell.

Berrell's face alone was befitting a restraining order. Slicked-back hair. Mean eyes set under dark, thick brows. "Horsey" lips barely closed over what would be a toothy grin should Berrell choose to smile—something he probably didn't do often.

Dallas couldn't imagine character witnesses claiming Jumbi was mild-mannered unless they'd been threatened.

Dawson said, "Any chance this's the guy took a pop at Mack Trial? He's about the right size. Five eleven, medium build."

Dallas shrugged. "Never got a look at his face."

Susan didn't recognize him either.

Dawson put away the photo.

Two detectives were also in the cabin. Tawes and Pritchett wore near-matching Sears poplin suits like backup singers in a tel-evangelist choir. Normally assigned to missing persons, they dou-ble-dutied at forensics on an as-needed basis.

Presently, they were dusting Crenshaw's cabin for prints. Vac-uuming for fibers came next. Tasks left undone when the original circumstances of Crenshaw's death tended to indicate an accident.

"The reason you're here," Dawson informed Dallas and Susan, "is because newspapers delivered after Crenshaw's death had been brought inside. There's two empty glasses in the sink. . . . I figure maybe you helped yourselves to a little look around after Bannister wrote out those charges against you. Seems like your style. If that's the case, I want to know where your fingerprints might turn up. Don't want to give that little peckerwood Bannister anything to hang you."

"I appreciate that, Rup."

"Bannister's a little know-it-all prick. It's gonna give me pleasure to tell him about the deer fuzz on your car. Carney Reuwer called about that."

"Speaking of my car, did you find out who joyrode in it?"

Dawson shook his head. "Been wiped clean of prints. What about in here?"

"We touched lots of stuff."

"I'm assuming you'd tell me if you found something good."

"We're working on it," Susan said.

While Tawes and Pritchett did their science project on Crenshaw's house, dusting for prints and vacuuming hairs that may or may not turn out to be Jumbi Berrell's, Dallas and Susan prowled around outside.

"Watch your step," Dallas warned, reminding her of the tripwire that had sent him sprawling.

Development had left the woodlands mostly undisturbed save a water and sewer easement that cut a cleared swatch through the northeast corner. That stripe of land, which crossed neighboring properties as well, was clearly marked with warnings not to dig or plant between red stakes. County work crews mowed it monthly during growing season.

Along with cut lengths of drying grass and shriveled weeds, the easement revealed the tire tracks of maintenance vehicles and mountain bikes, footprints and paw tracks. Residents made use of the casually restricted line as a path, like the two middle-aged women walking aerobically toward Dallas and Susan now. Outfitted in new sweat suits, breathing deeply, they nodded and continued on.

"Looks to run a long way," Dallas said of the easement. Checking both directions, he couldn't see where the narrow clearing ended. "Probably meets up with roads eventually. Whoever was snooping around Crenshaw's house had plenty of ways in and out. They could have driven in with a four-wheeler."

A few parcels away, one of Crenshaw's neighbors was having a cookout. Smoky hickory weaved its way through the trees.

Dallas pushed away low branches of soft white pines. Where the forest met a cleared five-acre building lot, a low metal barricade fence had been erected. The crosshatch pattern of dull silver was mostly concealed by aggressive honeysuckle vines.

The remaining boundaries of the expansive, manicured lawn were walled by knee-high brick topped with spans of ornate wrought iron. Polished Williamsburg lights crowned brick pillars at twelve-foot intervals.

The home "protected" by these fences was a three-story farmhouse estate, painted beige with a slate roof.

A family cookout was being held on a raised stone patio. Attended by three generations, the fifty-three-year-old patriarch of which manned an oversized grill.

A three-martini-lunch man, big and barrel-chested, the roar of his conversation and laughter carried across the lawn. A personality so powerful it influenced all those around him. He flipped burgers and steaks with authority, flames from the grill licking his arms, cooking for the twenty-plus group at the patio and swimming pool beside it.

The postures of all his guests, even those seated far from him, seemed to tilt slightly back from their host, a telling body language showing through happy smiles and pleasant chatter. This man ran the show. He knew it. And they knew it.

His name was Pete Marjani. Owner, developer, and builder of Hurricane Bay Country Club. The man who told Victoria Secrets he wasn't giving Judge Crenshaw five percent ownership in the club because Crenshaw hadn't finished what he was working on for him.

▽

17

"**N**OTHING," SUSAN SAID. "Not one blessed thing."

Back at the Ocean Tides, Dallas and Susan went through Crenshaw's files again—and in some cases, yet again. It was now nine-thirty, four hours after undertaking another search of Crenshaw's house (which had been objected to by the fingerprinting Tawes and Pritchett until a phone call to Rupert Dawson told them to stay out of Susan's way; Dallas having been cleared by inference).

In neither locale had they discovered so much as a reference to Pete Marjani or Hurricane Bay.

"Which means—" Dallas began.

Susan finished his thought: "Someone already snatched it from Crenshaw's house."

"Or . . . ?"

"It's in the office Crenshaw recently set up in the Hurricane Bay clubhouse."

"Which means . . . ?"

"Marjani could have it—whatever *it* might be—and will use or destroy it, as best suits him."

Dallas lay across the bed. The jalapeño peppers he and Susan had had with their Popeye's chicken dinner were still warm on his tongue. "I could always ask Marjani."

"Probably not a good idea. Someone with something to hide has an advantage knowing who might be looking."

Dallas reached for the phone. "I was hoping you'd say that." He dialed the lobby. "Herbie?" His frazzled-hair manager was on the desk. "You feel like doing some night work?"

"Dallas," Susan warned. "Don't!"

"We'll leave in"—Dallas checked the wreck/war room's wall clock, which only had a little hand. Close enough—"half an hour. Say, ten o'clock."

"Dallas," Susan repeated once he'd hung up the phone, "if Crenshaw left any evidence he was working on something for Pete Marjani, it could be anywhere."

"But probably at the clubhouse. Marjani's not the sort of man to take his work home. His wife could ask what he was doing and he might have to talk to her."

"But it *could* be anywhere."

"But it's probably in the clubhouse."

"Brent Bannister will love it if you get caught."

"Yeah, I know, but that's negative thinking. Think positive, Sus. Positive."

She tried. "I have enough money to lend you to make bail?"

"There you go."

"Well, I'd say we're a little underdressed for the occasion."

"Hell's bells." In the passenger seat of Herbie's VW, pulled onto the tilted shoulder of the Big Drive, Dallas looked two hundred yards ahead at the Hurricane Bay clubhouse.

It was lit up like a Fourth of July sparkler. Footlights lining the entrance drive shone across delicate fronds of palm trees Marjani trucked in every spring from a Florida nursery. Fountains—Marjani was big on running water—spewed excited squirts into the air that were caught in flight by green, orange, and blue floodlights.

Three flags were hoisted above the club's manicured lawn: the U.S. and state banners shouldering Marjani's own corporate logo.

Cars overflowed the parking lot and littered the grassy side not only of Big Drive, but her right-handed offshoot, Sliced Way. Most of the vehicles were oversized four-doors, late-model Caddies, Lincoln Town Cars, Buick Park Avenues, Olds Delta 88s. Big, eight-cylinder gas hogs that had been to Golf Mecca (Myrtle Beach, South Carolina) so often they could find their own way; which was good, seeing as their drivers were usually half inside a pitcher of Bloody Marys or blinded by cigar smoke while at the wheel.

Dallas said, "I've never seen this many cars here in my life."

"We should've called for reservations." Herbie took off his black baseball cap and let long hair fall over his shoulders.

He and Dallas were outfitted in matching Johnny Cash black. Herbie's little kit bag was also black; in it were many gizmos, some high-tech, some not, all designed to help penetrate a security alarm system without detection. The plan had been to break in.

"Son of a bitch." Dallas sighed, considering alternatives.

To their right was Hurricane Bay's swimming pool, an amenity Marjani built three years ago to pacify members whose wives complained there was nothing for them to do at the club (which had been Marjani's intention).

The members told Marjani that without a pool for their wives, they'd have to quit. Marjani barked that the members should be "real men and stand up to their old ladies." To which the members advised their wives would divorce them and they'd be left cash high and dry and unable to pay dues.

Marjani, figuring money and wives was better than no money at all—but not by much—built the pool. Built it his way: in the shape of a golf ball, right down to a dimpled concrete finish; he even got the Titleist company to spring for painting so they could splash their scripted logo across the pool floor.

As further insult, Marjani situated the pool so close to the driving range that errant practice shots zinged in like angry missiles, thereby discouraging swimming without a hard hat. That arrangement lasted only until a risk management team from Hurricane Bay's insurer had a group seizure upon inspection of the layout.

To keep his liability coverage intact, Marjani erected a fifteen-foot chain link fence around the pool. Very ugly. To make appearances even worse, he covered the chain with metal billboards (sold as advertising to golf companies). Now, not only was the fence unsightly, it blocked the sun. Also, whenever a sliced practice shot from the driving range hit a metal billboard, it sounded a frightening *clang-gh-gh-gh-gh-gh* that sent wives and children diving for cover under lounge chairs.

Marjani hadn't expected that. He considered it a dividend, and took such pleasure in watching the ladies scurry for cover that he installed a hidden video camera to tape daily activity around the pool. Highlights were compiled and shown at the annual members-only *men*-only Christmas party.

No doubt about it, Marjani thought his big Titleist golf ball filled with water was his biggest coup ever in the battle of the sexes. He was even working on plans to put a big fountain in the middle of it. Marjani did love that spraying water—reminded him of taking a good piss. "Which is something else," he'd grumble, "women don't know anything about."

After a brief think-tank session, Dallas decided he and Herbie should crash the party, get lost in the crowd, and sneak off to find Crenshaw's office.

Herbie said, "Uh-uh. Boss, there's no way I could ever get *lost* around a bunch of drunks older than my father, who weigh an average of two-forty and think any kid with hair longer than two inches is a communist, drug-fiend 'hom-ah-sexual.' " Herbie opened his door. "You help yourself. I'll take a walk and meet you in an hour."

Dallas wasn't that crazy about his own plan either. He preferred parties where he was the oldest participant by at least ten years, where the guy-girl ratio was minimally one-to-one and people were looking for any excuse to take their clothes off. If he went inside the club and some chubby bottled-water salesman so much as unbuttoned his collar to look for a string of puka shells he'd lost under all his chins, Dallas was heading for the border.

"An hour," Dallas called after Herbie. "And don't leave without me."

Herbie headed for a nature stroll across the golf course, trusting the moon to show the way once he was beyond the clubhouse lights.

Dallas walked the rest of the way up Big Drive.

The clubhouse was a sprawling, recently renovated, nouveau-stately fifteen thousand square feet of brick, wood, glass, and marble. Eye-pleasing touches included orange slice windows, richly stained and shellacked entrance doors, and intricate brickwork personally supervised by expert mason Pete Marjani.

The slate roof was identical to the one on Marjani's house. No doubt a truckload of shingles had "gotten legs" from his members'-dues-paid job site and ended up at Marjani's home near Judge Crenshaw's place.

Dallas could hear Marjani defending invoices to the fiscally conscious board members now: "Well, we gotta buy extree singles because of how many get busted by the cheap labor you guys make me hire."

An inscribed banner stretched between columns over the tile entrance announced tonight's gala as the FIRST ANNUAL MEMBERS GIMMEE. Right away, Dallas smelled a rat. A free party. Parties were like lunches with Pete Marjani; no such thing as a free one. Marjani giving away booze was like his members taking home flowers to their wives: either bribe or apology.

And Marjani was giving away lots of booze. The smell of house-brand whiskey and keg beer wafted through opened double doors like an alcoholic force field. You could get drunk just breathing.

There was no doorman, no bouncer, no activity in the lobby. All the revelry was down the long, carpeted hall where swing music, conversation, and laughter resonated from the Best Ball Ballroom.

Dallas, trying to act like he belonged in his jeans and black tennis shirt, stopped to consider a massive architectural drawing framed and hanging on the moss green lobby wall. It depicted the all-too-familiar layout of Hurricane Bay's golf course, which Dallas had played—always badly—a few times a year since its construction.

The drawing also showed an additional eighteen holes—eighteen holes that didn't exist beyond an architect's imagination. A printed sash draped across a frame corner read, TROPICAL STORM, 18 NEW HOLES IN 18 MONTHS! And in smaller print below that: A PETE MARJANI COMPANY PROJECT.

The proposed par-5 fifth looked like a bitch. Five hundred and thirty yards, double dogleg bordered by a wide stream that crossed the fairway at two strategic positions. Sand bunkers surrounded a long, but narrow, green. Dallas could see himself scoring a 10, no problem. Unless he got lucky and could keep his drive straight, which would be a miracle, but if he could, he might have a shot at laying up—

"Excuse me."

Dallas did a startled half-jump when the hand touched his back. A woman in a fashionable red gown. Even more startling than her having snuck up on him was that she may have been the first woman Dallas had even seen after dark in Pete Marjani's clubhouse who wasn't a hooker.

She was a very polite, handsome, fifty-or-so lady who'd put a great deal of effort into looking nice this evening. She didn't give Dallas's casual attire a second glance, assuming he was the help. Slightly embarrassed, she asked where the little girls' potty was. "My husband told me, but his directions weren't the best, and he gets aggravated if I ask twice."

"I'll show you, if you like," Dallas volunteered. "It is a little tough to find." He guided her down the hall, away from the ballroom.

She looked over her shoulder. "The men's room was back there." As though Dallas was giving her a bum steer.

"I know. But the only women's room is in the ladies' locker room."

"Where's that?"

"About half a mile from here."

"That's not very convenient."

"That's the idea. Not mine, though."

These were difficult times, men/women-wise. Guys like Pete Marjani who brandished the chauvinistic sword were written off as too set in their ways to change; young surfers who called girls "Bettys" were dismissed as too young to know better; which left guys Dallas's age dispatched to some wary emotional no-man's-land, worried about every sentence and nuance being taken the wrong way; conversations with the opposite sex were being homogenized like political mumbo jumbo—as boring as it was inoffensive.

Dallas had worried about that more when he'd practiced law full-time, but now he was at the beach. Rules didn't apply here because this wasn't real life, it was fantasy. A much better place to hang.

Dallas turned right at the bank of conference rooms, heading toward the darkened clubhouse restaurant that overlooked another Marjani-signature fountain spewing behind the eighteenth green. "Some party tonight, huh?" Dallas said, making small talk with the woman in red.

"It's a nice party," she replied without enthusiasm.

"Are you a member?"

"Yes. For a few years now. But this is only my third time to the club. They don't have many functions for women. The club we used to belong to back home had wonderful dances throughout the year. Here"—she made a face—"I came over once to use the pool after it was built, but they were taking away some woman in an ambulance who'd been hit in the ear by a golf ball. I didn't stay."

Score another one for Pete Marjani, Dallas thought.

"I'm not sure my husband is going to remain a member, either." She sounded exasperated—and slightly winded—trailing Dallas down a set of steps carpeted Bermuda-grass green.

The stairwell was evenly lit by sconces shaped like golf balls. The walls were papered in textured pale salmon—a very Florida feel to it. Music from the ballroom was barely audible.

Dallas asked why her husband might quit the club. "Raising dues?"

"Probably. They have every other year. But that's not the reason. It's so crowded on the course he can't get tee times to play." She sounded upset for him. "They bring in so many outside conventions and tournaments, the course ends up being closed to its own members. It started out as one or two days a week for a half-day, and the closed days were always advertised in advance in a monthly newsletter. Whenever that happened, 'A' members—that's what my husband is—were allowed to play any other area course for free." She shook her head. "But not anymore."

"Huh." Dallas didn't know the inner workings of the club; he didn't belong, just played as a guest.

At the bottom of the stairs, Dallas turned left. Way, way, way at the end of the hall, past the men's sports room, men's sports bar, men's lounge, and men's locker room, was the ladies' locker room.

"Gene's been very aggravated about it," the woman continued. "This spring the course was closed as much as three days a week, sometimes Saturdays and Sundays. Gene says he's tired of his dues being used to cover Marjani's overhead so Marjani can bring in tournaments to make more millions."

The relationship, Dallas realized, between the haves and the have-nots was always a tenuous one, especially when the have-nots were paying the haves. Sooner or later, resentment took hold and the have-nots realized what had been true all along: they were being ripped off through the gills.

"Now"—the woman's ire rankled a little in her husband's behalf—"this new course is supposed to be built for members only. That's what this party is for: to settle the angry 'natives.' A lot of Gene's friends have been threatening to quit, too."

Which explained the free drinks.

"Gene doesn't think the new course will make *any* difference. He figures Marjani will start filling that up with tournaments pretty soon too, and push the members out again." She took a breath. All this walking and talking. "Where *are* we going?"

Dallas pointed just ahead. Another woman, also nicely dressed in a backless gown, had just emerged from the ladies' locker room and was trying to find her way back to the dance.

"Thank goodness, I'm about to burst."

Dallas dropped off his red-dress friend and offered to escort Madam Purple Sequins back upstairs. "Are you a member of the club?" he asked—more small talk.

"Not for long, I don't think. My husband is ticked off with how things are being run around this godforsaken hellhole."

"Well," Herbie said, leaning against the curved fender of his yellow VW, "you didn't get arrested. Find anything?"

Dallas half staggered to the car. "I'm exhausted. I must've walked twenty women to the bathroom. I'd no sooner get one back than another one came out and asked where she could go to wee-wee. Look-at-this." Dallas pulled a handful of bills from his pocket. "I got tips."

"Neat."

Dallas got in the car. "Phew." He grabbed his knees. "I'm beat."

"So now what?" Herbie stuck the keys in the ignition, waiting for instructions.

"Well, I might have a new angle. On one trip to the ladies' room I passed Claude Taylor coming out of the sports bar. He said Ronnie

Ward dropped out of their foursome tomorrow morning." Dallas took a breath. "Claude asked if I wanted to join them."

"Doesn't Claude usually play with—?"

"Pete Marjani."

"Man, tips and a lucky break. Boss, you're on a roll."

"Now I gotta remember what I did with my clubs."

"You threw them in the ocean."

"Oh, hell. That's right. Did you get them?"

"As always."

"How much do you want for them?"

"One-fifty."

"One-fifty! Those clubs're fifteen years old."

"A hundred."

"Twenty. I've paid for them five times over buying them back from you."

"Eighty."

"Twenty."

"Seventy."

"Twenty or you're fired."

"Twenty," Herbie conceded. He'd have taken ten.

"Good." Dallas drew another breath. "Maybe tomorrow I'll get to ask Marjani about the new eighteen holes he's building."

"Tropical Storm?"

"How'd you know about that?"

"I'll show you." Herbie started up the VW, ground into first gear, and did a U-turn out of the club.

At the intersection of Big and Bayshore Drives, Herbie took a right and headed toward the bay that had been carved into the wetlands sixty years ago by the last big hurricane to hit Ocean City.

It was dark where the road ended. Ignoring a No Trespassing sign, Herbie braked to a stop on loose paving stones. His headlights, sifting through gravel dust raised by his tires, focused upon a large wooden sign posted on twin four-by-fours.

In neat, painted letters:

COMING SOON
TROPICAL STORM
18 CHALLENGING NEW HOLES OF CHAMPIONSHIP GOLF
A PETE MARJANI COMPANY PROJECT

But over this proud announcement, sprayed in dripping black letters, was a protest: LIKE HELL IT IS!

18

"WHERE DOES YOU WANT THIS?" the he-man asked Dallas. At the opened back of the psychedelic van, he tilted a beer keg in lumberjack arms. The van's interior was covered with multicolored shag carpet from the mid-seventies.

"What is it?"

"Natty Boh Light."

"Oh, my God." Dallas shivered from the prospect of what that beer might taste like.

"So where does you want it?"

"My guess," Dallas said, "is up there." He pointed to the third floor of the Ocean Tides where all the music and screaming were coming from.

Kids were packed on the balcony, dancing, playing Frisbee catch from floor to floor and the parking lot. A beer bong tube ran from the second to the first floor; suds poured in from above were drunk a level below.

"You payin' for this?" the beer lugger asked, following Dallas and Herbie toward the stairs.

"I would hope not, but probably. Who called you?"

"Somebody named Chad."

"Then unless he still has his father's credit card—"

"I don't take no credit! You crazy? This operation's illegal as hell already. Deliverin' beer to a bunch a underage kids?"

Somebody shouted, "Duck!" as Dallas reached the second floor.

A cooler was dumped out; what had been ice an hour ago came splashing down. Near miss.

"Sorry!" the same somebody shouted.

"No problem." Dallas continued up to the third floor.

Getting from the stairs to Chad and C.J.'s room through all the bodies was going to be difficult—

"Beer man!" the big guy shouted.

A path cleared more readily than the Red Sea parted for Moses, and the Red Sea probably didn't cheer Moses.

"Over here, over here!" An arm reached above the crowd, hand-tied beach bracelet around its wrist, fingers snapping. Chad, tall, dark-haired, shirtless, getting bulky from all the weight lifting and beer, waved for the delivery.

"You got money?" the delivery man demanded, keg on his shoulder.

"Seventy bucks, right here."

Dallas watched in amazement as Chad—Chad? The proverbial broke and borrowing Chad—pulled a wadded ball of cash from his shorts. "Seventy bucks, count 'em, seventy, cold hard American *dollahs*." It was getting near Chad's witching hour, when beer and the prospect of sex drove him toward hyperspeed. He stuffed his COD in the beer man's shirt pocket.

C.J. stood outside their room with two flashlights fitted with orange light cones. He waved the keg in like he was directing a 747 onto the runway.

Stomping feet and a unison chant, "Beer! Beer! Beer! Beer!" shook the Ocean Tides.

Every door on the third floor was open to the community party, except for Jas and Wendy's. They were so sleepy. . . .

But, speak of the devil, Jas's door flung open. He hopped up and down, looking over the crowd. "Dallas! Hey, Dallas! There you are. Come here! You're on TV!"

Dallas was joined by Herbie, who had already outfitted himself with a tub of beer and big bag of popcorn. They wedged into Jas's room.

"Hi!" Wendy smiled coyly from the bed, sheet pulled up under her arms.

A lot of interesting underwear in pretty colors was strewn all over the place, like someone had set a fuse to a lingerie fashion show and blown it up.

Jas closed the door and bolted it to keep anyone else out. "Look." He pointed to the color TV (well, it was two colors, anyway; green and yellow came in clearly).

The video was framed shakily, but there was Mack Trial, thrown over the front of Rupert Dawson's Crown Victoria, screaming that an innocent man was being arrested. Someone adept at electronic special effects had "painted in" the back of Trial's head to cover his hair plugs.

And there was Dallas, in Dawson's cruiser, holding up his wrists, but through the windshield it looked like he *had* been handcuffed.

Jas turned up the sound.

"All in all," the Baltimore newscaster reported seriously, "a very bizarre and unusual happening in Ocean City this morning as an attempted assassination of high-profile attorney Mack Trial ended with Trial running to defend a wrongly accused suspect."

"Unbelievable," the coanchor said seriously. "When danger infects even our vacations . . ." Shaking her head somberly.

"Now," the anchor stated, "for a look at sports, here's Ronnie Elvis."

Fifties dance music blared raucously as the sportscaster, donning an Elvis wig, danced, played air guitar, and rattled off baseball scores.

Jas turned down the sound. "Aw, damn, you missed the best part. They showed you coming out of an alley and this cop running toward you with his gun drawn."

Dallas rubbed his temples. He suddenly didn't feel very good. "Swell."

A warning fist pounded on Jas's door, followed by frantic activity on the balcony. "Police! Police!"

The party was clearing out in a hurry. These were mostly good kids from respectable families whose parents had no idea how their progeny acted when unsupervised. Care had to be taken, because getting caught slide-stepping through a wilder life could blow their parents' fantasies to hell. (Although the really deluded moms and dads, called by the police in the middle of the night, always claimed the cops had the wrong person: "Not my so-and-so. He/she would never do anything like that." "Yeah, lady, right, then you come down here, take the panties off her head, and tell me whose daughter this is with regurgitated clam fritters in her shoes.")

Wendy, wrapped in a sheet, put her glasses on. She parted the curtains and peeked out at the boardwalk. "It's just two cops. But they aren't coming up here."

"Hey, Dallas," Jas said, looking under the bed where Dallas was hiding. "It's okay. The cops're down on the beach."

Herbie said, "Hey, boss, maybe you better go down there."

Dallas recognized the trio immediately. Standing by the volleyball net were the two bodyboarders and photographer girl he'd seen earlier in the ocean. Away from sunshine, not riding waves, they looked bad. Tired, thin, worn out, and still in their bathing suits: damp trunks that hung low on the boys' hips.

The girl wore a ripped sweatshirt and acted as spokesman. Having a little standoff with a pair of cops.

"Look," she said, "we weren't sleeping, okay?"

But they had been. Her hair was tangled and caked on one side with sand. Her eyes blinked against the strain of a street lamp behind the policeman questioning her.

The cop asked for ID.

"We don't have to give you that," she replied aggressively.

The pale-haired kid—Blond—was looking really scared, eyes darting from side to side.

Dallas nudged Herbie. "Go find Bobby. Hurry up!"

Herbie sprinted back to the motel.

The taller, older officer kept his voice calm, but there was control and determination behind every word. He was doing his job by the book—maybe *too* by the book. "Where are your parents?"

"Why?"

"Do your parents know where you are?"

Blond's hands became jittery, playing with the loose front of his swim trunks.

Dallas thought, Don't do it, kid, don't do it—help's coming. Dallas hurdled the retaining wall and jumped down to the beach on bad ankles.

The officer talked mock-casual, as though trying to be their friend. "Where are you from? Around here? Maryland?"

She wouldn't answer. The darker South Seas boy kept his head down. Blond fiddled with his trunks.

"Came down for a few days, right? Couldn't find a place to stay? All the hotels are so expensive."

No comment. Indicted politicians should keep so quiet.

"You have a car?"

The second officer began to round up the kids' things. Bodyboards. Knapsacks. The girl's soft camera bag. Three sleeping bags.

"Man, please," South pleaded, "that's our stuff, don't take our stuff, okay?" When he stepped toward the second officer, the tall cop roughly grabbed his arm and held him back.

"Son, we're just trying to help you. We're just going to take you—"

Blond bolted. Turned and ran, kicking up sand.

"Damn," Dallas cussed.

"Get him, Charley!" the tall cop ordered.

His partner chased after Blond, holding his gun belt to keep it from flapping against his thigh. Crossing soft sand, his hat flew off. Blond ran toward firm beach along the water's edge and started pulling away; running scared beat plain running most every time.

The tall cop took charge of the girl and South. "Sit down!" Not wanting to lose either of them.

"Hey." Dallas waved to the kids. "South, Photo." He assigned them names.

The cop turned his authority toward Dallas. "Sir, please stay where you are. Don't interfere with the situation."

Dallas kept coming. "I'm their lawyer."

The cop looked at him like, Sure you are, some uncombed beach jockey in a black shirt and jeans.

Dallas reached into his pocket. Miracle: he had a business card. Bent, but it was a card. How long had that been in there?

The cop looked, but didn't take it. "What bar'd you get that in?" Very unfriendly now. Looking over his shoulder, he saw his partner had given up chasing Blond and was coming back. He muttered *"Dammit"* under his breath.

Dallas said, "You arresting these two?"

"It's a misdemeanor to sleep on the beach, in case you didn't read that in law school."

Oh, okay, so the cop believed he was a lawyer, he just didn't *like* lawyers. Well, he and Dallas had that much in common.

"They're not sleeping on the beach. They're sleeping in that motel." Dallas pointed to the Ocean Tides.

The cop smirked. "Okay. Then all they have to show me is a room key and we're—"

Dallas tossed the girl the key to room 301.

Startled, she caught it between her fingers.

"Show it to him."

Unsure, she held the key out.

"Hey, bozo!" This shout came from the boardwalk.

Damn, it was Bobby. Dallas tried to wave him off. This might not be necessary.

"Yeah, you, Bozo Cop!" Bobby pointed at the officer. "You know who I am? You got more warrants out for me than the rest of this beach put together. And you know why you can't catch me? 'Cause I'm smarter than you." This from a twenty-year-old in cutoff jeans, ripped T-shirt, no shoes, double-fisted drinking cans of Old Milwaukee in public (which, of course, was a violation of two laws: underage possession and public consumption).

The tall cop sensed he was losing control of this situation and wasn't sure how to handle it. No one ever told him that in a town of at least two hundred thousand kids, he'd never had control in the first place. "You're under arrest," he had the foresight to tell Bobby.

"You can't arrest me." Bobby's patented line.

The cop started toward Bobby, handcuffs coming off his belt.

91

"Watch me *not* arrest you!" He hoisted himself up and over the retaining wall onto the boardwalk.

Bobby was sporting enough to give him that much of a handicap. Then, he took off running with *both* cops in pursuit. Fleeing and eluding was Bobby's specialty. If the boys in blue thought Blond was fast—Bobby was the demon in "speed demon." He instantly had a half-block lead and never lost his beers.

The girl handed Dallas back the key. South was gathering their belongings. "Thanks," she said, barely looking at him.

In a mere glance of reddened eyes, Dallas saw far more suffering than someone her age should have experienced. He didn't take the key. "Keep it. Stay."

Fatigued, she reached for her photo bag. "We gotta go."

"It's not going to cost you anything."

She looked at him accusingly, as though he had seen what she most wanted kept private.

"Actually," Dallas smiled, "you'd be doing me a favor. I run the motel and your taking this spot just about fills the place up. Now, if any lawyers want to stay here, there's no room."

She, of course, had no idea what he was talking about, but blamed her lack of comprehension on being so tired. She ran her hand through her hair, brushing out sand that fell over her torn sweatshirt.

"We'll find your friend, too," Dallas assured.

South said to the girl, "Let's do it, okay, Gina? We can't handle the police."

"Whaddaya say, Gina?" Dallas urged, picking up on her real name.

She kept scratching her hair as though the motion was relieving hypnosis taking her away from all this. Finally, she said, "Yeah, okay. For tonight . . ."

"This way." Dallas led them toward the Ocean Tides.

Police proximity had broken up the party, leaving behind a wake of plastic cups and beer cans like a tornado had struck a college frat house. It was quiet, but Dallas guessed South and Gina wouldn't have had any trouble sleeping under train tracks. They were out on their feet by the time Dallas got them to their room.

From there, Dallas went up on the roof alone with his CD Walkman and *Chicago's Greatest Hits*. He sat in his lounge chair and stretched out his legs. He'd regret this in a few hours when Claude came by to pick him up for an early-morning eighteen with Pete Marjani, but he wouldn't be able to sleep now.

$\triangledown$

19

WEBBED FEET SOFTLY EMBEDDED on the silt floor of tidal wetlands, the elegant blue heron craned her long neck, extending her vantage point above placid pale green water.

As early-morning sun cast a misty gold tint over the low country, the heron's trained eyes remained ever alert for the darting silver fish she hunted for breakfast.

Perfectly motionless, the tiny circumference of the heron's stilt legs offered little underwater warning of her presence. Her reflexes would be quick, a lightning strike of beak slicing into the water for her prey.

Often, it was a long, tedious process that left her poised like a graceful statue. Patient, focused, deliberate . . .

The Titleist DT 100 spun a sharp *fffssssssss*. Scientifically perfected dimples rotating the ball with a violent displacement of air, it zipped right by the heron's raised head and splashed a deliberate *kerplunk* that rippled the still salt pond.

"Duck farts!" Pete Marjani slammed the head of his Ping one-wood to the ground, forming a crater in soft sod.

The heron squawked with surprise. Expanding long wings, she took flight, drawing stick legs to her body like an airplane retracting landing gear.

"Gimme another ball!" Marjani barked.

Frog-faced Jack Hayes, Pete Marjani Company's senior vice-president in charge of sucking up to the boss, rushed to Marjani's side with one of three extra balls he kept handy for such occasions. Each ball was imprinted with the stylish Hurricane Bay logo and, in block letters: P. MARJANI. Anyone caught using a lost Marjani ball was subject to immediate expulsion from the club.

As the veins in Marjani's thick neck bulged and his red face deepened to violet, he teed up his fifth "mulligan" in as many holes. Ready to hit again, he wiggled his large frame ridiculously over the ball, took a backswing as though preparing to drop a tree, and swung mightily. The club head ripped up a vicious foot-long trench of grass.

The ball, having been glanced by little more than the top of

Marjani's driver, popped up in the air and landed with a *thunk* about five feet short of the ladies' tee.

There are many golf jokes about a man's drive not carrying beyond the red tees, but no one kidded Marjani with them. The last person who unwittingly made such a comment had his neck sized by the graphite shaft of a two-iron Marjani had been swinging at the time.

"You see that?" Marjani complained to Jack Hayes. "I kept my goddamned wrists quiet like Bucky told me and the ball pulls that shit on me. *Goddamn!*" He slammed his driver into his bag.

Marjani had been taking golf lessons for years and never got any better. He'd been through twenty teaching pros, 114 sets of clubs, different balls, shoes, hats, shirts, stances, grips, gloves; he'd tried hypnosis, meditation, acupuncture, sex before, during, or right after a round; using a caddy or not; drinking alcohol or not; walking the course or using a power cart; teaming with guys who were better, the same, or worse than he was. He'd auditioned all the excuses: I don't play often enough; I'm playing too much; I'm playing in spurts.

Presently, his rationale was what Bucky Connors, Hurricane Bay's club pro, told him: "I'm too big. My barrel chest gets in the way of my swing. Won't let my arms extend."

Bucky had been a genius to think of that one: using physical proportions Marjani was proud of as an excuse. A negative caused by a positive. Like saying you couldn't understand the poor because you were so rich. Bucky might actually stick around longer than the 6.2-month average of Hurricane Bay's former pros by keeping Marjani appeased with lines like that.

The bald truth of the matter, however, was that—short of his high school football days as a seventeen-year-old brutal two-hundred-pound defensive lineman—Marjani was not that well coordinated. The only way he'd ever break ninety-five at Hurricane Bay was to cheat even worse than he already did.

But Marjani refused to face this fact. There had to be a way for him to be a good golfer and he was going to keep trying to buy—in terms of lessons and equipment—what God hadn't graced him with. And he *was* going to buy it, goddammit. If there was something Marjani hated more than anything else it was not being able to buy what he wanted.

Two holes later, Marjani took eleven more mulligans out of a sand trap. A shower of sand blasted into the air each time he swung his wedge. Balls hit fat went four feet, half the distance he sprayed the sand. Balls hit thin zinged over the green and into the backyards of Pete Marjani–built patio homes, chipping mortar out of brick walls, denting vinyl siding, and smacking loose roof shingles.

Jack Hayes became winded from running back and forth to the golf cart for more Hurricane Bay–logo balls.

Dallas and Claude watched silently. There was nothing safe to say.

Dallas felt like he'd been playing surprisingly well (for him); he might've broken 50 on the front nine, but would never know for sure. At the end of each hole, Jack Hayes asked for scores and Marjani announced them for everyone. "Give Claude a six. You had seven. I had five." (Actually 12.) "And what's-his-name . . ." (Dallas) " . . . had a seven."

A sum that was rarely correct.

By the turn, Marjani was ready to call it quits. "Worse goddamned golf day in my life," he roared, face the color of hundred-degree temperatures on *USA Today*'s weather maps. "Goddamned awful."

Conversation having been completely monopolized by Marjani, Dallas was yet to work in a single question about Judge Crenshaw or the planned new course, Tropical Storm. Which had been the entire purpose of waking up at dawn this morning. Now, it looked as though it might all go for naught.

Ripping off his lambskin glove, Marjani told Claude and Dallas, "You boys go ahead and finish out." As though being gracious not to make them stop because of his sorry play. "Jack, take my clubs up to storage."

The bug-eyed, fleshy-jowled Hayes was also through for the day. Who knew, Marjani may have needed some pencils sharpened.

"I don't know, Pete," Dallas said. Seated in the gas cart beside Claude, he pointed to number 10. "I got this feeling about you and this par three up here. Like an aura, you know."

Marjani glared at Hayes. "What the shit's he talking about?"

"Might be hole-in-one time," Dallas said. "You never know."

Marjani ground his granite jaw. It was almost as though a cartoon thought bubble had been drawn over his head. A little cloud of consciousness connected to his brain. Dear Lord, how he had dreamed of having his name on the hole-in-one plaques hung in the clubhouse. How many times he'd been tempted to inscribe his name anyway, make it another lie he'd get so used to telling he'd soon be convinced it was true.

Jack Hayes had driven the golf cart halfway around the putting green and a spewing fountain when Marjani shouted him back.

"Get your ass over here, Jack! I'm gonna hole this duck fart bastard!" Thumping his temple with two fingers, he peered at Dallas. "All this worrying about my swing, I forgot about positive thinking. Goddamned!" Determination steaming from his ears, pieces of macadam cart path grinding under his cleats, Marjani stalked toward the tenth tee.

A very "doable" hole. Ninety-five short yards, all downhill, a half-swing pitching wedge to a soft, forgiving green.

"Nice and easy," Marjani coached himself, approaching the tee. "Nice, easy swing. Bring your wrists through. Finish high, hands aiming for the hole." Taking a few clubless practice swings mid-stride, he reached the tee before Jack Hayes could navigate the cart around another fountain. "Let's goddamn go, Jack. I'm in a groove. *I can feel it!*"

Hayes sped the cart up, took a turn on two wheels, and came screeching to a stop beside the tee. He hustled Marjani's club to him.

"A ball, too, Jack. I need a goddamned ball."

Hayes dug into his pockets, a fifty-year-old man who'd made a long career playing step-'n-fetch-it.

Marjani pushed a tee deeply into the grass, just enough to give his ball a slightly elevated line. Standing behind the ball, he lined up his shot, then moved in place to hit.

About this time, Lowell Javitz—Hurricane Bay resident, retiree, and lost golf ball hunter—emerged from the woods along the right rough. He poked around tall grass with the same hickory stick he used to ward off snakes. A soft bag containing his morning find of balls was looped to his belt.

Marjani wiggled his powerful torso. Stared down at the ball. Eyes burning through it.

Jack Hayes was about to say, "Watch out for old man Javitz," but cut his sentence short, fingers touching his lips as though pushing the words back down his throat.

Claude was adding up scores from the front nine, doing a little editing for his own tally.

Dallas was telepathically signaling Marjani's ball, *Go on the green. Go on the green. Somewhere near the hole if not in it.* Needing Marjani to keep playing so he could ask about—

Swoosh. Marjani swung.

Thhhhukkkk. The club head hit some grass.

Dink. He toed the ball.

Sssssttt. The ball flared violently to his side, no arc, on a line like an arrow. Heading right for . . .

Plunk.

Lowell Javitz couldn't have heard the telltale sizzle of a ball in flight for more than a millisecond. Still, it was enough time for him to look up and get a Titleist right between the eyes.

The ball appeared to lodge in the soft furrows of Lowell's brow as though glued there. When Lowell dropped like a stone, the ball hovered for a second in the air above him, as though it might still possess enough energy to travel a few more feet. But once Lowell hit the ground, the ball was only a second or so behind, settling into the impression it had made on Lowell's forehead upon contact. An unlikely resting place that made Lowell's face resemble an elaborate tee.

Marjani, always quick under pressure, thrust his pitching wedge into Jack Hayes's grip, and yelled, "For God's sake, Jack, you hit that man." Heading back to the clubhouse, he ordered, "Call an ambulance. I've got work to do."

Dallas's tee shot on fourteen started out straight and high, then made a wild yip way right as spin induced by an outside-in swing took hold. If a cop had been around, he'd have ticketed the ball for making a turn without signaling. Dallas's wicked slice: a banana ball. His X-out Top-Flite sailed off over a line of cedar trees into an adjacent field.

Dallas stared in disgust. If Herbie had been around to fetch his clubs, he'd have thrown them somewhere. "Crap."

"You didn't finish your swing, you damn dummy." Claude's critique came from behind Dallas. "You quit on it. Your arms went to jelly."

Dallas and Claude were playing the back nine as a twosome. Marjani and Hayes were holed up in the clubhouse; Lowell Javitz was on his way to Peninsula General with paramedic escort.

Claude walked to the cart, his stride a somewhat rakish series of angles in motion. Six two, slender, a young sixty-eight, he constantly fought the pain of bad knees ruined forty-five years ago while quarterbacking for William and Mary. His fingers, broken but never set during that same era, bent from his knuckles at more slants than the hands of a clock saw during an entire day.

Claude's toupee was less than inconspicuous, though Dallas had known him so long he never thought of it as a piece. His pants were bright yellow, stitched with dozens of crossed blue golf clubs. Acceptable golf gaudy.

This was "Uncle" Claude, as Dallas first called him over twenty-five years ago, when he was a kid and Claude a family friend and industry fixture selling TV advertising in Baltimore.

A lot of golf between then and now.

"You gotta finish your swing." Claude was a patient amateur teacher who had a knack for spotting the many things Dallas did wrong.

Dallas was glad Marjani quit early. This was much better. Even if you were playing badly, there was nothing like being out on the course with someone you liked.

Halfway down the 415-yard fairway, Claude stopped the cart and made a dismissing arm motion toward the cedar trees. "Never find your ball over there. Just drop one."

Dallas dug into his bag, found an old range ball, and managed to send it thirty yards short of the green with an okay four-wood. So he was looking at another 7. . . . It *was* a beautiful day, an earlier golden mist having burned off. Soon, it would turn hot.

Claude hit a two-iron toward the big trap that guarded the green. "Go left, dummy," he hollered after his shot.

The ball hit grass just short of the trap and bounced left, rolling onto the fringe.

"Luckeee," Dallas said.

Riding to the green, Claude said, "See over there." He pointed through a break in the cedars to acres and acres of unfarmed field dotted by compact forests of tall, aged trees. Land danced with wetlands out to the bay after which Pete Marjani named his country club. "That's where the new eighteen holes—Tropical Storm—may never be."

"What do you mean, 'may never be'? What was the party about last night?"

"Between us and the grass," Claude said, stopping the cart, "a merry ruse."

Dallas pulled his wedge and putter from his bag.

Claude said, "The members have been complaining so much about crowds on the course, Pete knows he has to keep them happy or they'll quit. He's got to build that second course."

Dallas lobbed his pitch shot thirty feet past the hole. "So what's the problem?"

Claude putted from the fringe, sent his ball over a roll in the green, and body-Englished it to within three feet of the hole. "Guy won't sell."

"Marjani doesn't own the land yet?"

Claude shook his head. "Between you and me . . ."

Dallas lined up a downhill putt. "So how's he gonna build this new course with no land?"

Claude shrugged.

Dallas stroked his putt too hard. It ran by the hole and kept going. "Come on, baby. Stop. *Stop.*" It finally did, fifteen feet down a nasty slope. "So what's Marjani gonna do? Come up with more money for the land?"

"He's already offered the guy two times market."

"Sure. The guy knows Marjani wants it, so he's screwing him." Dallas decided to hell with lining up this next putt—he never knew what he was looking at anyway—he just hit it. It almost went in. "Damn!"

Claude picked up both balls, two liberal gimmees within three feet. "Rollie Gunderson just plain hates Pete Marjani's guts. When Marjani first built this course, right back along there"—Claude pointed to a barbed-wire fence behind the fourteenth tee—"Gunderson used to have manure brought in by the truckload and dumped there. You should've seen it, this big mountain of cow and horse poop drawing flies and smelling up the place." Claude laughed. "It was awful. That's why this hole's called The Stinkpot."

Back in the cart, Claude sped them toward a shady paved cut through the trees and the fifteenth hole beyond. "Gunderson used to be a real good guy. Or so people say. He's a lawyer—*was.* You don't know him?"

"No."

"He might've quit by the time you came along. After his wife left him—twenty years ago, I guess—he started coming apart. He split up his law partnership and bought this land down here. It was all backwoods at the time. Supposedly lives like a hermit. Fishes for his dinner every day, some damned dumb thing like that."

Claude braked the cart at the fifteenth tee. A murderously long par-4 with a pond in front of the green. "You know," he said, dropping his Pinnacle Gold into the ball washer and spinning it around, "Gunderson's ex-partner just died the other day. You know crazy Judge Crenshaw?"

$\triangledown$

20

DALLAS LOOKED INTO THE bodyboarders' room through opened jalousie windows. "You guys hungry?" He rustled the carryout bag. "I got cheeseburgers."

Nonresponsive, Gina stood at the far end of the room, looking at the beach through the screened balcony door. Arms folded, she wore her bikini top and oversized sweatshorts.

South opened the door. Much more affable. Toweling thick black hair, his gaunt suntanned body was dotted with water and smelled of soap. "Felt good to take a real shower." He seemed to be apologizing, for what Dallas had no idea.

"You want something to eat? On the house?" Dallas said it loudly enough for Gina to hear over the breakers and kids' happy cries carrying up from the beach.

She didn't so much as turn toward him. Nothing.

South said, "She's worried about Cutback."

"What?"

"That's his name. The guy who was with us last—"

"Oh, yeah, your friend who ran off. He hasn't come back, huh?"

"He scares kind of easy." South spoke without teenage flip. No *uhs*, *ums*, or *like, you know*s. He paused at the end of each sentence as though weighing if he'd spoken enough—or too much. "So she worries about him. . . . What he might do."

"I'll keep the gang looking out for him. We'll track him down." Dallas aimed his words for Gina, but still didn't get a response. Oh, well. "Here." He opened the Alaska Stand bag and pulled out two cheeseburgers. "If you haven't already tried these, you're missing the world's best. I've been eating 'em since I was five. Rare with mustard and onions."

South hesitated, but took them at Dallas's insistence. "Thanks."

"You need anything else? Herbie's going on a grocery store run later. We can get you some stuff if you like."

"That's okay."

"Really. It's not a problem."

"Maybe some milk and cereal. Just don't get the milk in the

cartons." South grinned when Dallas looked puzzled, said, "Sorry, private joke."

"Tell it to me sometime."

He almost nodded. "Thanks again for the burgers. And for last night. *And* the room. From Gina, too."

"Anytime. Stay as long as you want." Dallas backed out the door. "Maybe we'll get some waves later on."

"I'd like that." South had a sincere smile.

Dallas hoped before too long Gina might smile, too.

"How was golf?" Susan asked. She sat on the bed nearest the war room's balcony, relentlessly rereviewing Judge Crenshaw's files for leads.

Dallas sat on the floor and leaned back against the paneled wall. "Pete Marjani hit a lowell-in-one."

"*Lowell* in one?"

"Yeah, he hit Lowell Javitz with his tee shot on number ten." Dallas yawned. Waking up early was unnatural. Here it was just after one and it felt like midnight. He was tired and hungry, more hungry, though. He opened the carryout bag and took a big bite of Alaska Stand cheeseburger; au jus and mustard ran down his hand. "You meet the bodyboarder kids yet?"

"No. Herbie said they were still sleeping as of an hour ago. Why? Is something wrong?"

"I think so, but I don't know what. They're real defensive. Very edgy. Although the one who looks Hawaiian is a little looser."

"Who knows, Dallas," Susan said. Not looking up from an opened file, she made a few notes. "There's a million things that can affect kids."

"That stinks, doesn't it? When you're growing up, you should be having a great time. Take advantage of the fact you haven't figured out how scary this planet really is."

"Maybe they've figured it out already."

"Jeez. I hope they don't tell me something *I* haven't thought to worry about yet. That would really stink." Dallas chomped more burger. The way he saw the rest of his day, he was going to catch a four-hour nap, ride some waves, then settle in for a couple nice rum drinks on a bayfront deck, watching the sunset. . . .

"You want to hear about this?" Susan said, lifting the legal pad from her lap. A third of the yellow pages were rife with notes.

"I'm awful tired. Already put in damned near a full day on the golf course."

"You want to hear how Crenshaw had it in for Mack Trial? How he's representing at least six clients with malpractice claims against Trial? Looking for *boh-koo* damages?"

Eating, Dallas said, "Vicky said something about Trial duking it out with his insurance company, trying to get them to settle malpractice claims before the media found out. She didn't say anything about Crenshaw handling the cases."

Susan tried not to react to the mention of Vicky Sterrett. She tapped her gold pen on the short stack of files tilted against her leg. "Two of the six had filed malpractice suits against Trial with other lawyers, but went with Crenshaw midway through discovery. Their original lawyers were not pleased about the switch. One fellow in Talbot County was considering a complaint to the ethics committee until I told him Crenshaw was dead. He didn't seem too upset by that."

"Nor anyone else," Dallas pointed out, taking another bite of cheeseburger, which was exceptional. He should've bought more. To hell with cholesterol, this was the beach. Some days you shouldn't read the fat content of a bag of Fritos, just eat them.

Susan said, "The other complainants hadn't filed suits against Trial until Crenshaw recruited them."

"Recruited?"

Susan's dark eyes widened for emphasis. "He went out and found them. How, I don't know. Unless he had someone inside one of Trial's offices feeding him information."

"Interesting."

"But it makes me wonder . . . why Trial? It's as if Crenshaw had a vendetta."

"Maybe he did." Dallas's reply came without much thought. He was more concerned that his cheeseburger was now finished and he needed something to wash it down with. He crawled to the refrigerator on all fours; standing required too much energy.

"So what did Trial ever do to Crenshaw?"

"Nothing I know of." Dallas opened the fridge. Yum, Bacardi Rum Breezers. He waved a bottle at Susan. "Want one?"

"No, thanks."

Dallas crawled into bed beside Susan, shoved aside some files, and stretched out. She smelled wonderful, wearing expensive perfume with her plain white T-shirt and jeans. Style.

Dallas unscrewed the bottle top and drank about half of the rum quick; if it outraced the burger to his stomach lining he might sneak a cheap buzz—an often underestimated pleasure. He renewed his offer to Susan. "Sure you don't want some?"

"Well . . . why not?" She took a swallow.

Dallas enjoyed being a bad influence. He considered it his most rewarding trait. "Any correspondence in there from Crenshaw to Trial or the clients or the insurance company?"

Susan offered an example. A very nasty letter to an adjuster on one of the malpractice cases. Dated three weeks ago, it demanded a quarter of a million dollars. It was coherent, pointed, direct, borderline abusive—vintage Crenshaw.

"No typewriter in the judge's cabin," Dallas recalled. "He was getting these typed somewhere." Turned on his side, he held the page to sunlight coming through the balcony door. "Good-quality typing. No corrections, no Liquid Paper spots. Maybe done on a laser printer." The bottom line of the page was coded in standard secretarial form: RCC/pm. "RCC. Raymond C. Crenshaw, typed by someone with initials PM. Any idea who?"

"No." Susan drank a little more Breezer.

"I see he's using a PO box as his business address. How about this phone number?"

"Home line."

"Hmm." Dallas traded Susan the letter for the rum. He closed his eyes. Nap time.

"I also checked in with Rupert Dawson. Nothing new on Jumbi Berrell—he's still 'at large.' They're waiting on fingerprint results from Crenshaw's house. And no witnesses have come forward who saw Crenshaw get hit by the car; his neighbors either didn't know him or didn't want to know him."

"Sound like logical folk. How 'bout Crenshaw, the junior? Anything new on that front?"

"Interesting you should mention him. Did you read Crenshaw's will?" Susan reached across Dallas to the other bed for the appropriate file.

With her lean weight pressing against his thighs, Dallas opened his eyes to find her T-shirt had lifted halfway up her side. Fighting grab-ass beach instincts, he interlocked his fingers to keep his hands from committing a misdemeanor. Holding on so hard that blood stopped reaching his fingertips, he sighed.

"*Did* you read the will?" Susan asked again, straightening her top.

"I . . . uh . . . *reviewed* it." Dallas wanted her to lie on top of him again.

"You catch this? 'Item Five'—after he tends to taxes and funeral expenses and offers you fifty grand to find out the circumstances of his death. 'Item Five. I give, devise and bequeath the rest and residue of my Estate, of whatsoever kind and whatsoever situated, real, personal or mixed, that I may own or have the right to dispose of at the time of my death, unto my only child and beloved son, Harvey C. Crenshaw, of Wilkes-Barre, Pennsylvania. All I can say, son, is that if you're seeing this will, I'm sorry.' "

"Crenshaw, sorry? There's a first. Sorry for what?"

"Doesn't say."

"Anything else in there?"

"Boilerplate. Vicky probably charged him a grand to have her secretary run it off disc." Susan flipped through her notes. "As for Crenshaw being at Hurricane Bay . . ." She produced a standard white letter envelope. "I found this. No return address. No stamp. One line typed on the front: R.C.C."

Without looking, Dallas said, "The judge's initials again."

Susan pulled out four stapled pages of shiny paper. The print was smeary black against a gray background. Paper either from a fax, early-generation copy machine, or microfiche. A duplicate of a district court lawsuit. She jabbed Dallas so he'd open his eyes.

"What?"

"Read this."

Dallas did: *Lawrence Invernitti* v. *Lawn Care International, Ltd.*

"Look at the resident agent for Lawn Care."

"I'll be damned. Pete Marjani." Dallas checked the date of filing. "This case's sixteen years old. What's Lawn Care International?"

"A pyramid scheme. According to this complaint, Pete Marjani bought lawn fertilizer from a wholesaler, had it rebagged under his Lawn Care logo, and sold it to distributors, who marked it up and passed it on to second-level distributors, who marked it up and passed it on to third-level, and so on and so on. The trouble was, by the time it hit third-level, it was the highest-priced fertilizer on the market. The only people who bought it were those who had other distributors further down the line.

"Invernitti was six levels down. There was no one he could sell the product to. In fact, half the people in his neighborhood were Lawn Care distributors, all *higher* in the chain than him. He sued Lawn Care for fraud and breach of contract. This was before pyramid scheme protection was on the books." Susan leaned over Dallas to deliver the clincher: "Crenshaw was the judge on the case. And Crenshaw not only awarded judgment to Invernitti, but wrote the attorney general's office *and* the IRS about Lawn Care. Marjani was out of business in nine months."

"Crenshaw bangs Marjani in court and now, sixteen years later, Marjani hires him?"

"Do we know for sure Crenshaw wasn't working *against* Marjani?"

"Marjani did call Vicky to say the five percent stock deal was off."

"But Marjani's hardly a disinterested witness. Maybe he's lying about that to cover up something else."

"Yeah, you know, I asked Claude this morning and he didn't know anything about Crenshaw and Marjani, and if Claude doesn't know—a man who Marjani plays golf with three days a week—it's either not happening or is some secret."

"It makes more sense Crenshaw being against Marjani, doesn't it: a man he knows as a fraud from the past?"

"Especially since Marjani's doing it again." Dallas told Susan about the new eighteen holes, Tropical Storm, for which Marjani hadn't yet bought the land from Rollie Gunderson, Crenshaw's ex–law partner.

At the mention of Gunderson's name, Susan said, "I know him."

∇

21

No Trespassing signs lined the crooked dirt driveway for half a mile to Roland Gunderson's tiny ramshackle house: red-and-white warning placards staked into dry earth like reflectors at a bad curve in the highway.

Susan barely slowed the Benz in the face of these legal notices.

"Yeah," Dallas said, "I wouldn't worry about it. Signs like this aren't enforceable unless they say, 'This means you.' " With his elbow perched out the window, raised road dust stuck to perspiring skin.

The gentle ocean breeze that had kept the beach bearable today hadn't found its way ashore. The air was parched like a blister. If someone stuck a pin in the sky, Dallas figured it would ooze.

A rock thrown off Gunderson's driveway by the Benz's front tires pounded the car's underside with a hard thud.

Not far to their right, through Pete Marjani's cedar trees, Dallas saw the fourteenth hole of Hurricane Bay. He should've brought his ball shagger and looked for his sliced tee shot.

"Beautiful spot back here," Dallas said of mostly unspoiled fields and wetlands. He started singing a few bars of *Give me land, lots of land, lots of* West Ocean City *land*, messing with the lyrics as he contemplated the serenity of four hundred acres of fertile earth touching the bay and forest.

"But this house," Dallas complained, "looks like what Jed Clampett left behind to move to Bever-lee—Hills, that is; swimming pools, movie stars." Dallas sang a little more.

Roland Gunderson's dilapidated abode made a prima facie case for poverty. A small cottage of aged graying wood was lifted three feet above the ground by creosote pilings; a separate barn-wood garage larger than the house itself sat fifty feet off the home's rear corner.

There weren't any cars in sight, but they could have been in the garage. The cottage's windows were shut and covered by yellowed shades. An exposed propane tank positioned dangerously close to the house was nearly covered with rust and bright green vines. A solitary rocking chair on the tilted front porch looked to be all the weight the structure could bear.

"A few gallons of paint," Dallas said, "and you could upgrade this place to an eyesore. Pete Marjani buys it, the first item of business is gonna be to tear it down."

Susan stopped the Benz short of the house and tapped the horn.

A deer neither of them had seen broke her frozen pose a hundred yards left and sped gracefully across the open field, white tail making her stand out against brown earth.

Susan beeped the horn again, longer this time.

Nothing.

"I'm going inside."

Dallas grasped her forearm. "As someone who has paid his fair share of unannounced visits to people who obviously don't want to be bothered, let me warn you this guy might turn out to be something less than you have in mind."

"To the contrary. This is exactly what I expected."

"You're kidding. How could you anticipate something like this? A setting to a slasher movie. *Psycho* meets *The Texas Chainsaw Massacre*. Look at this place, Sus. What kind of person would live in this squalor if he didn't have to? Or want to?"

"A lot of people say that about your room in the motel." Susan might have had him on that one.

When she turned off the engine, it seemed exceptionally quiet. Deadly quiet. Dallas checked for buzzards overhead. Seeing none, he followed Susan to the front door. The porch squeaked, but it felt sound beneath their feet.

Susan knocked loudly. "Mr. Gunderson?"

Dallas rapped a windowpane. "These are new," he noted of an insulated square of glass.

"Mr. Gunderson?" Susan rapped again.

Dallas leaned over the porch side and looked back to the garage: a barn-style structure of faded red wood with a door wide enough to accommodate farm equipment. Driveway stone was laid in front to provide firmer traction on wet days. Loft doors set beneath gables of a high-pitched roof accessed what could be a second level.

"Mr. Gunderson?"

Dallas hopped the porch rail and checked the side windows and rear door of the house—all closed, locked, and covered from inside by roller shades.

A sturdy frog leapt from tall grass near the propane tank and landed on the dirt in front of Dallas, who stepped around him.

"Mr. Gunderson?" Susan kept working the front door.

Dallas checked the garage. Small hinged windows set at eye level were dotted with tiny specs of varying colors, a buildup over time of sprayed paint having drifted from its intended surface. One of four windows was slightly ajar. Dallas lifted it on squeaking hinges and peaked inside.

Organized on workbenches and a dirt floor was a decent inventory of auto tools and equipment that looked to have been picked up used from gas stations and service departments. Probably enough gear to do everything from engine retooling to body work. Two vehicles were inside, one on blocks, the other with wheels; both were covered with tarps.

Either Gunderson had a new sideline in lawyer-retirement or rented the barn to someone with cars in their blood.

Dallas was about to pull the window shut when something near the garage door caught his eye. Bales of hay were stacked above the door, perched precariously on a single two-by-six, one end of which was fitted with a wire connecting to the door handle.

"Cute."

Gunderson had rigged the door so intruders would have bales of hay dropped on them. The man was serious about his No Trespassing signs. Although bales of hay were a far cry from a spring gun.

Dallas closed the window and headed back to the house.

Susan wasn't on the front porch. The door remained closed.

"Hey, Sus?"

The only response was the distant cry of a blue heron. Dallas wondered if Pete Marjani was back on the golf course, assaulting nature.

"Susan?"

He looked beneath the house and had a clear view from front to back and all sides with the structure raised on pilings. Nothing under there except a bunch of cut tiger lilies looking to have been blown in on a windier day.

Where the hell was Susan? Her Benz was still there. Nothing but open field around them.

Dallas stepped up onto the front porch. Yelled, "Hey, Susan! Sus—!"

"It's okay!" She opened the front door a few inches from inside.

He moved to enter, but Susan wouldn't let him in. "What the hell's going—?"

"Wait in the car a little while, okay?" Her voice was a firm whisper.

When Dallas tried to peer inside, Susan closed the door to an inch of its frame. "Just wait for me, okay? Here." She dug into her jeans pocket for car keys. "You've been wanting to take it for a ride. Go ahead. Maybe half an hour, forty-five—"

"What're you doing? Is Gunderson—?"

"It's okay."

"Sus—?"

"It's *o-kay*." She dropped the keys when he wouldn't take them. Closed the door and locked it.

$\triangledown$

22

"**H**EY, RUP. IT'S DALLAS." Car phone wedged against his shoulder, Dallas drove Susan's Benz seventy-five in a forty-five zone, chewing up single-lane Route 611. Pushing eighty-five on the straightaways.

Trees, trailer parks, and convenience stores were blurs in his peripheral vision. He burned past cars that didn't pull off the road at the sight of him in their rearview mirror, a sleek white Mercedes bearing down on them like a maniac.

"You know a guy named Roland Gunderson? Owns a farm—well, sort of a farm—next to Hurricane Bay?"

"Yeah."

"Tell me."

"He's a retired lawyer. Lives alone, keeps to himself mostly. Not too happy about having a country club for a neighbor." The telltale squeak of springs coming over the line evidenced Dawson's office chair struggling mightily to hold his weight. "Marjani's about the only thing I know brings Gunderson off his property unless it's to complain about his tax bill. That a horn I hear?"

"Yeah. I'm using a car phone." Dallas blasted the horn again. "You got any radar traps set up on six-eleven today? 'Cause I got this drag-ass Chevy Cavalier doesn't want to get out of my way. I might have to do a hundred to get around him." Dallas hit the horn, flashed headlights. "Never mind, there he goes. You oughta send a car to check that guy out."

"Gunderson?"

"No, the Cavalier. Anybody drives the speed limit on this road must be drunk."

"I'll pass that right on to dispatch," Dawson grumbled. "What do you want to know about Gunderson for? This got anything to do with Crenshaw?"

"Maybe I'll know a little later. Susan's in Gunderson's house now."

"Susan?" Dawson sounded concerned.

"You're not making me feel any better. Is Gunderson some kind of whacko? Susan says she knows him, but wouldn't say how."

"Not like her to be mysterious."

"Should I go back there and wait for her?"

"As a precaution."

"Yeah, okay. How come you're never this concerned about me?"

Dawson didn't say anything.

Dallas hit the brakes and spun the steering wheel with deft coordination, days of racing with the Marsh Runners coming back to him. The Benz went into a controlled 180-degree turn, wheels screeching, leaving a rubber tattoo across the roadbed. Facing the direction from which he'd come, Dallas punched the engine and sped back toward Hurricane Bay. "And he never lost the phone!" Dallas announced.

"Goddamn!" Dawson screamed. "I'm not fixing any tickets you get."

"When we were in law school—and for a few years after—I worked phones at U of B fund-raisers, pestering alumni for money. One of my first-ever calls was Roland Gunderson." Susan affectionately touched the shoulder of the short, chubby man shaking Dallas's hand. "It was always a highlight of my year."

"Mr. Henry, nice to meet you."

"Dallas."

"Okay . . . Dallas. Sit on down," Gunderson invited, a pleasant enough man.

Gunderson was what Santa Claus might look like if you sawed him off to five five and changed his profession to outdoorsman. Late sixties. Bald except for short white hair pressed to the side of his round skull by tonic; a face made leathery from decades of work in the sun. His firm muscle tone belied the series of round parts that made up his body.

Judge Crenshaw's ex-partner wore a threadbare long-sleeve work shirt rolled one cuff length above his wrist. His pants were cheap discount-store jeans still stiff from drying on a line. Only his deck shoes were reasonably new.

"I don't get a lot of company. People warned me when I was younger that would happen if we didn't have children. But, you don't listen much when you're young, do you?"

Susan was visibly charmed after her half hour alone with a man she had only previously known by phone. She sat forward on an antique sofa, her expression alive with interest.

Gunderson settled onto an oak log box. His motions were easy, seemingly unencumbered by the routine aches and pains of age.

He leaned against a masonry fireplace that dripped hardened mortar between chalk red brick.

The inside of his house was a vast improvement over the exterior. Walls were paneled in the old-style knotty pine that was an early Ocean City trademark: shellacked yellow wood burled with dark brown grain and knots the size of silver dollars. Wide-slat oak floors were gnarled and beaten with age. The furnishings were older than Gunderson, mostly dark woods and wood accents, many refinished by Gunderson's talented hands.

A worktable occupied one corner. Gunderson's current project was a wreath fashioned from grapevines. Dried flowers hung near the window to be added later.

Dallas sat on a cane chair a museum would probably have paid a few hundred bucks for; they could have it, as far as he was concerned, it was uncomfortable as hell.

Susan said, "Whenever I called for the fund-raiser, Roland said, 'That time of year already, eh, Miss Vette.' We'd talk about my courses or cases I was working on. Roland could cite authorities like people quote Shakespeare. Some of them were *his* cases. A few he'd won before the court of appeals."

Gunderson appreciated the fawning.

Dallas was jealous. "So why'd you quit practicing law?"

"I should've quit years before I did. I came from a simple background, Dallas. My family never had much. Father and grandfather worked the land way down near Bishop's Head. God's *real* country. But I was a restless kid. Had big ideas about becoming rich."

Gunderson's accent was mostly cleansed of Eastern Shore roots by years in Baltimore. His patter was unhurried. Clearly a man who'd stopped checking his appointment book years ago.

"I went to law school, U of B, just like you two, only well before your time. I clerked for Judge Willis awhile, then went into practice with a classmate." Gunderson stopped as though not wanting to say the name.

"Judge Crenshaw," Susan filled in.

"Raymond Crenshaw," Gunderson repeated with the ease of passing a kidney stone. "Raymond Crenshaw . . . Ten, twelve years, we did good. And the more we made, the more I wanted. I went home to Bishop's Head one time with pockets brimming with cash. A real show-off. Only the people I'd known all my life suddenly weren't so friendly. I assumed they were jealous. It didn't occur to me it was because I was acting like a horse's ass.

"I met a girl at a USO dance in Cambridge that weekend. A

pretty—*beautiful*—country girl. Nineteen. She'd always wanted to leave the shore, just like me, only never had the means. I flashed all my money and showed her the sports car I was driving. Two weeks later, she came to Baltimore and moved into a rooming house for girls. Stayed there until I convinced her to move in with me.

"That was hot stuff back in 1957. Living with someone you weren't married to was *un*thinkable. But I loved it. The attention, the scandal . . ." Gunderson shook his head. "It was like being a celebrity. I'd walk into restaurants and people would buzz about this hotshot young lawyer *living* with some girl. Only I was so busy being a star, I never saw the impact it had on Penny. Goddamn, Dallas, folks were calling her a harlot.

"When her family found out, they disowned her. But, hell, I even brushed that off. Good Lord, but I was crass. So caught up in it all. Penny and I finally married, but it was never the same. Like the spark we'd had burned out. Eight years, we argued over the dumbest things."

Gunderson shook his head with regret. "I was unfaithful, I won't lie about that. Penny had reason to leave me. Not long after she did, it *all* started coming apart. Cases I should have won went against me. Raymond Crenshaw, who had always been my friend, forced me out of our partnership. He swindled me, took it all, the clients, the money, *everything*. He saw I was down and he kicked me until all the stuffing was out. Went right for the jugular."

Gunderson's speech slowed, as though he couldn't believe his own history, even having lived it. "And what scared me most was when I finally realized that if Raymond Crenshaw had been the one who'd fallen down and out—not me—and I'd had the opportunity to do to him what he did to me, I'd have probably done it. Being a lawyer trains that in you." He jabbed his sturdy, round gut. "It's planted deep in your gut like a poison seed, and even as your stomach burns, you keep at it because winning, getting ahead—*screw the method or cost*—that's all that matters."

Gunderson looked at Dallas. "*That's* why I quit. And if I'd done it a few years earlier, Penny might still be with me. I mourn her leaving every day. It's why I built this house. An exact replica of the house Penny was raised in."

Gunderson pointed to a restored sepia-toned photograph on the wall behind Dallas. "That's her folks' place. Right there in Bishop's Head. See in the background? That big flower patch? Most all of those were tiger lilies. Penny's favorite. I got a crop of them out back myself."

Voice growing quiet, Gunderson turned his hands atop his knees as though scouring them. "Yeah, Dallas, I thought maybe Penny'd find out I built this place and'd know I was apologizing. That maybe she'd come back." He looked up. "I'm still waiting."

Out of the house, swamped in afternoon heat, Roland Gunderson's spirits lifted somewhat. He rolled his shirtsleeves a few more turns and, with immeasurable pride, gave Susan and Dallas the "short walking tour" of his land.

Quarter-acre vegetable farm, tended by hand, flourishing with silver queen corn, tomatoes, zucchini, carrots, potatoes, and beets. The tiger lily patch was beside another large flower garden dotted with blossoms like Dallas had seen drying at the window. The garage where he worked on cars. Gunderson confessed he had the door rigged to drop bales of straw on someone's head if they came prowling around. "Not enough to hurt them, just scare them off." He had a small pier for his fishing boat: a "glorified" rowboat with a five-horsepower Evinrude engine.

Walking near the water's edge, Gunderson exclaimed, "It's all you need, really. All anyone needs. Life's not complicated when you analyze it. It's pure simplicity." Gunderson pressed his finger and thumb together as though measuring off a pinch of spice. "A body needs two things: nourishment and physical labor. Nothing fancy about that. I grow crops for myself, fish these waters. During the warm months I am entirely self-sufficient. Maybe you didn't notice, but there's no electricity in my house. Propane for cooking, that's all. I heat with the fireplace in the winter. Just like Penny's parents."

Susan linked her arm inside Gunderson's as they looked across Hurricane Bay—the actual body of water, not Marjani's country club, which had stolen its name.

Along the shore, claw scratches from sandpipers, egrets, gulls, and ducks were fossilized in dry earth, a surface of mud baked crisp above wetter ground like the fine ceramic shell of an egg.

Nearer the marsh edge of the bay, the soil turned soft and squishy, and their shoes left signs of a presence contrary to the wildlife there before them. Red-wing blackbirds fluttered inside the cover of tall grass and reeds.

Gunderson said, "A few years ago, Federal Wetlands Commission boys were all over this place. Testing water, taking measurements, marking tides. I filed an injunction to keep them off, but was dismissed. I knew it wouldn't work," Gunderson confided, "I just wanted to hassle those bastards."

Dallas asked why.

"Because they were here to reclassify this land. Take away its wetland protection. You can't build on wetlands, you know, can't develop it, can't bulldoze so much as a spoonful. You have to leave it *as is*. Makes it damned inconvenient for developers like Pete Marjani.

"Two years *before* the federal boys showed up, Marjani tried to buy this property from me. Tried to steal it, really. Because it was wetlands at the time, it wasn't worth much. But I knew that wouldn't last. Because Marjani was going to bribe those federal boys. Sure enough, wetlands protection disappeared and Marjani tried to buy it from me again. I turned him down." At the water's edge, Gunderson turned them back toward his shanty home. It was a spectacular view, even including the ramshackle house. Serene, Eastern Shore Waldenesque.

"Marjani kept offering more and more money. And I kept saying no. I must admit, one of the great pleasures of giving up a life of possessions and money is standing in the way of those still driven by it. And Pete Marjani is that kind of man.

"One day, though—last fall—I thought I might have taken my fun a little too far. Marjani screamed at me. Called me an old fool. Demanded to know what it was going to take to get this land. When I said there was no amount of money he could pay me . . . well . . ." Gunderson took a quick breath. ". . . Marjani's a very big man— much bigger than me. And his face got so red it looked like he was going to explode. I thought for sure he *was* going to kill me. He grabbed one of the logs I had stacked on the porch and smashed my front window with it. He went away right after that, but I don't think I stopped shaking for days. I was scared he was going to come back, but he hasn't set foot on my property since. Maybe the No Trespassing signs worked."

Susan's anger made her bold. "If Marjani comes back here again, you call us. What he did clearly constitutes assault."

Gunderson smiled. "Next time . . . I'll call the police."

Dallas said, "Good idea." Damned if he wanted any more middle-of-the-night phone calls from retired lawyer-judges. "If Crenshaw had called the police instead of me, maybe they'd have found out who he thought was trying to kill him."

Gunderson shook his head. "You're not the only one thought he was crazy. Raymond Crenshaw *deserved* to be crazy. I'm glad I outlived him," Gunderson admitted frankly. "Every sunrise since his death has seemed brighter to me and every sunset more peaceful."

Susan's cellular phone was linked to an answering service so if
someone tried to reach her while she was out of the Benz, they
could leave a message. When she started the car outside Gunderson's house, the phone sounded its birdlike notice: messages.

In this case, Herbie, calling from the Ocean Tides for Dallas.

Susan handed over the phone for Dallas to listen to the play-
back.

"Boss, big, big news. Rupert Dawson called. They had a mess
of prints lifted from Crenshaw's house they couldn't ID at first.
Then, about an hour ago, Harvey Crenshaw, the judge's son, gets
arrested for DWI. They process him, take his prints, and Dawson
thinks to check them with what they lifted from Crenshaw's
house. . . . Bingo."

$\triangledown$

23

"TECHNICALLY," Assistant State's Attorney Brent Bannister advised, "it *is* breaking and entering."

"Which you won't be able to prove," Dallas said.

"Because," Susan continued, "his father is dead and you need his father's statement that Harvey didn't have permission to be inside the house."

Bannister smugly adjusted his seersucker suit jacket. "Since the house is part of Judge Crenshaw's estate, the personal representative can advise whether or not Harvey had permission to be inside."

Susan said, "Crap, too."

Bannister's head tilted back as though she'd spit at him.

Dallas grinned. Legal arguments brought out the beast in Susan. And though he knew it was physically impossible, Dallas swore her hair got blacker, and thicker, and wilder, when she was mad—turning to tentacles that might grab Brent Bannister and rip his lungs out.

Bannister, his fear of aggressive women notwithstanding, held his ground. "None of this matters, however, because you *are not* his attorney—attorn*eys*," he corrected, shifting his gaze to Dallas as though such description applied loosely in his case.

"The only reason we're not his attorneys is because he doesn't *know* we're his attorneys," Dallas said.

Susan crossed her arms. Boy she looked tough in that T-shirt and jeans. "We're volunteering our services to him."

"That's unethical. The solicitation of legal representation is—"

"Perfectly proper if you take the case pro bono."

"That's not one of Sonny and Cher's kids, by the way," Dallas said. "So, Brent, why don't you move your fat bureaucratic ass out of the way and let us see our client."

Susan and Dallas had no intention of representing Harvey Crenshaw, but that was the best lie they could think of to get Bannister to let them see him.

A sheriff brought Harvey to a windowless room in the Dorchester Street police station and sat him on a metal chair. Left to his own coordination, Harvey half slumped over a card table forfeited from outlawed Lion's Club poker nights.

The late judge's son smelled of vomit. His black hair was tangled as though whipped by the same blender that had processed the melon piña coladas he'd slurped down with 151-rum shooters.

His dress shirt was buttoned rakishly, tie bar dangling from one stiff collar tab like a rock climber who'd lost his grip. Presumably, the tie he'd been wearing was now a piece of mangled debris somewhere along Ocean Highway, making motorists wonder how the hell that got there just as they wondered about a solitary shoe lying cockeyed on the median strip.

No doubt Harvey Crenshaw was drunk; what he was *not* was dupeable. He was a lawyer. He knew con jobs. Even through crossed eyes he saw this one coming down the block.

"Christ," he swore at Dallas, enunciating better than the other night in the parking lot, "you're the prick who conned my ol' man outta fifty grand. Tellin' him someone's tryin'a kill 'im." Harvey's face and hands were puffy with water weight. Splotches of adult acne mottled his cheeks. His skin was oily enough to fry eggs.

Susan said, "What were you doing in your father's house, Harvey?"

"Who're-you-bitch?"

"I'm a lawyer and I'm trying to find out how your father was killed."

"*Woman* lawyer." Harvey tried to straighten up, but his hand slipped off the table and he banged his elbow hard. "Shit. Shit-shit-shit!" He winced, grabbing his arm. "Goddamn, that hurts."

Susan asked if he was all right.

"Like you care." Harvey's maturity seemed to have derailed somewhere short of tenth grade.

"Why were you in your father's house, Harvey?" Susan asked again.

"None of your business—for old time's sake, okay?" He continued to rub his elbow.

"Your fingerprints were all over your father's desk drawers and closets and picture frames."

"Maybe I'm an art collector."

"Or maybe you thought he had a safe built into the wall."

Harvey took a shot at rubbing his face, but his hand missed his head and breezed past his ear as though throwing an imaginary palm of salt over his shoulder. "Look . . ." He tried to gather himself. ". . . how my ol' man ended up dead is because *he*"—pointing at Dallas—"got him all worked up thinkin' someone was tryin'a kill 'im. Get some clause put in his will to get paid fifty grand for doin' nottin'. Meanwhile, my old man gets scared and goes out roamin' the streets in the middle of the night with a shotgun lookin' for bogeymen."

"Maybe we should try again once he sobers up," Dallas suggested.

Harvey grunted, "Humph," then mumbled something unintelligible as his slouch worsened and his butt was all the way off the chair.

"Last time, Harvey," Susan said. "What were you looking for in your father's house? If it has to do with why he was killed, it could help us find out how he died."

"You wanna help me, honey?" Harvey banged the tabletop with his palm. "Whyn't you get rid a your friend and hop on up here. Lemme pry you loose of them pants."

Susan turned calmly to Dallas. "Maybe you're right."

They stood in unison and headed for the door.

Harvey Crenshaw tilted his head back and made slobbery gestures with his tongue, licking the air in Susan's direction.

Susan yanked the legs of his chair out from under him.

Harvey was on the floor so fast he must've thought the ground came up to smack him. He hit hard tile with a mean thud.

None of the sheriffs was too eager to respond to Harvey's screams.

Down in the lobby, Rupert Dawson stood near the door. The sound of Harvey's cries was less distinct at that spot. Dawson followed Dallas and Susan out into late-afternoon heat.

Dallas loved leaving a police station without having to post bail. Susan wasn't so cheerful. "What a jerk."

"He tell you what he was doing in his father's cabin?"

"No."

"Kid was looking for something." Dawson walked a step behind, too wide for the sidewalk to accommodate them as a threesome.

Two little kids having a squirt-gun battle dodged between parked cars. A teenaged girl walked by smelling vibrantly of suntan oil.

Dallas contemplated waves, naps, and sunset drinks, only to be rudely interrupted by a relevant thought. "Hey, Rup. You never did find Crenshaw's shotgun, did you?"

"No."

"Harvey"—Susan realized, picking up Dallas's lead—"just told us his father had a shotgun with him when he was killed."

"And how would he know that . . . ?" Dallas said.

". . . unless he was there." Susan turned back to face Dawson. "Where's Harvey been staying in town?"

Dawson's girth cast a wide shadow. "I don't know, but I'm telling Commissioner Hammerman not to release him until he tells us."

Dallas, not necessarily speaking from experience, said, "You could check his car for temporary parking permits."

"And when you find out where he's been sleeping," Susan added, "don't limit your search warrant to looking for that shotgun. Use language like any fruits of a theft of the premises of Raymond Crenshaw, and list things like cash, insurance policies, antiques, other valuables. Things of different sizes so you can look everywhere."

The chief nodded and headed back to the Dorchester station.

Dallas didn't move for a few moments; then he shuddered. "This is dangerously close to acting like prosecutors."

Susan unlocked the Benz. As she started the engine, the car phone tweeted.

Dallas picked it up. He loved these high-tech gizmos.

Another call from Herbie.

Dallas dialed the motel.

"Hey, boss, you know that woman you call Victoria Secrets?"

"Yeah."

"Now I know why. She stopped by to see you. You should've seen what she was almost wearing. How it stayed in place defied every law of physics in this book I'm reading."

"What . . . uh . . ." Dallas didn't want Susan to know the subject of this conversation. "What happened next?"

"What happened next? Well, I told her you weren't here."

"Uh-huh . . ."

"You want to know what happened next?"

"Uh-huh . . ."

"She asked for a key to your room."

"Yeah . . . ?" So nonchalant.

"And I gave it to her."

"Uh-huh . . ."

"What happened next: Chad asked her for a date. She said maybe."

"And . . . ?"

Susan glanced at Dallas, wondering what this cryptic chat was about.

"As we speak, she's in your room. The curtains are closed. Which leaves the question, boss, are you going to tell *me* what happens next?"

24

Dallas OPENED THE DOOR. "Vicky . . . ?"

A swatch of sun slipped over his shoulder and cast a stripe of light into his otherwise darkened room.

Dallas ventured one foot and half a hip inside. "Vicky . . . ?"

No response. Maybe she'd gone back to her Coconut Malerie's suite, leaving the balance of Dallas's afternoon to be just another of life's *what ifs*. What could have been. Damn.

Even though actual history was no more tangible than a memory once over and done with, having lived the experience was so much more rich and, in this case, potentially perverse (which beat the hell out of rich nine times in ten). Or was Dallas merely pretending to want her now that she wasn't here? What happened to those hurt feelings? Knowing she'd left him before and might do it again. Was that memory fogged like water laced with cheap whiskey by her claim *he* had left *her*? Or did it take that much?

Maybe all he really cared about was a chance to feel what he had years earlier. Which he was *always* trying to do anyway. Like having Herbie put on a blue serge suit and wingtip shoes and walk the beach like Nixon used to do so Dallas could pretend it was 1972.

Living at the beach was *not* as simple as it seemed sometimes. It got damned complicated.

Dallas closed the door and reached for the light switch. The standing lamp didn't come on—he'd been meaning to replace that bulb—but at the other end of the room, the bathroom light popped to life. Vicky Sterrett emerged with sultry stealth.

How long had she been waiting for him? How long would she have kept waiting? Quick questions that spun through his mind only to be flicked away like pesky ants on a picnic blanket. What she wore was all he cared about at the moment.

Dallas felt desire surge through him. How gratifying. What a relief. He was back to the hedonistic basics, no longer concerned about what had been, but enthralled by what was about to be.

Vicky stood boldly in the light, a very downtown move. A full lace body stocking clung to her from provocative shoulders to delectable toes. It was perfectly sheer save paisley designs of sexy black; sparsely placed emblems that didn't dull the garment's prurient appeal nor attempt to conceal that she wore nothing beneath it. Her blond hair was brushed to one side and draped along her neck.

"Sorry about yesterday," was all she said before she started toward him.

Dallas had flashbacks of law school days. For a few seconds it was difficult to separate past from present; his mind was so routinely tangled up in memories there were times he honestly couldn't answer how old he was without thinking about it. But then Vicky touched the side of his face—her flesh scented with exotic perfume—and Dallas was launched into the immediacy of now as though fired from a catapult.

"So let's not talk about what used to be . . . okay?" If that had been more than a rhetorical question, her tongue probably wouldn't have slipped into his mouth, preventing an answer.

Heart thumping, Dallas still managed to fall asleep, enthralled by the scent and feel of her, his more vital parts aching. It could have been days later when he finally awoke, or was it just minutes? And where was Vicky? Oh, God, it hadn't been a dream, had it?

In the dark, he frantically searched beneath the covers. Maybe she'd shrunk. His fingers touched nylon—her bodysuit. Ah, it hadn't been a dream. He felt wonderful.

The shower was running in his bathroom. Well, for land's sake, catch it, Dallas thought, bare feet and bare rest of him heading in that direction.

He opened the door and warm steam billowed into his face. The light was off, the window open, allowing in the pale purple cast of sunset along with the eyes of any snoops who might walk by. In the shower, Vicky was covered by no more than an opaque glass door and soapsuds.

Dallas got in with her.

Vicky hummed pleasantly as Dallas touched her slick hips and moved up. "You want to do it again?" She pressed her hands where his response was obvious. Human body braille.

By the time they managed to untangle themselves, it was well past dinnertime. Vicky suggested the Waves, one of the resort's more fanciful restaurants. Dallas counteroffered with Ponzetti's pizza, a place on the boardwalk where they could buy sloppy slices, dash on hot peppers and oregano, and people-watch.

Vicky said maybe tomorrow. Tonight she wanted tablecloths, silverware, candles, and an ocean view. All of which the Waves offered. The Waves also happened to be located in the Sheraton, where the lawyers' convention was at near fever pitch, heading into the weekend like an airline disaster those litigious bastards would mortgage their children to get a few wrongful-death claims out of.

No doubt Vicky wanted to play celebrity and have fellow attorneys gnashing prime rib between angry molars as they unavoidably admired and envied the beautiful success that was Vicky Sterrett Callere (accent on the *re*).

Dallas was reminded of Roland Gunderson saying how restaurants used to buzz when he showed up with his live-in girlfriend. Law could get dangerously like show business, a breeding ground for a new twelve-step program perhaps, Narcissists Anonymous. Maybe Gunderson was right: the only cure was to ditch it all and live like a repentant hermit.

Dallas was picking through a pile of semiclean clothes for something he could shake out and pretend was befitting the Waves when Vicky handed him a garment bag embossed with the Saks, Tyson's Corner, logo.

"A little present," she said, still not wearing anything herself. She unzipped the bag—Dallas loved hearing things unzip around Vicky.

Holy *GQ*, Batman, it was a Hugo Boss suit. Summer silk. Double-breasted jacket, pleated pants. Taupe fabric that glimmered on the hanger. Forty-two long. Thirty-four–thirty-four pants (a little snug, but long enough). She put it on him; a slow, deliberate process that included lots of adjusting and groping. A few laughs. He felt like he was wearing money.

"This's great." Dallas hardly recognized himself in the mirror. He should probably shave.

"I had it overnighted for you. A little more apology for yesterday. I'm good at guessing sizes." Her hand pressed along his leg. "And now, each time you take a step and this silk flows over your body . . . you'll think of me touching you." Vicky laughed provocatively when a certain shift in Dallas's physique threatened to interrupt crisp pleats. "Maybe don't think of me *that* much."

She slipped into her body stocking, adding a short beige skirt and oversized man's blazer that buttoned only once at her waist.

As though cued, headlights flashed against Dallas's window from outside along with two taps of a rich horn.

Vicky said, "I got us a limo."

"That's how I usually travel." Dallas linked arms with her and, like two polished diamonds, they stepped into the parking lot from his landfill room.

The white stretch nearly blocked the Ocean Tides parking lot. Tourists stopped to stare.

Ashley—half-owner of Door Dings Incorporated—hopped out of the driver's seat wearing a suit he looked to have stolen along with the limo. Ashley was average height, but his pant legs dragged along the ground like the robes on Snow White's dwarfs. "Damn," he whispered to Dallas, closing Vicky's door, "I thought this car was hot until I saw your date."

Ashley pulled the limo to the Sheraton's entrance. He stumbled over his pants getting out to open doors.

"What luck," Dallas said, "we didn't pass a single cop."

Ash opened Vicky's door and immediately went to work wiping the car's interior with a buffing rag. A thoughtful felon, eradicating his customers' fingerprints. "Car'll be over there." He pointed vaguely across the parking lot. "I'll be somewhere nearby."

In other words, if the car got pinched, Dallas and Vicky were walking home.

They entered the lobby; a good whiplash lawyer could have made a bundle from all the necks snapping to look at Vicky. She and Dallas crossed the marble foyer to Waves.

The restaurant wasn't crowded; its tables were separated at luxurious distances amidst soothing peach and pale blue decor; New Age music was piped through ceiling speakers with just enough volume to carry over the murmur of conversation and tinkling of plates being cleared.

Phil Burke, maître d' fixture and double-talk practitioner extraordinaire, stuttered legitimately at the sight of Vicky.

"So," Vicky asked, opening her menu to pale candlelight, "what are we having?"

"One helluva good time."

Her smile was warm, almost cozy. "Me, too. I think about you a lot. I've thought about calling you at least a hundred times, but . . . well, you know how it is." She set the menu down and leaned forward. Forearms crossed gracefully on the table, she spoke quietly. "You know, when Raymond Crenshaw came to my office and included that provision in his will for you to investigate his death, I saw there would be reason for me to call you and—this is terrible to say—but I liked knowing one day I'd

124

have an excuse to call. I just didn't expect it would be so soon."

Dallas touched her hand. "You're positive Crenshaw didn't mention anything about who he thought was out to get him?"

Vicky shook her head. "He said he couldn't."

"*Couldn't?* Not wouldn't."

"I know: the semantics. Sometimes I think we lawyers get too caught up in spoken words. We read definition into what someone said as though conversation is a contract that's gone through twenty careful drafts and revisions. Who knows if what Crenshaw said is what he really meant. But the words he said to me—I wrote them in my file notes—were, 'I can't tell you.' *Can't.* Not won't."

"That doesn't make sense."

"It's what he said."

"I'm not questioning your memory, just *why* he would say something like that."

"It crossed my mind it was a joke. He had that reputation."

"That's what I thought this whole deal was. But it's not. . . . So why does a man worried someone may try to kill him not say who or why?"

Dallas looked out at the ocean. The hotel lights shone across the shoreline catching the white foam of cresting waves as they rolled toward the beach. When he turned back toward Vicky, he found that not having looked at her for a mere ten seconds made her an even more dazzling sight. "God, you're pretty."

She smiled with appreciation. "You, too. Must be the suit."

"Yeah," Dallas tugged at the silk, "stuff like this makes me wish I had money."

"Speaking of which . . ." Vicky's soft lips tightened briefly. "I have some bad news."

Dallas braced for the worst; she was getting back together with one of her ex-husbands, or some guy who'd returned from safari or a stint in the foreign legion.

Vicky said, "Crenshaw died broke."

Dallas felt like a bullet had whizzed by his heart, not into it. "What?" Asking even though he'd heard what she said.

"There's no money in the estate. He's got nothing except household possessions and that old car. His house was mortgaged to the hilt. No stocks, no bonds, no real cash to speak of. Maybe ten grand, tops. Unless there's something I haven't found, but I've been to the bank and to— Are you all right?"

Dallas was gripping the table for support. Good God, the prospect of her saying their little frolic today was a one-shot deal, that she was off to the Riviera with some guy named Jules or something like that, had actually traumatized him. He felt light-headed, a sensation only now starting to pass.

So much for hedonism, living for the moment. He was right back where they'd left off over a decade ago. Aching as though diagnosed with a disease he thought he'd beaten.

"Dallas, are you okay?' She clasped his hand firmly. "I'm sorry about the money. If I'd had any idea, I would have told you sooner."

"It's not . . ." He tried to laugh. "Ah, the hell with it. It's just uh . . . just uh . . ." He waved it off. "Forget it. I'm fine. Nothing a dozen drinks won't cure."

Vicky snapped her fingers and a waiter appeared, springing into place like a pop-up in a children's book. The lady got service. "Dallas?" she asked.

"*Two* gin and tonics."

"One for me. Premium brands."

"Certainly," the waiter responded to her cleavage.

When he bopped away to fill their order, Vicky said, "And it's not just that Crenshaw died without money. There's another problem."

"I'm too woozy to guess."

"Harvey Crenshaw."

"No kidding." Dallas was about to report Susan's recent tussle with Harvey, but stopped short—always uneasy talking about one woman while with another. There was a strange loyalty to his lust.

Vicky said, "Harvey came by my hotel this morning about his father's estate. I understand his alienation at being replaced as personal representative in the new will, but his accusations . . ."

"What accusations?"

"Harvey claims his father was a wealthy man and I've stolen all the money."

$\triangledown$

25

Vicky's RED LIP GLOSS left a sticky imprint around the rim of her gin glass that gave Dallas what a televangelist would term an impure thought. In fact, it gave him lots of impure thoughts. An army of them.

"When Harvey arrived this morning," Vicky recounted, "he was already half trashed. I think he must have spent the morning at the convention's Bloody Mary buffet."

Listening, Dallas finished his first gin and started on a crock of sherry-tinged cream of crab soup. His equilibrium returned, but he anticipated the leveling-off period would be brief; he was about to dive into his second drink and order a third.

"I explained to him there wasn't any money in his father's estate, but he wouldn't listen. He screamed at me. He called me a thief and a few other things I won't mention, but if your imagination is half as good as I think it is . . . well, you get the gist."

"He thinks you looted his father's net worth."

"Yes. He asked about his father's stock in Hurricane Bay. He knows about this somehow, so I figure the judge told him about his five percent stake. But I can't find any evidence of it. No certificates, no dividend checks, nothing. Not even in his safe-deposit box. So I called Pete Marjani and he says he doesn't know anything about it. I reminded Marjani that *he* called me the other day saying he was withdrawing the stock deal because Crenshaw hadn't finished working on some matter for him. Marjani denied we'd ever had the conversation."

"As possible explanation, it may be Crenshaw wasn't working for Marjani." Dallas told her about Marjani promising Hurricane Bay's members a new golf course in eighteen months and that he didn't even own the land it was to be built on; also about the sixteen-year-old case where Crenshaw had ruled against Marjani and ended Marjani's pyramid scheme.

"But," Vicky said, "what does Marjani accomplish by calling me in the first place?"

"Maybe it was a lead-in, or a trick question—a roundabout way to find out what you know about Crenshaw and Hurricane Bay.

My bet is Marjani was taking a shot at something. Some con. He's lots better at fraud and cheating than golf. Maybe Crenshaw found out Marjani was pulling a fast one on the members and was out to expose him."

"Do we have any proof of that?"

"I'm big on theory, thin on proof." Dallas set his spoon in his empty bowl, then took it out and laid it properly to the side. "There's another thing about the judge's son."

"I'm sure there's *lots* of 'things' about Harvey Crenshaw."

"Don't you find his being in town strange? The timing of it? He just happens to come down from Pennsylvania right before his father's killed?"

"I checked. Harvey registered for the bar convention months ago. He's licensed to practice in Maryland; he just ended up working in P.A. because of his father. Well . . ." Vicky reached for the basket of breads, then decided not.

"Go ahead, have one," Dallas urged. "You've been eyeing them up since the waiter almost dropped them in your lap."

As Vicky pulled back the linen cloth, rich steam rose off homemade breads. She settled for a poppy seed muffin. "I really shouldn't."

Dallas loved those words. What life at the beach was about.

"Anyway . . ." Vicky took a dainty bite of muffin, bits of which crumbled moistly over her lips. ". . . how Harvey ended up in Pennsylvania . . . By the time he got out of law school—a few years after us—his father was the most hated judge on the bench. You never practiced in front of him, did you?"

"A few times."

"He was wild. When he was a lawyer, he was pretty well liked. But once he took the bench"—Vicky shook her head—"he came apart. Crenshaw'd have a civil case, each side represented by a lawyer he was friendly with. When he had to make a decision and one lawyer left mad, Crenshaw got paranoid whoever he found against was smearing him out in the halls."

"Which he probably was."

Vicky nodded, joyously chewing her muffin. For all her fashion indulgences, she was boringly cautious about what she ate. "But that happens. It's part of the territory. There's no doubt judges withdraw from other lawyers. They're not one of the guys anymore, only Crenshaw couldn't accept that. Once a few attorneys started bad-mouthing him, he thought we *all* were against him. He started going out of his way to nail attorneys. He'd have a fifty-case traffic docket that was going to take all morning and he'd wait to call defendants with lawyers dead last. Just to make the lawyers waste half a day for a hundred-fifty-dollar traffic case."

"There's a certain poetry to that."

"Everything he did became a hatchet job against lawyers. It was a vendetta for him."

That was the second time today someone had analyzed Crenshaw's behavior as a vendetta. The first was Susan talking about Crenshaw going after Mack Trial with malpractice clients.

"What made this even worse for Harvey was that when he got out of law school—your basic my-father's-a-judge arrogant shit—he couldn't even get a job clerking. Forget he had to take the bar exam four times before he passed it. People hated his father so much Harvey was your literal fruit of the poisonous tree. Combine this scenario against a background of Crenshaw, divorced father, who never saw much of his son growing up and spent piles of money trying to sway him from his mother, and you've got an emotional powder keg."

"Which doesn't explain how Crenshaw ended up broke."

"True. But at least now I know why he put the line in his will about being sorry. That part about 'Son, if you're seeing this will, I'm sorry.' Did you catch that?"

Because Susan pointed it out to him, Dallas thought, but didn't confess. "That's what Crenshaw was sorry about? That he died without any money?"

"Looks like it could be," Vicky said. "But notice the language: Crenshaw says 'if you're seeing *this* will.' "

"As in, there's another one?"

"Maybe it's just semantics again, but he set out that clause specifically, had it typed for me to insert word for word. And I don't know why, but I got the feeling this was only a temporary will. That something might happen soon that would cause him to change his will again."

"That he might leave enough money so he wouldn't feel he had to apologize?"

"Maybe." Vicky glanced at the muffin basket the way men who walked by tried to glimpse inside her blazer.

Dallas pushed the muffins closer, the bad influence again.

Vicky succumbed. A pineapple one this time. "If these end up on my hips . . ."

"I'll lick them off."

"Pleasant thought." Vicky opened a packet of margarine.

"So the question is: What was Judge Crenshaw doing that might have made him some new money? Something with Hurricane Bay? Pursuing cases against Mack—?"

Vicky warned, "Shhh," with muffin on her lips. "Speak of the devil." She chewed quickly, swallowed, and stood, buttoning her blazer just when it seemed like she might forget how little she wore beneath it.

Dallas turned in time to see that famous TV lawyer pronounce, "Hi, I'm Trial, Mack Trial," as he gleamed at Vicky, shook her hand, and pulled a third chair to their table for two.

Lost, Dallas thought. Get lost.

"Be right with you, honey." So everyone would notice, Mack Trial waved theatrically to his dinner date: not his wife, but his makeup girl from the set yesterday.

Being seated in a cozy booth across the room, she glared angrily at the back of Trial's head, laser beam eyes that looked capable of uprooting his hair plugs. She obviously wasn't used to being tossed aside for Trial to make a mad dash across the room for someone he thought he could impress. She was new.

"How'd you like us on the news last night, huh, Dallas? Good footage, wasn't it? The way I threw myself over that *speeding* police car." Trial's memory was conveniently sensationalistic. "You catch it?" he asked Vicky, flashing teeth he'd had polished for this week's convention.

"I did," she replied, pretending to be impressed. "A little early for you to be on TV, wasn't it? I usually catch you around three in the morning those nights I'm coming in late from Georgetown. Do you get any clients out of those *cheesy* ads that aren't insomniacs?"

Trial may have sensed he was a little out of his league, but his ego was so tightly wedged between Vicky and Dallas he couldn't pry himself loose without busting something. "Three weeks ago," he reported pompously, "a million-dollar lead paint case was settled that I got from one of those *cheesy* ads. Not exactly limberger, huh?"

"I heard about that case. The only work you did was to turn it over to one of the big firms downtown you pretend to loathe. Because you knew *you'd* screw it up."

First Susan body-slammed Harvey Crenshaw, now Vicky thrust a verbal sword right between Mack Trial's eyes. Dallas was lucky not to be bloodied catching such action from front-row seats.

Trial forced a smile. Too many people in the restaurant, some of them lawyers, were watching, whispering—"Hey, isn't that . . . ?" "Yeah, the moron lawyer on TV." He couldn't let this develop into a scene even if none of these folks were the unemployed junior high dropouts he usually ripped off as clients. He had his pride. "Dallas . . ." He heartily grabbed Dallas's hand and managed to make it look as though Dallas was honored to be touching him. "We'll have to get together sometime. Just the two of us. Mano a mano."

"Mano a dweeb." Vicky smiled mock sweet at Mack Trial.

Trial stood and tried to suavely push back the chair he had borrowed from a neighboring table, wondering how Sean Connery would do it. Trial was so enamored with being watched he didn't do much watching himself, didn't see the woman crossing the room like a poison dart spat from a blowgun.

"You don't want to return my phone calls!" she yelled angrily, her harsh voice interrupting the room's quiet ambience.

Everyone looked, including Trial, who no doubt would have paid a month of contingency fees to melt into the carpet fibers and disappear when he realized who she was. And he did know who she was.

Fear, yellow panic seized him, threatening to crack the phony smile he wore like a mask. Each of his feet turned in separate directions, searching for an escape route, finding none.

"Two days I've been calling! Two days and you ignore me! You think you can ignore me! *That I'll go away!*" She was a handsome woman, with short practical hair, who didn't look like she'd had an easy life. Her mid-level manager's suit was unflattering. Creases around her eyes were stitched with worry. Forty-five or so, brimming with summoned anger and, Dallas suspected, dare.

A touch of hesitancy in her posture contradicted her aggression. She had no doubt built up courage for this confrontation, maybe rehearsed it dozens of times, telling herself she could do it. She didn't look like a screamer, and the volume of her assault seemed alarming to her own ears. "I want an answer! And I want it soon! Tomorrow. Or I'm getting another lawyer. You understand me? This is no bluff."

Trial stared, too mortified to attempt salvage.

The woman left as abruptly as she'd arrived. As she exited the restaurant, a few people began to clap. Soon, the entire room was applauding. A couple of guys stood.

Mack Trial, visibly shaken, face white as a dinner plate, rushed out through a side door and set off the emergency alarm.

Over the din of clanging sirens, Dallas reached for his drink. "We should come here more often. The floor show's great."

26

Full of gin and tonics, lobster thermidor, and the quadruple-quadruple chocolate cheesecake they'd shared, Dallas opened the lobby door for Vicky.

They stepped out into a late evening so glorious even humidity had taken the night off. A full yellow moon was encircled by pale haze, a sign of good weather tomorrow.

Vicky put her arm around Dallas and looked across the parking lot. "What's going on with the limo?"

Three cops were circumnavigating the white stretch. One officer was quite active with his flashlight, inspecting. The other two questioned prospective witnesses.

Dallas adroitly steered Vicky in a different direction.

"Dallas . . . Someone might have run into it. And I don't see the driver."

"You might want to walk a little faster," Dallas suggested.

"Sir?" a voice called from behind.

"Do much running?" Dallas whispered, hurrying Vicky along.

"Dallas, what's the matter?"

"Sir? Hey, sir!" Someone trotted after them: a Sheraton parking valet with surfer-blond hair, dressed in sleek black and white. He came in stride beside Dallas, offering an envelope. "Some guy left this for you."

Dallas kept his head down, not wanting the valet to get a decent look at him. "Thanks."

Vicky peered curiously as Dallas tore open the slim parcel.

"Bus tokens," Dallas said.

Vicky said, "It'll be fun."

"I hate these things. Big, diesel-regurgitating hunks of steel on wheels."

"Like we used to ride downtown when we were in law school, remember? We went to Harborplace to Christmas shop. God, that one night right after Thanksgiving? It was late, all the stores had closed, and it was so damned cold. The heat on the bus didn't work, so we snuggled together in the backseats and made out." Vicky, leaning against a street sign, grabbed the lapels of Dallas's suit and pulled him straight into her, cocking her leg around his to hold him close. "Remember?" She kissed him.

Kids on the waiting-for-the-bus bench watched.

"Remember?"

"Yeah." How could he not smile? "I remember."

Hugging Dallas, Vicky spoke over his shoulder to the teenaged voyeurs. "We would have probably gotten married once, but he left me. Now I've got him back."

One of the girls sighed, "Awwww," like, wasn't that romantic.

When the bus arrived, Dallas and Vicky packed into SRO conditions. They were the only riders old enough to buy beer with legitimate IDs. The plastic and metal interior smelled like a high school lavatory half an hour before homeroom: cheap perfume, deodorant, hair spray, and sneaked puffs of cigarettes. They reached the back of the bus and stood body to body.

Vicky's laugh gave away the exact moment Dallas stuck his hand inside her blazer. "You're going to get us arrested."

"I know a good lawyer."

"But *she's* not going to do you much good with no clothes on."

"Hey, it's the beach." Dallas struggled with her body stocking. "How does this damned thing work, anyway?"

Vicky ran across the lobby, still laughing hysterically from the bus ride. Her heels clicked against shiny marble.

Dallas chased after her, much to the alarm of the Coconut Malerie desk staff, who debated calling security.

"You're bad!" Vicky accused. Pointing at Dallas, she announced to a dozen stunned witnesses: "Don't fall in love with this man. Don't do it!" She passed beneath a row of potted palm trees, holding her blazer closed to conceal how Dallas had worked her half out of her body stocking on the bus.

Midway up the open staircase, her skirt fell to her ankles, and suddenly her blazer was the miniest of miniskirts by default. Vicky laughed even harder. "How did you do that?"

Dallas was ten yards behind her. "Wishful thinking." He collected her skirt, scooped her into his arms, and did his best Rhett Butler up carpeted steps to the third floor. "Key," he gasped, reaching her room.

Vicky dug into her blazer pocket and pulled out her possessions: American Express Gold Card, receipt from dinner, room and car keys. Dallas opened the door and, as Vicky crossed the threshold, removed her blazer like a slick magician.

"You are stunning." He kicked the door shut.

"Bedroom's this way," Vicky invited, backing toward it, arms crossed over her breasts, hair tangled, kicking her shoes at him like harmless missiles.

He ducked the high-heeled assault, charged across the room, and tackled Vicky onto the king-sized bed. The headboard banged the wall. They kissed furiously.

"It smells so good in here," Dallas said between gropes. "Soapy."

"Mmm."

"Do I hear splashing?" He did. Dallas sat upright and looked over his shoulder to the bathroom.

The door was half-open; the mirror mounted to its face reflected an image of the Jacuzzi tub filled with water and suds. Herbie was in there taking a bath.

"Heya, boss." Herbie waved a lathered arm. His frazzled blond hair was tied in a knot atop his head—the world's skinniest sumo wrestler. "Figured I'd find you here. And if I called you guys wouldn't answer the phone."

Vicky covered herself with the bedspread.

"Herbie, get the hell out of here."

"Don't shoot the messenger."

"You're no messenger, you're a prowler."

"*Au contraire, mon frère.* Chief Dawson wants to see you."

"Now? Tonight?"

"ASAP. Wants you to ID a shotgun."

"What the hell's that girlie smell?" Chief Dawson sniffed his own office through congested nostrils.

"Ask him." Dallas pointed at Herbie.

"Clair De Lune bath gel, I think it was called." Herbie offered a half-salute from the hall, having driven Dallas from Vicky's suite.

Dawson's brow creased as he considered a follow-up question, but decided against it. Bear-paw hands grasping worn arms of his desk chair, he pushed his bulk to a standing position.

A wall air conditioner groaned deeply, visibly expelling chilly air like frosty mist.

"Got something for you," Dawson said.

Dallas saw the shotgun leaning against the paneled wall, wrapped in a long clear bag and tagged EVIDENCE. Remains of fingerprint dust clung to its stock and barrel.

Dawson handed Dallas the weapon. "Recognize it?"

Dallas turned the gun over in his hand, no expert on such things by any means. "You want to know if it's Crenshaw's?"

"You lawyers would call that a leading question. I just want to know if you recognize it."

"I don't know, Rup, it could be. I wasn't paying that much attention."

The chief went back to his chair; there was always a sense of relief about him once seated. "We pulled it out of the trunk of Harvey Crenshaw's Jaguar."

"Prints?"

"The judge's mostly. But Harvey's, too. Just around the middle of the barrel, right hand only, like he was carrying it alongside while walking." Dawson gripped the handrails and rocked his chair a few squeaky inches. "Been fired recently, too, but no other buildup. Like it was cleaned between shots."

Dallas set the weapon on the desk. "What's Harvey say about that?"

Dawson picked at wax in his ears. "I believe you're familiar with the Fifth Amendment."

Back at the motel, Susan left a Post-it note stuck to Dallas's headboard: *Check what I got from Parole and Probation. Fax page on top files re: v. Mack Trial.*

"Okay," Dallas replied to the note. He headed for the war room.

Life was quiet tonight at the Ocean Tides. No parties. No loud music. Dallas didn't like it. Even if he wasn't with the kids, he missed them being around. Their absence made him feel old.

In the war room, no one was home, but lights remained on. It was a little stuffy with the balcony door and windows closed, but the lack of air exchange caused subtle remembrances of Susan's perfume to linger. As much as Dallas had enjoyed being with Vicky tonight, there was no one like Susan. Maybe one day . . .

The board game Clue was open on the bed. Three hint pads were scratched with notes. Susan, Jill, and Jill's sister Meghan had been playing. They'd renamed the Clue crime scenes, weapons, and suspects to fit a beach motif. The last murder had been committed by Lifeguard Hunk with a surfboard in Marty's Playland. Jill had figured it out.

Dallas found Crenshaw's case folders concerning Mark Trial. Scotch-taped to the top file was a fax Susan had received from Parole and Probation: a copy of a letter sent to the parole board two months ago by Mack Trial, addressed to each board member individually.

Re: Jumbi Berrell
Dear Board Members:
I was the Assistant State's Attorney originally assigned to the prosecution of this case. Although Mr. Berrell's guilt was indisputable, the imposition of sentence, I feel in retrospect, was too severe.

Mr. Berrell did not intend to harm Judge Raymond Crenshaw. His actions were borne of frustration with the judicial system. Undeniably, his firing of a weapon in a public place was regrettable. However, it was an act of protest, *not* attempted murder.

I believe that, this event having taken place in a courtroom, the sentencing judge may have been overly eager to make an impression that those causing courtroom disturbances would be severely dealt with.

While I feel the point was well made (and well taken), to continue to incarcerate Mr. Berrell is to punish him unduly for what was an aberrant act on his part.

To assure my opinion is based on fact and not memory alone, I have gone so far as to meet with Mr. Berrell and members of his family. I discussed this matter with them in great detail.

Mr. Berrell shows the utmost remorse for his acts and I am sure, under the supervision of your department once released, he will be a model citizen.

I therefore respectfully request that you grant Mr. Berrell's release at his upcoming parole hearing.
Very truly yours,
/s/
Mack Trial

Susan had penned a note at the bottom of the page: *Collateral issue resolved? Would J.B. have shot at Mack Trial after this? Doubtful. But: Does this give Crenshaw motive to go after Trial w/ malpractice cases? Also: Could Berrell have hired Trial to write this?*

Dallas hadn't thought about Jumbi Berrell for a while. Movies aside, it was rare for a convicted criminal to seek revenge against the judge, prosecutor, or jurors who'd put him away. Mack Trial must've been thinking along the same lines; he didn't seem too concerned, traipsing about Waves with an adulterous dinner date, more fearful of an angry-client-ignored than another attempt on his life, perhaps by a felon he'd prosecuted.

As for what made Susan think to call the parole board to dig further into the Berrell-Crenshaw link, Dallas would have to congratulate her. Two heads *were* better than one, especially if one of the heads was smarter.

Dallas put the fax back on the file pile. He was about to pick up the phone and call Vicky, but decided against it. With Susan's sensuous smell still in the room, he'd feel like he was cheating on her. That love logic again.

He idly scanned a few other notes Susan had made on her legal pad. One page, dated today, was marked at the top: *Mrs. Roland Gunderson*. And beneath that: *Locate and surprise Roland?*

Swell, just what Dallas needed, setting up a little episode of "This Is Your Life" for a reclusive old lawyer. Dallas, being the mature adult he was, remained jealous of Susan's interest in Gunderson.

Sudden hollering outside drew Dallas to the curtain. He looked out at the beach. The kids were starting a volleyball game. The high school girls—three Ls and an M—versus Chad and C.J.

C.J. spit into his hands and jeered, "Come on, serve it up. We don't need more than the two of us to whip a bunch of Bettys."

Chad did a few stretching and flexing exercises in his muscle shirt.

Dallas had to see this. Macho beer bravado was about to get slammed into the sand.

$$\bigtriangledown$$

27

"LET IT GO! Let it go! It's going out!"

Chad let Laura's serve hit the sand.

"In!" all four girls shouted in unison. They formed a circle; each put one hand in the center and brought their other hand to the middle in a sweeping arc, slapping skin. "*Ace!*" they cheered.

Chad glared at C.J.

"Okay, so it didn't go out."

"Shut up and play the net."

Laura served a shot down the line. Chad dove for it and missed.

"In!" Another ceremony. "*Aaaace!*"

C.J. looked back at Chad. "I didn't say that one was gonna be—"

"Shut up and play the net." Chad whipped off his shirt, bent into a ready position, and adjusted the legs of his baggy shorts.

Laura's 2–0 serve arched a little higher than her first two. Chad settled under it, bumped it to C.J.

C.J. jumped. Swung his arm mightily. "*Arunghhhh.*"

The green and black jungle ball sailed over the net and kept going for about fifty yards.

"It's outta there!" C.J. called. "Home run!"

"You idiot." Chad threw sand at him. "You're supposed to set for me."

"You never set it for me. You always hit them yourself."

"I'm taller."

Meghan chased down the ball. It was 3–0.

Dallas used to think the reason the girls won all their games was because of the cute outfits they wore: tight bike shorts and fluorescent elastic tops. That was before he realized how skilled they were. As for Chad and C.J. . . . . "You guys are really bad."

"Get your ancient ass in here, then," Chad challenged.

"Okay," C.J. taunted through the net, "let's go, let's go. Come on, Laura, serve that hummer. It's coming back at you. Down your throat. Here we go."

Dallas knew he should change out of his new suit, but figured the game would be over by the time he got to his room and back. He stripped down to his pants and rolled the legs up.

"Okay, okay," C.J. kept chanting, "what're we waiting for here? What's happening?"

"Will you shut up."

C.J. turned at the waist, University of Maryland hat worn three-quarters backwards. He saw Dallas for the first time. "Hey, all right. Now we're ready. Send that ballie over here, Laura."

"First chance you get," Chad instructed Dallas, "knock him down." Pointing to C.J.

Laura served a rope. Chad dove, dug it with his fist. Dallas bumped it to C.J. C.J. knocked it over for a kill.

"All right! Side-*out*!" C.J. dropped to one knee and pumped his arm. "Yesss!"

Lisa rolled the ball under the net toward C.J. Chad grabbed it.

"Hey!" C.J. protested.

"You're not serving."

"Gimme the ball!"

"Forget it." Shove. "Get up there." Harder shove.

C.J. shoved Chad back.

Dallas asked if he'd have time to change.

"You guys need a fourth?" It was South, the Hawaiian bodyboarder.

"Come on in," Dallas invited. "You play this much?"

South shrugged. "A little."

Dallas made introductions. "Guys, this is South."

The bodyboarder didn't question nor mind the moniker.

C.J. and Chad shook his hand, C.J. apologizing for the spit on his palm. The girls huddled to discuss strategy and how cute South was. Laurie said she was going to ask him out.

Chad served it into the net.

"Yesss!" C.J. celebrated.

Chad picked up the ball and pegged C.J. with it. It bounced off C.J.'s back and went over the net.

Meghan collected it. Her serve. A beaut.

South dug it. Chad bumped it for Dallas. South jumped between Dallas and the ball, knees bent, thirty-inch vertical leap, and nailed a vicious spike.

Lisa dug it. Meghan set. Laura drove it over the net.

The ball struck C.J.'s fists and sailed way over the end line. South sprinted after it, dove, saved it back inbounds. Dallas tapped it over the net.

Meghan bumped it. Laurie spiked it.

South, back at the net, blocked it.

"Yesss!"

Dallas looked at Chad and grinned. "We got a ringer."

The girls looked serious.

Dallas dove for the ball. Meghan had dinked it. A cheap little dink. A cheap little strategically placed game-winning dink.

Dallas laid out flat against the beach, sand sticking to his sweaty body. "Crap."

A small enclave of boardwalk spectators clapped and slowly dispersed. The girls' undefeated streak survived a scare, 15–13. A game that took forty minutes.

"One less gin," Dallas mumbled, spitting sand, "and I'd've had that ball." His heart was thumping madly.

Chad helped him up. "Next time." Chad pointed at the girls. "Rematch tomorrow night."

Chad was about Dallas's height these days, an easy twenty pounds broader. Dallas remembered when Chad was ten. Nights on the boardwalk when arcade games were amusement enough. Too much time had gone by between then and now; time Dallas wanted back.

Dallas brushed himself off. His pants were covered with sand, pockets filled with it.

South handed him his shirt and jacket. "I saw you leave in a limo tonight with a very pretty lady. Your girlfriend?"

"Used to be. A long time ago."

"Very pretty," South said again. He stood silently, but acted as though he wanted to say something else.

The rest of the kids gathered by the net, figuring out where tonight's party was going to be.

"Your friend hasn't shown up yet, has he?" Dallas asked. "Cutback?"

South shook his head.

"Maybe he went home. Sometimes a scare with the police makes home seem not so bad."

South started to speak, but stopped.

"If you want to call his folks and check, go ahead. If it's long distance, that's okay. You're not calling Alaska, right?"

"No."

Dallas had hoped for a little more personal information than that, but didn't want to come out and ask. "Gina doing okay?"

"She spent most of the day looking for him. She's asleep now."

Dallas nodded.

South looked at Dallas, but upon meeting his eyes, averted his gaze to the ocean. Another period of silence.

"You guys have everything you need?" Dallas asked.

"Yes. Herbie . . . with the long hair? He got some groceries for us."

"Jugs of milk, not in cardboard cartons, right?"

"Yes. It's . . . it's very nice of you to help us like this. Gina might not say so . . . might not seem like she cares . . . but she's very thankful, too."

"Glad you're here. We'll get your friend back."

Laurie jogged over and asked South if he wanted to go barhopping with them. They knew some bouncers who'd let them in with the measly fake IDs Chad bought off a kid at school.

"I'd like to, but . . ." South shrugged.

"We never get caught if that's what you're worried about." She was always cheerful, her sisters, too.

"I'll still pass . . . thanks."

"See you tomorrow night, though? For the rematch?"

"I'll be here."

Dallas looked across the boardwalk at the Ocean Tides. Gina wasn't sleeping. She was on the balcony. As soon as Dallas noticed her, she retreated inside.

The other kids came over to collect Laurie and encouraged South to join them.

Dallas pulled Chad aside. "Do me a favor."

"Yeah."

"Don't do bars tonight. I'll send Herbie out for a couple of cases for you."

"No Old Milwaukee."

"You pick it, I'll pay. Just get South to tag along and find out what his story is."

"Easy enough. You coming with us?"

"Nah. I'm going up on the roof for a while. Catch you tomorrow. Maybe we'll do the General's for breakfast. One o'clock sound good?"

Dallas walked into the lobby, said, "Hey, Herbie. Two things. First, go get three cases of beer for Chad."

"Money." Herbie held out the hand that wasn't clutching a drippy steak sub.

"It's in my room."

Herbie withdrew his "demand" hand.

"Second thing: tomorrow, crack of dawn, go down to the Third

Street post office and check out Judge Crenshaw's PO box. He's been using it as his business address. About time I figured we should see who's been sending him mail, huh?"

Herbie put his hand out again. "Key."

"That's where you come in. We don't have the key."

The hand dropped. Eyebrows raised. "You want me to pick it? A U.S. government mailbox? As in committing a federal offense?"

"It's only a crime if you get caught."

28

DALLAS WAS HAVING A nightmare. It was 8:00 A.M. and someone was calling him on the phone. It kept ringing, and ringing, and ringing. . . .

It was no dream. He grabbed the phone. "Yeah?"

"Heya, boss. Wake up." Herbie.

"Whaddayou want?" Dallas snapped. "It's early."

"I'm down here at your friendly neighborhood post office, reporting in."

Post office? What the hell . . . ? Then Dallas remembered: Crenshaw's PO box. Dallas propped his head on his hand; getting his eyes parallel to the floor helped clear his brain. "You get the box open?"

"Simple."

"Good. Take out whatever's in there and bring it back. Susan and I'll go—"

"There's nothing in there."

"Oh . . . Really? What's today?" Dallas tried to remember.

"Thursday, but today's mail hasn't been put in yet."

Dallas forced his thoughts into gear. "Crenshaw died early Monday morning . . . that was before the post office opened . . . so we've got Monday, Tuesday, Wednesday. . . . No mail in three days?"

"I don't think that's it," Herbie said. "Some old-timer came in here just after I picked Crenshaw's box. The oldster opened his box and had a fistful of junk mail. He griped about it to me—how mail-order businesses should have to pay triple postage, not get a discount. He asked if I believed he got that much junk mail in two days. He dumps these fliers in the trash, so I took a look. It's all carrier presort stuff that gets delivered to *every* address in this zone."

Dallas didn't get what Herbie was saying, because midway through Herbie's report his thoughts had drifted uncontrollably to Vicky.

"Boss"—Herbie brought him back from fantasyland—"someone's been picking up Crenshaw's mail."

Dallas snapped to. "You at a pay phone?"

"Yeah. Right inside the post office."

"Gimme the number."

Herbie did.

"Hang on, I'll call you right back."

"Don't leave me standing here too long with nothing to do. Someone'll mistake me for a post office employee."

Dallas hung up and called Coconut Malerie's. "Miss Sterrett— Miss Callere's room, please. Even if you've got to let it ring a hundred times before she answers."

She picked it up on the second ring, sounding awake and alert.

"Vicky?" Dallas thought he had the wrong room.

"Hi, baby." She sounded very glad to hear from him.

"You up already?"

"I'm up every day at five. You don't impress clients getting to the office *after* they do."

"Well, when we get married, you'll have to sleep in the other room."

"I'll be so-o-o lonely," she pouted. "When are you coming over? It seems to me we didn't quite finish what we started last night."

"Tempting . . ." Dallas lay back in bed, preferring the dreamy quality of this conversation to dealing with Herbie's realities. "Very tempting."

"I hope so."

"But . . ."

"Mmmm?"

"Vicky, I've got to check one thing on the case."

"Case? Dallas, I told you last night, there's no money in the estate to pay you."

"Ah, I'd only have to pay taxes on it, right? They still make you pay tax in this country for making money, don't they? It's been so long since I've had an income, I've lost track."

"Forget about the case. Come over here with me. I'll give you what money can't buy."

Suddenly, Dallas was uncomfortable. Something had shifted in Vicky's tone. Sincerity was being overtaken by an incoming tide of hard sell.

"Dallas . . . ?"

He sat up. "Do you have Crenshaw's post office box key?"

She exhaled displeasure. "You're not coming over, are you?"

"Vick . . . do you have the key?"

"I don't care about any post office box. And I wish you wouldn't care, either."

"What's the matter?"

"I miss you, goddammit. I want to go to bed with you. I want you to—" She proposed a long list of deviant behavior.

Dallas listened, then asked, "Where am I going to get a saddle and five gallons of maraschino cherries at this hour of the morning?"

"Herbie?"

"What took you so long? It's getting ugly around here. There's a long line of customers and only one person on the desk selling stamps. All the other employees are placing phony home pickup orders to sabotage UPS."

"Vicky doesn't have the key to Crenshaw's PO box."

"Neither do we."

"Yeah, but someone does. Whoever's been coming by to—"

"Oh no. Ohohoh no-o-o! I'm not waiting around here all day to see who picks up some dead guy's mail. Pass-adena!"

"What magazines do you want? I'll stop by Hazel's and get them for you."

Herbie groaned.

Dallas was disappointing a lot of people this morning. And it was so damned early. "I'll bring food, too."

"Not food, doughnuts. The kind with a lot of creamy filling. And a Big Gulp. And some beef jerky."

"I'll be there in half an hour."

"Great," Herbie replied sarcastically. "The post office'll pension me by then."

Dallas hung up. This was why he slept late. People were damned ornery in the morning. By noon life was easier to deal with.

He struggled out of bed, took a shower, got dressed.

Outside, the clouds were puffy and white, just enough to offer welcome shade breaks from the sun. Tourists had already begun to crusade to the beach, toting umbrellas, playpens, blankets and towels, coolers, and straw bags full of sundries. Riders of all ages traversed side streets and the boardwalk on aged rental bikes—real bikes, not those fancy zillion-gear things people rode wearing goofy outfits and alien aerodynamic headgear.

Dallas went up the stairs to the second floor and knocked on the volleyball girls' door.

"Open," a clear voice chimed. Jill was kneeling on the kitchenette counter, having boosted herself to reach the cabinets. She pulled out a box of sugared-up cereal. "Oh, hi." She grabbed a bowl. "Want some breakfast?"

"It's too early to eat."

"No, it's not."

The other girls were still asleep. Clothes were strewn all over the place along with curlers, hair spray, and myriad plastic bottles of shampoo. Wet towels had been optimistically draped over the backs of kitchen chairs to dry.

Dallas asked Jill to watch the front desk until Susan came in.

"Sure. That way I can ask her about her date."

Dallas was staggered by this news—like a stake had been driven through his heart. "Susan went on a date?"

"She said it wasn't a date date."

"No?" Renewed hope.

"Just some man she used to know. Some old guy." Jill poured out colorful cereal balls that danced into a plastic bowl.

"What's his name?"

"Something funny." She hopped off the counter.

"A funny name?"

"Yeah." She got out the milk and poured a little too much, splashing it over the side of the bowl. "Oops." She grabbed one of her sister's T-shirts and wiped up the spill, realizing what she'd used after it was too late. "Oh, well." She gave a little laugh, tossing aside the milk-sopped top.

"This guy . . . ?" Dallas asked.

"She said she met him on the phone when she was in law school."

"Gunderson?"

"That's it."

"Here." Dallas dropped the grocery bag onto the passenger seat of Herbie's VW. The contents shifted in protest.

"You mad at me for not staying inside the building?" Herbie gestured to the bland brick-and-tile post office across the street.

"No, screw it. You can see from here."

With the sun not yet above a condo two blocks east, there was no glare across the plate-glass window that looked into the lobby and box area.

Herbie dug into the goodies. "Vanilla cream. These are great." He took a big bite of doughnut. Powdered sugar dusted his face, matching his skin tone. For all his love of Ocean City, Herbie could not overcome genetic dice that rolled him out with sun-sensitive skin.

Dallas rattled the bag. "There's also a book in there about the beginning of the universe. Hazel had it on the dollar table. She said no one's understood it yet. I figured it'd be perfect for you."

"Neat."

"And here's the portable cellular. Just in case."

"Dusty," Herbie observed. They hadn't used it since last summer.

Dallas squatted beside the VW, resting his arms where the window was rolled down. "Did Susan say anything to you about going out with Gunderson?"

Herbie reached for his Big Gulp and drew in a long swallow of Coke while his mouth was still full of vanilla cream and doughnut. "I don't think it's anything to worry about."

"Yeah, well, I've called her condo five times and she doesn't answer. I even stopped by her place on the way to *and from* Hazel's. She's not home. Her Benz, either."

Herbie said, "Ohhh," expelling a smoke ring of powdered sugar.

Dallas grimaced. "You think she spent the night with him?"

"Uhhh . . ."

Dallas pounded Herbie's door with his palm. "I hate this."

"Boss, maybe this is a bad time to bring this up, but didn't you go out with Victoria Secrets last night?"

"I wouldn't have if Susan would go out with me. All she has to do is say the word and I'm hers forever." Agitated, he stood. "I'm going over there."

"Where?"

"Gunderson's."

"You're gonna make a fool of yourself."

"What else is new?"

29

ROLAND GUNDERSON STEPPED FROM his rickety boat onto the small gray pier, fishing rod in one hand, string of three flounder in the other. He considered Dallas from across the unplanted field, not waving, just looking, as though expecting a confrontation.

Dallas felt a little dumb worrying if Susan had slept with her former phone mentor. Being here now, that seemed so unlikely. Besides, what business was it of his, really? Still, he was going to ask—somehow. And then what?

"Morning," Dallas called, friendly enough.

Gunderson showed relief. He raised his catch just hooked out of Hurricane Bay's bounteous waters. "A truly *good* morning." He started across the field.

Behind him, the bay's tidal motion rolled his little boat gently against the creosote pier.

"Took me a while to get used to fish for breakfast instead of bacon and eggs. Now, with all the health news what it is, looks like I've been doing my circulatory system a favor. Quit smoking nearly thirty years ago, so, who knows, I might live to be a thousand." Gunderson gestured to the house. "Come on in if you're so inclined. Company two days in a row. I might get spoiled."

Gunderson stepped onto his creaking porch. The front door was unlocked. He left it open for Dallas to follow.

Beneath the house, Dallas saw another collection of bright orange tiger lilies, cut from the field and left in the shade. A soon-to-be element of Gunderson's craft projects, no doubt.

At the kitchen sink, Gunderson made quick work of scaling the flounder. He was sure and efficient handling the flat bottom dwellers, chopping off tails and heads, slitting them width-wise and turning out clean fillets. He took a tub of margarine from a compact refrigerator, scooped out a dab with his finger, and flicked it into a cast-iron skillet. Turned on the propane burner and, as soon as the oleo sizzled, laid in the fillets.

The only seasoning used was flecks of parsley removed from a stalk drying at the window and ground by his fingers.

"So," Gunderson said, his back to Dallas as he tended his breakfast, "you're here about something." Direct enough.

"We can't find Susan." Dallas made this seem a collective effort, not jealous obsession on his part.

"She was here last night."

"Until what time?" Dallas asked a bit too quickly.

"Ten-thirty, perhaps eleven. I'm not sure." He gestured across his small shack/home. "I don't have any clocks." Alerted by the popping sound of frying fish, he flipped his meal with a metal spatula. After a pause, he said, "Did she tell you she was coming here?"

"No."

"I didn't think so."

"Why's that?"

Gunderson looked out the window. "Well . . . I asked her if she was living with you—just being curious, not meaning anything by it other than wondering what the relationship was. Yours and hers. She said you were just good friends."

Dallas caught the reflection of Gunderson's smile in the window.

"She just brought over dinner," Gunderson said, a tone used to deliver reassuring news. "Chinese carryout. We ate and talked. That was all." Gunderson's smile remained. He turned off the propane and slid his fish onto a worn piece of china. Not offering Dallas any, he ate standing by the sink. "I'm glad you came over," he said, chewing.

"Really?"

His expression quite knowing, Gunderson nodded. "It's been a long time since I was suspected of sleeping with someone. I've missed it."

Herbie was right. Dallas had made a fool of himself . . . again.

Gunderson said, "You should know she's not the kind of woman to give herself willy-nilly. I could tell that talking to her on the phone all those years. She's very serious. Not that she can't have her fun, but some things mean more to some than others."

Dallas resented Gunderson telling *him* about Susan. Dallas was the one who'd seen her nearly every day for the past three years. Not Gunderson.

"If your Miss Vette feels strongly about someone, she's going to approach that relationship with a great deal of care. Nurture it. Let it unfold naturally. The way you prepare and raise a garden. Those," he said, waving his fork at Dallas, "are the relationships that last. I learned that the hard way with Penny, my wife. We were like a meteor hitting the earth's atmosphere. We lit fast, burned bright, and crashed. Meteors don't last. Gardens do. They come back every year." Gunderson finished his two fillets with the abandon of someone who ate to live, not vice versa; a trait acquired living alone and cooking for one.

He rinsed his plate and stuck it on a wood rack to dry. The fish he hadn't cooked was wrapped in brown paper and stowed in the fridge. "I've got some gardening to do. Can I interest you in some cantaloupes? Got a good batch coming in."

Dallas followed him from the house, across a field left to rest this growing season. Gunderson's active crops were five hundred yards from the house and garage. Rows upon rows of flourishing vegetables.

Bending with a teenager's agility, Gunderson lopped two melons from viny entrails and handed them to Dallas. Their pale brown skins were so much more natural than the hard greenish ones in grocery store bins. Sweet aroma drifted off their navels.

"Now you see?" Roland Gunderson asked, looking at Dallas with pride in his eyes that made him seem the same height, not eight inches shorter. He tapped the melons with the butt end of his knife. "Land that can produce food this wonderful should never be in the hands of a man whose only interest in life is conning money from people."

"Pete Marjani?"

Gunderson nodded. "Now if I could outlive *him*"—he breathed deeply as though anticipating a pleasant smell in the air—"imagine how wonderful *that* would be."

"Duck farts!" Kneeling on freshly cured concrete, the echo of hammering still ringing in the warm breeze, Pete Marjani glared at the nail he'd just mishit.

Driven through the base two-by-four of a newly framed wall, the nail had protested meeting concrete and ended up bent at a ninety-degree angle.

Marjani dug the claw end of his hammer under the ruined nail and ripped it out viciously. "Corky! Bring me another box of nails, goddammit!"

Marjani's three-man work crew looked as though the new patio home they were building was a carton of eggs. They tiptoed about cautiously, terrified of doing something wrong around the big boss man. Probably wishing he didn't feel these Sam Walton urges to show he was one of the little guys. They liked it better when Marjani stayed in his office and wrote checks.

Corky, a leather-faced fifty-or-so cowboy who looked to have swum the better part of his life inside a bottle of cheap whiskey, hustled a fresh box of masonry nails to Marjani.

Dallas said, "Hey, Pete."

Marjani squinted into the bright sky, his stern expression growing angrier when he recognized him. "Hey, goddammit." He aimed his hammer at Dallas as though it was a loaded .45. "Lowell Javitz sues me for hitting him with that golf ball, I'm naming you as a codefendant. I'd've been in the clubhouse if it weren't for you."

Behind Marjani, his work crew hammered noisily. Two men studded a wall that would soon be in place atop a concrete slab; the third man sunk landscaping ties with twelve-inch spikes.

Dallas squeezed "into the house" between exposed two-by-fours.

Marjani growled, "And I told Claude I'm suing him too for suggesting you play with us. Goddamned, but I hit the ball so poorly it carried over this morning. I played seven holes and goddamned quit. I play and play and practice and practice and it never gets any goddamned better. Damn how I hate this game." Marjani grabbed a fresh nail and pounded it with his frustrations, sinking it through wood and into concrete with six slams of heavy forearms and powerful wrists. "Damn, damn, damn!" He drove in another nail, his face reddening deeper than a scoop of salad bar beets.

For as poorly as he swung a golf club, Marjani was right at home with a hammer; no Harry Homeowner tap-tap-tap, he drew the tool behind his ear and sent it toward the nail with a mean wallop.

Dallas squatted beyond Marjani's reach to ask what he'd never gotten around to discussing yesterday. "Hey, Pete . . . ?"

Marjani looked over as though surprised Dallas was still there. "What?"

"I want to ask you about Raymond Crenshaw."

Marjani drove in a fresh nail. *Bang-bang-bang-bang-bang-bang!* Grabbed another one.

"Pete . . . ?"

Marjani slammed in the nail. Hollered, "Corky!"

"Yes, sir." Corky came skidding across the foundation, work boots kicking up concrete dust.

"You and the boys take an early lunch."

"Yes, sir."

Corky and crew loaded into Corky's pickup truck faster than a trio of hound dogs cut loose on the hunt. Their hammering stopped, it was quiet along the eighth fairway, save moans of golfers' failures and errant iron shots hitting distant trees.

Marjani stood, knees of his blue jeans chalked with concrete. His gray T-shirt, soaked with sweat, stuck to his massive chest and arms. He came toward Dallas with the hammer gripped like an axe by his side.

Dallas took half a step back and looked for a loose piece of two-by-four, something big he could swing.

▽

30

"JACK! GET YOUR ASS OUT HERE. I'm at four-oh-seven Hooked Lane." Marjani slammed the portable cellular phone back into its soft-sided case.

Dallas felt silly holding a length of two-by-four, having thought Marjani was coming after him when all he'd wanted was the "goddamned phone." Dallas pretended the two-by-four was a golf club and took a few easy practice swings before setting it down.

Not noticing Dallas's would-be defensive pose, Marjani went back to his hammering, hitting nails so hard the entire foundation shook. The nearest Richter scale probably recorded tremors.

Working, Marjani said nothing save one or two "Duck farts!" when he bent a nail.

Within five minutes, a Lincoln Town Car came speeding down Hooked Lane, road dust raised in its wake as though leading a cattle drive. Frog-faced and rumpled, Jack Hayes burst from behind the wheel. He scuttled across the dirt yard, navigating discarded rolls of wire mesh and rusty lengths of rebar. Hurrying to Marjani, Hayes barely glanced Dallas's way.

"Duck farts!" Marjani fouled a nail. He ripped it out and stuffed it into his pocket with other mishits. "Construction site should always be clean. Like a kitchen and a bathroom. But tell that to these morons I got working for me. Leave enough materials scattered around to build a whole 'nother house." Barking this to no one in particular.

Hayes stood attentively in his sad brown suit, waiting to be advised why he was here, a wish Marjani finally granted.

"Jack"—Marjani jabbed his hammer toward Dallas—"Mister I-Think-You're-Due-For-A-Hole-In-One wants to know about Raymond Crenshaw."

Like a good frog, Jack Hayes remained perfectly still, as though blending into his surroundings might save him from predators.

Marjani grabbed the car keys Hayes held in his hand. He headed for the Lincoln, leaving Hayes to respond to Dallas's questions.

Dallas would have preferred hearing from Marjani himself, but he'd tossed that two-by-four a little far away to press his luck. He looked at Hayes.

Hayes swallowed.

"Was Crenshaw working here at the club?"

"Here at the club?" Hayes repeated the question to give himself time to work on an answer. "No."

"He didn't have an office here?"

"Office . . . ? No."

"But you did know him?"

"Know him . . . ?"

"Raymond Crenshaw? You knew who he was?" Dallas demanded impatiently. "You know that he's dead."

"Dead . . . Yes."

Marjani got inside the big Lincoln and slammed the driver's door. Started the engine. It died when he shifted into gear. He started it again, foot all the way down on the accelerator. The tail pipe belched a cloud of oily smoke. Marjani revved the engine louder than a jet. It quit when he shifted into gear. "Duck farts!" A shout heard through the sedan's windows. The smell of sulfur drifted across the homesite, expelled from the car's catalytic converter. Marjani ground the engine again.

Jack Hayes winced.

Over the pained engine, Dallas said, "I'm a lawyer and . . ."

Hayes's expression registered a definite uh-oh.

". . . Raymond Crenshaw's estate has hired me concerning his rights to five percent ownership in Hurricane Bay."

Hayes said, "Ummmm . . ." as though physically afraid to repeat words concerning Crenshaw owning part of the club.

"We'd like to make a deal to sell his interest back to the club. At a discount. On the qt. No admissions of liability, no admissions, really . . . about anything." Dallas was a good liar.

"No liability . . . ?" Hayes's eyes twinkled as though someone was tickling his scrotum with a boa feather.

Marjani got out of the Lincoln and kicked the door shut. "Jack! This goddamned miserable rental piece of shit is worthless. You take it back and tell the goddamned body shop my car isn't ready by five I'm coming down there to rip out their duck fart hearts!"

Hayes backed from Dallas like a skittish puppy afraid his choke chain was about to clamp down on his throat.

"Ask Pete if he wants to talk details," Dallas urged, trying to contain a minor swell of euphoria at the prospect of connecting Marjani and Crenshaw.

Hayes politely gestured with his pointer finger for Dallas to wait one minute. He crossed the debris-cluttered yard and saddled up beside his much-larger boss.

As Hayes relayed the message, Marjani's gaze shifted from his amphibious gofer to Dallas. He looked mad . . . but interested.

A team of twenty-plus Hurricane Bay and Pete Marjani Company employees shared the entire second floor of the newly improved Hurricane Bay clubhouse. The sprawl of offices was sectioned only by glass walls so Marjani could determine in one sweep of eyes who was working and who was working harder.

Secretaries, bookkeepers, architects, contractors, and salespeople worked with a sense of energetic accomplishment that turned up a notch when Marjani roared in.

The boss knew everyone by name and touched base with six or seven staffers, checking on bookings for upcoming golf tournaments, current financing plans offered by local banks for Hurricane Bay home buyers, and a planned improvement in employee health benefits.

Immediately, Marjani was up to speed on all fronts.

What surprised Dallas the most was that the male-female ratio was dead even. And that Marjani's conversations were carried out without regard to gender; no honey or sweetheart references for the women, be they young or middle-aged, attractive or plain. For not wanting club members bringing their wives to social functions, apparently when it came to getting the job done, Marjani only cared who did the best work.

These on-the-fly briefings lasted a total of ten minutes. Throughout, Marjani didn't introduce Dallas to anyone, nor was he asked who Dallas was.

Afterward, Marjani led Dallas to yet another level of offices. The top floor.

Windows lined all four walls of Marjani's private office. Two thousand square feet that included an indoor putting green and computerized practice tee. The decor was Southwest influenced, with bulky furnishings of washed oak and Aztec-patterned fabrics and wallpaper. Pale green, dusty rose, and gray colors throughout.

Pleated shades were lowered over the northeast window wall, not, Dallas surmised, because of sunshine, but because that view, although a splendid vista of the bay, included Roland Gunderson's land. Marjani, apparently, could not stand to see that which he wanted so badly and could not have.

Suddenly gracious, he gestured Dallas toward his indoor practice tee, where, instead of driving the ball into a net as was the
usual golf-shop setup, the target was a wide white screen.

Marjani flicked off overhead lights and hit another switch that
projected the photographic image of a fairway onto the screen. He
kicked a logo Hurricane Bay ball across the AstroTurf; it rolled to
a stop by Dallas's sneakered foot.

"Go ahead. Hit away." Marjani offered a Ping driver and gestured to the screen. "Recognize it?"

Dallas hadn't oriented himself yet. He'd read about these inter-
active golf games, but never experienced one firsthand. He looked
closely at the projection screen. "It's the first hole."

Hurricane Bay's number one: a short par 4, slight dogleg right
around a wide sand trap.

"Give it a shot."

Dallas took a practice swing. The Ping was much lighter than
his wood driver. He settled behind the ball, as self-conscious here
as on any first tee shot. His swing was decent, sweeping the ball
off the plastic tee. A split second later, it hit near dead center on
the screen, impacting with a quiet thud.

A digital display appeared.

"One-ninety-five out, thirty yards right," Marjani read. "Should
be just short of the trap."

A computer mechanism whirled behind the screen. Having mea-
sured the speed and accuracy of Dallas's drive from sensors
mounted around the tee, microprocessors searched through thousands of photographic images to best depict where Dallas's drive
had come to rest.

"Guess I know my own course, huh?" Marjani said when the
next slide was displayed.

The kidney-shaped sand trap was just ahead, directly between
Dallas's line to the green. A new digital read showed the distance
to the pin as 145 yards.

Marjani handed Dallas a seven-iron and kicked over another
ball. Asked, "How much are we talking about?"

"One-forty-five, right?" Dallas nodded toward the distance display.

"One-forty—?" Marjani cut off his sentence, realizing what Dallas was talking about. *Not* what he'd been referring to. "Not distance," he said. "Dollars."

Dallas eased his grip on the seven-iron and leaned on it like a
sporty cane. Marjani wanted to get to business: how much Crenshaw's estate was willing to take to sell back its Hurricane Bay

interest. Dallas opened the negotiations. "How about half a million?"

"Half a million!" Marjani roared. "You're out of your mind. These are Hurricane Bay Country Club shares, not Marjani Company stock. Hell, the company owns all the land. The club just leases it. There's no real equity. You don't know what you're—" Marjani stopped, and grinned. "Hell, you *don't* know what you're talking about, do you?" Calling Dallas's bluff.

"You're defrauding your members, Pete. Telling them a new eighteen holes are coming in eighteen months and you don't even own the land."

"The hell I don't."

Dallas was surprised Marjani would try sustaining this lie. "Roland Gunderson hasn't sold you his farm."

"That senile bastard. What the hell do I need his land for?"

"He said you've been after him to sell it for years. One day you smashed his window when he said he wouldn't sell at any price."

The natural pink tint of Marjani's face deepened a half-shade. "He told you that? Did he tell you I apologized? That I replaced *all* the windows in that goddamned outhouse he lives in for free? How I gave him leftover lumber to build that garage he tinkers with those cars in? He didn't tell you that part, did he? Because then he'd have to admit I'm a good neighbor." Marjani's face was touring the color spectrum, heading toward the reds.

"You'd think this golf course was the worst thing in the world. Gunderson's been trying to get me out of here for years. Didn't want me here in the first place. He comes around here at night spray-painting graffiti over my new houses and signs like some juvenile delinquent. He doesn't think I know it's him, but I've got guards who've seen him do it. He busts windows, pokes holes in drywall. Cut goddamned electrical wire in one house; I hadda redo the whole place. He's senile."

"So you don't want Gunderson's land?"

"It would've been nice, having the new course right next door, but if I can't buy it, I can't buy it. That's why I got another farm five miles west of here. Settled on it three months ago. That's where Tropical Storm is opening *as planned* in eighteen months." Marjani lifted a telephone extension, barked, "Kenny, bring over the layout for the new Tropical Storm."

It was all there, covered to the smallest detail: a true test copy of the recorded deed conveying title of a four-hundred-acre farm to the Pete Marjani Development Company. A plat of the property matched a series of transparencies that, placed in turn on the map, showed proposed changes in elevations, drainages, and how Tropical Storm's eighteen holes were going to be laid out.

Marjani told Dallas, "Now what were you asking me about? Someone named Raymond Crenshaw?" Marjani looked at Kenny Pete, his course architect, a sturdy man about Dallas's age with academic wire-framed glasses. "You ever heard of Raymond Crenshaw, Kenny?"

"No, sir."

Marjani shrugged and did a slow, triumphant turn toward Dallas. "Me neither."

Dallas had that empty feeling in his stomach like a big algebra test was coming up in an hour and he'd forgotten to study: a dream experienced since high school haunting him in his waking hours.

What a morning: first Gunderson makes him feel like a fool for thinking Susan slept with him, then Marjani has him feeling equally stupid for missing the link to Crenshaw.

Dallas plunked a quarter into a pay phone in the Hurricane Bay clubhouse bar.

"Ocean Tides," Jill answered.

"It's me."

"Oh, hi."

"Any word from Susan?"

"Nope."

Damn. "Anything else going on?"

"Herbie called. He said he needs to talk to you right away."

Dallas jammed the 280 into fifth and roared past a Cadillac full of old-guy tourists in golf hats reading a map. Herbie had something: a woman who'd picked up mail from Judge Crenshaw's PO box.

31

"**G**ET OUTTA THE WAY!"

Dallas shouted uselessly, sweeping his arm across the inside of his windshield, trying to wave a puttsing Oldsmobile sedan off the single-lane road. He wasn't even sure anyone was driving it. From behind, all he saw was a blue pile of fuzzy hair barely clearing the driver's seat.

He would have gone around, but every time he reached a straightaway, cars were coming at him from the other direction. Finally, he couldn't take it anymore.

A Toyota 4Runner passed him going south. Dallas cut into the opposing lane a little too close to a curve. He punched the accelerator.

Brrraaaaaaappp! A horn blew shrilly. A yellow VW coming right at him.

Dallas hit the brakes and jerked the 280 back in behind the snail's-pace Olds, nearly ramming its bumper. He looked at the oncoming car he'd almost hit and got a brief glimpse of Herbie, frazzled hair blowing out the opened window, screaming at him, but not stopping.

Cars trailing Herbie drove off the road, fearing a maniac—maybe one of Dallas's clients—was about to smash them head-on. Their acts of escape cleared the way for Dallas to swing onto the shoulder and spin a loose 180-degree turn that nearly pitched him into a ditch.

Horns blew, and people screamed obscenities hot enough to melt paint off a church.

Dallas floored it in pursuit of Herbie.

Herbie followed the red 4Runner as it turned off Route 611 onto Bayshore Drive. Keeping a safe distance, Herbie stopped at Big Drive when the sporty jeep/truck proceeded up the palm-treed entrance to Hurricane Bay.

Dallas pulled in behind him.

Herbie jumped out of his yellow Beetle, agitated. "You could've killed us back there."

"It wasn't that close."

Beside them, a stray practice shot struck the metal billboards surrounding Pete Marjani's golf ball swimming pool. *Thwang!* Women and children bathers took cover.

Herbie flinched, nerves tangled, yelling at Dallas, "And you said *I* drive too fast! At least it's on the right side of the road." Herbie clasped a hand to the chest of his wrinkled T-shirt and leaned against his door. "I got the pulse rate of a hummingbird."

"Probably all that sugar you had for breakfast." Dallas pointed toward Hurricane Bay. "Who was in the truck? The woman who picked up Crenshaw's mail?"

Herbie nodded. He wheezed panicky breaths, trying to calm himself.

"Who is she?"

"I don't know." Gasp. "That's what I was trying to find out when you auditioned me for a hood ornament." Herbie took a big gulp of air and gestured to the dent in Dallas's hood. "You know, I think maybe you ran over Crenshaw after all. When your trial comes up, don't call me as a character witness."

Dallas got back into his car and opened the passenger door for Herbie to get in.

"Oh, no," Herbie protested. "I'll *follow* you."

They drove wagon-train style to the Hurricane Bay parking lot. Most of the spaces were taken by the big cars favored by Marjani's golfing set. The 4Runner was easy to locate.

Dallas and Herbie stopped nearby.

"You see the driver?"

Herbie looked around and shook his head.

Dallas sidled alongside the late-model four-wheeler and peeked inside at a stick shift, front bucket seats, bench back seats, and an open trunk. Neat and clean save a little sand on the floorboards and a stack of mail on the passenger seat.

Dallas, very casually, opened the door. One of the pieces of mail looked familiar: a small, square cardboard box identical in size to what Crenshaw had given Dallas hours before he was killed. Only this box had been addressed to Vicky Sterrett Callere in Raymond Crenshaw's handwriting; postmarked last Saturday.

The box was stamped in post-office red: INSUFFICIENT POSTAGE—RETURN TO SENDER. Being a cheap bastard was a hard habit to break.

Dallas shook the parcel. It felt about the same: something small and solid inside a shipping liner of some sort, crumpled newspaper perhaps. No sense guessing. Dallas ripped open the box.

He saw something white and round through opaque bubble wrap. A golf ball. A Hurricane Bay–logo golf ball. With the imprint P. MARJANI.

The small white sphere appeared comically puny in Rupert Dawson's hand as the chief idly rolled it between his fingers. "So what you're saying," Dawson interpreted, turning the Hurricane Bay logo faceup, "is this ball proves Pete Marjani killed Raymond Crenshaw."

"No." Dallas sat across from the chief's desk; the window air conditioner blew frigid mist across the back of his neck. "I'm just providing a fact. That this package is similar to the one Crenshaw gave me right before he was killed, and he'd written on my box the same instructions he gave me verbally. Not to open it unless he 'ended up dead.' "

"Nothing like that on this box." Dawson examined shredded remains marked RETURN TO SENDER. "And no note inside."

"Maybe he called Vicky ahead of time and told her."

"You ask her?"

"I tried calling her suite, but she was out."

Dawson rolled the ball like a round worry stone. "Still doesn't explain why he didn't come right out and tell you. Besides, you don't know this exact type of ball was in the box he gave *you*."

"Hey, Rup, congratulations." Dallas clapped. "You're finally thinking like a defense attorney after all these years. And you're right, I don't know if it was the same kind of ball, or even a golf ball. I'm just keeping you informed."

Dawson scowled suspiciously. "Now I get it. You want something."

Caught in the act, Dallas handed the chief a slip of paper on which was scribbled the 4Runner's license plate. "Can you run this tag for me? I rummaged all through that damned truck and couldn't find a registration."

"Cindy!" Dawson shouted for his niece/secretary.

She appeared promptly, a bikini contest winner many times over, much to the chagrin of her protective uncle. Despite his size, Dawson found that where children were concerned he was as powerless as the next guy to make them always "do right" in his eyes. "Cin." Leaning forward with effort, he handed her the paper. "Run this plate, okay?"

"MVA computer's down."

"What else is new?"

"Hi, Cin," Dallas greeted happily.

"Hey, Dallas." She was equally chipper.

Dawson shooed her from his office. "Go do something." Then told Dallas, "Off limits," as Dallas watched Cindy head down the hall.

Dallas would have turned right back around, but a new sight caught his eye.

A cop entered the station with a young kid in handcuffs. Cutback, the blond bodyboarder—the third angle of Gina and South's triangle.

"Wasting your time," the arresting officer told Dallas. He was a big guy named Morris with a Dick Tracy jaw and bulldog underbite. "He doesn't say anything. Not his name, his address, where he's from. Nothing. Right, kid?" Morris shook Cutback roughly by the elbow as though trying to dislodge words caught in the boy's throat. Morris told Dallas, "See?"

Cutback kept his head down. He looked even worse than night before last. Still wearing the same bathing suit, he had haggard dark rings under bloodshot eyes. He was scared, but fighting hard to hold it together, twisting his fingers where his hands were cuffed behind his back.

"What'd he do?" Dallas asked, trailing along to the booking room.

"Theft."

"Of what?"

"Cheeseburger and fries. He walked out on his check."

Dallas reached into his pocket and pulled out five bucks. "Here."

Morris turned his head to the side; the tip of his cap cast a shadow across his nose like a sundial at two-thirty. "Is that for me?" Thinking Dallas was bribing him.

Dallas wondered where Dawson found these guys. "To cover the food he didn't pay for. Give this to the hamburger joint and let the kid go."

"No way." Morris shook his head tightly. "Place's manager says it's time to teach these kids a lesson. You know how much pilferage costs honest citizens every year?"

Dallas couldn't handle being an captive audience to some other stuck cog in the legal system's rusty wheel. He jammed the fiver in Cutback's pocket, said, "Hang in there, kid. I'll get you out."

Dallas's day improved immeasurably upon returning to the Ocean Tides. There was Susan's Benz.

"Thank God."

Susan was in the lobby chatting with Jill. Wearing an expensive Adrienne Vittadini bronze blouse and pleated cotton pants. Her conversation was animated, very charged up.

Dallas smacked his forehead. "I forgot again, didn't I?"

Susan was too enlivened to really care.

"You were on some panel discussion group at the bar convention, right? Another environmental law kind of thing." He set a half-gallon of milk on the counter.

"That's all right, Dallas. We're only talking about saving the world." She *was* a little burned after all.

"You give that talk again somewhere when there's no lawyers around and I'm right there—in a flash."

She cocked her hip aggressively as though listening to an opposing witness lie through his pearly whites. "The whole point *is* lawyers, Dallas. Getting them involved in litigation and lobbying efforts against corporations that try to sell consumers on thinking globally and living locally while at the same time *they're* dumping hundreds of thousands of gallons of waste into the Pacific Ocean. Surfers out there are riding waves that turn black from refuse." She was riled with the cause. "Lawyers are always getting shafted because people think all we do is defend criminals and chase ambulances. This is an opportunity for the legal community to do something truly positive."

Dallas thought, but didn't dare say at this particular moment, that if the legal community wanted to do something positive it should take the proverbial long, long walk on a short pier. Instead, he gestured to the door behind him. "How about I'll go out and come back in and tell you I didn't forget your panel this morning, but I've been working on Crenshaw's case?"

"I've been doing that, too."

"Oh." Dallas felt like a puppy who'd just tinkled on the Oriental rug and didn't have any cute faces to save him.

Susan said, "Two things."

"Yeah?"

"First, Harvey Crenshaw got bailed out of jail this morning by . . . ?" Waiting for Dallas to guess, which he didn't. ". . . Vicky Sterrett."

"Vicky?"

"Two," Susan continued through Dallas's shock, "I think I know who PM is."

"PM?"

"The person who typed Crenshaw's letters."

▽

32

"P AMELA MEYERS. PM." In the war room, Susan picked through samples of Judge Crenshaw's business correspondence, confirming the secretarial code at the end of each typed letter: RCC/pm. "The same initials every time. PM . . ." She turned a page. ". . . PM. PM again."

"So," Dallas asked, "who's Pamela Meyers and how'd you find out about her?"

"After the conference this morning, we got to talking about Judge Crenshaw. I said I was surprised he'd gone back into practice and asked if anyone else had heard."

"Uh-huh . . . ?"

"J. Phillips said that a couple of months ago, a woman he knew from the courthouse in Baltimore stopped by his office. She asked if J. knew any condos she could rent for the season that wouldn't cost her an arm and a leg. J. gave her a few names, then they chatted about this and that, and when J. asked what she was doing moving down here, she said she'd gotten a job at Hurricane Bay. She also said she might do some secretarial work on the side. She mentioned Judge Crenshaw, but no details. Just that Crenshaw was a 'maybe.' "

"Did J. say what she looked like?"

"Mid-forties, plain to attractive. Brownish hair."

"Sounds like who Herbie saw pick up Judge Crenshaw's mail this morning."

"His mail?"

Dallas explained the PO box and how Herbie presently had the woman staked out at Hurricane Bay.

Considering all this, Susan said, "There's one other coincidence for the it's-a-small-world department. You know who Pamela Meyers used to work for in the court system?"

"Crenshaw."

Susan shook her head. "The state's attorney's office. Child Support Division. She was in charge of enforcing delinquencies." Susan allowed this to register. "You know who else was working in the state's attorney's office at that same time?"

"Mack Trial."

Susan nodded. "Mack Trial."

The jalousie door insets to Gina and South's room were open. Dallas looked inside and saw them at the dinette table eating peanut butter sandwiches and a bag of Oreos.

He knocked. "Can I come in?"

"Open," South said with a mouthful of peanut butter. He sat on a towel, his bathing suit and hair wet from a swim in the ocean.

Elbows on the table, Gina held her sandwich with both hands. Her Big-Dog T-shirt stuck to wet triangles of an orange bikini worn underneath. Her Nikonos camera was on the table beside an opened loaf of white bread.

Dallas set the half-gallon of milk on the veneer table. "Hi." Smiling, but serious. He turned the carton until the panel featuring a notice from the Missing Children's Network faced them. A boy's picture: Lawrence Jenkins, last seen in New Orleans two years ago, believed kidnapped by his noncustodial father.

South and Gina didn't move.

Dallas sat on a cheap vinyl chair, one of three featured in every cramped Ocean Tides kitchenette. He reached for an Oreo and leaned back. "I love these things. Always eat them at once, though. The whole thing." He popped it into his mouth and licked chocolate crumbs from his fingers. Talked while chewing. "So"—tapping the milk carton—"this is it, right? Your private joke from the other night. About only buying milk in jugs, not cardboard containers."

Gina got up from the table, went determinedly to the closet, and started stuffing belongings into her duffel bag.

South stared straight ahead.

"Cutback's in jail," Dallas said. "He got picked up for skipping his tab for a cheeseburger. He's too nervous to keep quiet for long. The cops're gonna figure it out."

Gina kept packing; South staring.

"Why don't you let me help you?"

Gina's silence broke in anger. "What can you do! Any better than any of the state agencies did! We're underage. The law says we can't be on our own. Everyone feels sorry for us, but the bottom line's always the same: we go back to our parents. *My* father who spends more time with a belt wrapped around his fist than holding up his pants." She pointed to South. "*His* drug-addicted parents. We get sent back because they're not proven to be unfit. And even if they were, then where do we go? Some foster home where a nasty old lady's got six of us sleeping in one room. Guys and girls together so she can collect checks from social services." She jammed a sweatshirt into her sack. "No, thanks. We'll take our chances on our own. You try to help us, you're just going to get us sent back. That's what *the law* says has to happen."

Dallas picked up a fresh Oreo, studied it. "This is the beach, you know." He popped in the Oreo and chewed. "We don't have those kind of laws around here."

Dallas left Gina and South to discuss it between themselves, assuring them that whatever they decided was fine with him. They could stay indefinitely, he'd get them jobs in town if they wanted, or, if peanut butter sandwiches were good enough, they could bodyboard out the summer and not worry about paying him rent.

In the meantime, Cutback was going to have to wait it out in jail. Dallas had to pay a little visit to Victoria Secrets.

He found her in a shady section of the Sheraton parking lot. Vicky wore a white man's-styled shirt and ice-blue cigarette-leg jeans. Professional-on-vacation style.

Blond hair blowing in the breeze, Vicky shared a laugh with an attorney Dallas recognized by face, not name.

"Dallas, hello!" The heels of Vicky's pumps clicked warm paving as she hurried to him, wrapping both arms around one of his. Her breasts pressed against his side. She smelled wonderful. "You know Joel Katzman?"

Vicky guided Dallas to the other lawyer, a curly-haired cherub who'd made a name for himself successfully defending pilfering S&L presidents. What Katzman and Vicky had been amused by was the new bumper sticker on Katzman's showroom-fresh Corvette: CRIMINAL LAWYERS GET YOU OFF.

"Cute." Dallas put on his nice-to-meet-you-(asshole) smile and shook hands.

Katzman had the grip of linguini cooked twenty hours in a Crock-Pot. He'd spritzed himself with enough cologne to intoxicate low-flying sea gulls.

Still on Dallas's arm, Vicky said, "Joel's got to leave the convention early. He's got a *major* RICO case starting in Richmond Monday." Vicky's tone was the usual lawyer blend of envy and congratulations.

Katzman made a clicking sound of acknowledgment from the side of his mouth. The kind of guy who frightened dating services by noting on his application he liked to disco. "Read about me in the papers," he bragged to Vicky. Nodded to Dallas, "Nice meeting you." Katzman got into his car, revved the engine, and laid rubber across the parking lot.

In a cloud of catalytically converted exhaust, Dallas shook his head.

"What a jerk," Vicky griped, suddenly honest. "I can't believe he got the Hindle case. God!" Neck and shoulders tightening, she shuddered in revolt. "Tell me"—she squeezed Dallas's arm—"you're here to take me away from this. That we're going someplace wonderful for lunch and then straight to bed." She rubbed against him in a manner that was borderline obscene.

Dallas couldn't help grinning, but couldn't help asking, "Why'd you bail out Harvey Crenshaw?"

Her eyes closed with disappointment. "Forget that case, Dallas. *I am*. I've spent most of the morning looking for another attorney to take over as PR of the estate. You know what four percent of nothing is, don't you? That's going to be my commission."

Kissing her ear, he whispered, "Did that answer my question?"

"What question?" Vicky became a little irritated.

"Bailing out Crenshaw's son?" Kiss. "Why did you do it?" Kiss-kiss. "He had his father's shotgun in the trunk of his car. Possibly removed from the scene of his father's death."

"Who cares?"

"Vicky, come on. Crenshaw came to you for representation. I don't think he'd want you to feel—"

Vicky didn't so much release her hold on Dallas as she threw his arm from her body. "Representation? Let's talk about how Raymond Crenshaw *represented to me* he had some money. That there'd be a fee in handling his estate. Not that his screwball substance-abusing son would start threatening to sue me and/or have me arrested *and/or* report me to the ethics committee for stealing money from his father. I want *out* of this case, Dallas. I want as much distance between me and *it* as possible. If you were smart, you'd do the same." Before Dallas could ask his question a third time, she took a half-step toward the tall glass and steel hotel. "I'm going to the Beach Bar for a few drinks. I'd like to have them with you. But if you're inclined to spend your afternoon some other way . . ."

When Dallas didn't reply, Vicky stalked off, hotter than the day itself.

She'd never had a hard side back in law school. Which was part of what had placed her in such attractive juxtaposition to class-rooms and hallways clogged with would-be attorneys. Now, set her in a conference center filled with lawyers, she blended right in.

Every time Dallas tried to turn back time, he ended up breaking the clock.

"Herbie's nervous," Susan said.

Dallas spoke to her from a pay phone along Coastal Highway. It was stuffy and cramped, hard to hear with traffic so nearby, but beat being any closer to that damned lawyer convention. "Nervous about what?"

"He's on his way back from West Ocean City and wanted to make sure you weren't on the road."

"Very funny. Is he following the Four-Runner?"

"Yes. And Pamela Meyers is driving it. Chief Dawson ran the tag and IDed her as the owner."

"How long ago did Herbie call?"

"Twenty, thirty minutes."

"Ring him back. He's got the portable phone in his car. Ask what direction he's headed. I'll try meeting up with him. Go ahead and put me on hold, I'll wait and—"

"Hey, boss."

"Herbie?"

A breathless Herbie, sighing with remorse, had taken the extension from Susan. "Just walked in."

Dallas leaned his head against the glass phone booth wall. "You lost her, didn't you?"

$\triangledown$

33

DALLAS WAS A KID when the first building lots for Ocean Pines were carved through towering forests of oaks, junipers, and (of course) pines. Originally a solitary setting, Dallas still referred to it as Lonesome Pines, which was what Uncle Smoke called it. Dallas even made up a little ditty he sang whenever he left OC by the Route 90 bridge and passed by. A sort of western, cowboy tune:

Hel-looo, dear, I'm calling you from Lonesome Pines;
just me, dear, and my conifer friends.
So lonely, me here with my evergreens,
just waiting, so forsaken without you.

Haunting.

The development, like Judge Crenshaw's neighborhood ten miles south, was originally a refuge from the high prices and traffic of the island. Slowly, it had become a wooded minimetropolis with enough year-round residents to support various shopping plazas and service industries.

Winding roads fed through inland lots like a gradual funnel to splendid waterfront homes directly on Assawoman Bay.

Dallas sang his Lonesome Pines tune, looking for 117 Sea Faring Court. That was the address MVA showed as Pamela Meyers's residence.

He found it a mile from the Ocean Pines entrance and eight hundred thousand dollars short of the bayfront homes. Meyers lived in a compact cedar-sided rancher with a steep-pitched roof and skylights. The windows and curtains were shut. A small front porch sported one Adirondack chair and clay pots of begonias that weren't getting enough sun through the pines. The small lawn was tidily kept; healthy green shade grass trimmed short; quaint mulched planting areas bordered by red bricks turned on end. A newspaper, rolled and banded, lay in the driveway.

Quite a contrast was the blue house next door. A little Cape Cod under siege by at least ten out-of-control tots aged five to ten. Yelling and screaming, running more bare spots into an already struggling yard, their Big Wheel bikes, skateboards, jump ropes, and balls were scattered all over the place. A little informal, unlicensed, zoning-violation day-care center.

Herbie, upon seeing this, said, "Swell. Anyone sees me watching Meyers's house they're gonna think I'm a child molester waiting to nab one of those little bastards."

"Well, get one that does windows." Squatting beside Herbie's VW, Dallas looked at the Meyers property. "Four-Runner's not home. Seems pretty quiet."

"How can you tell with all this damned racket?"

The day-care kids were loud. The late-thirties-or-so woman supposedly watching them was seated on the front stoop, hip deep in a twenty-ounce paperback romance on the cover of which was yet another bronze, pectoral-busting dark-haired stud embracing a damsel in distress whose dress was shredded like she'd been in a cat fight.

Dallas continued to survey the area. Near Pamela Meyers's house, a perpendicular dead-end lane meandered deeper into virgin woods. Hammering and sawing was going on back there.

Dallas got in the VW and directed Herbie to that cul-de-sac. Two houses from the corner, a work crew was framing a small cottage. Dallas said, "Perfect."

"You wanna buy it?"

"No, but if someone catches you sitting inside, tell them *you* do." Dallas motioned for Herbie to keep going when one of the hammerers saw them from the roof. "Leave your car somewhere else and walk back here with the portable phone. It's not a great angle, but you can see Meyers's house. These guys"—thumbing toward the workers—"oughta be ready for a couple six-packs and shots of Jack soon. It's gotta be close to three."

"And when she comes home, all I'm doing is watching her?"

"Yup. And following her if she goes anywhere. And keeping me posted."

Herbie grumbled something about overtime.

Dallas took the long way back to the Ocean Tides. Wanting an in-person look at the land Pete Marjani had shown him on the plat that morning. The new—alternate—site for Tropical Storm.

Something had been bothering Dallas about that. He knew what when he saw the property. Hands on hips, he looked around.

This was a flat, nondescript cornfield, two acres of which had been left cleared for a chicken coop since burned out. No trees. No contour to the land. Just acres and acres and acres—four hundred hot acres—of boring. At least to the golfer's eye.

What *made* a golf course was blending fairways with nature, carving a sporting contest through scenic hummocks, along streams, up and down hills. There was none of that here. Just corn and the old coop. Land so dry each of Dallas's footsteps raised dust.

Dallas pulled back the husk from an immature ear of corn and found big, yellow kernels. No buttery silver queen or sweet corn, this was horse corn. A feed crop stuck on a hunk of land not good for much else.

But then again, Dallas wasn't a farmer or golf course architect. Maybe it just happened there was an unglamorous crop here; feed corn properly sold for good money. And there might be some way Pete Marjani could invest a couple million bucks in this old field, landscape it with some quick-growing trees and shrubs, and let it mature into an established course in ten or twenty years. But that was a pretty long wait for someone as impatient as Marjani. And a far cry from the picturesque Gunderson property.

Sweat ran down the back of Dallas's neck. He shook his head. No way were Hurricane Bay's already restless members going to like this. Marjani looked to have bought himself a million-dollar grave.

Dallas started back for his car when he heard someone cussing. A quick "Damn!" that sounded like self-scolding on the far side of the chicken coop.

Three hundred yards was a long way to walk when there were waves to be ridden ten miles east, but Dallas figured he'd come this far . . .

Walking a narrow dirt trail just wide enough for a pickup truck, Dallas approached the coop. Blackened wall studs had turned to brittle charcoal; flecks of gray took wispy flight in the hot breeze. All that remained of the roof was a few charred trusses sticking into the air like singed fingers.

The voice cussed again. A man's shrill "Damn!"

Dallas walked around back of the narrow coop. The acrid smell of a recent fire hovered like a specter. "Having trouble?"

A scraggly guy about forty-five, wearing a straw cowboy hat, dirty jeans, work boots, and a flannel shirt with ripped sleeves, looked up. The flesh on his arms and hands was as leathery as his face. Cigarette between his lips, shovel handle in his hands, shovel *blade* snapped off in the ground, he answered. "Trouble? Yeah, you could say that." He leaned the busted end of his shovel to the ground.

The hole he'd been digging was about two feet square and a little deeper. A layer of dry earth that gave way to dirt, then sand, then . . . then what?

Dallas looked closely.

"Limestone," the digger said, pronouncing it *lahmstone*.

Dallas reached down and rapped it with his knuckles. "Hard."

"Bet'cher ass it's hard." The cigarette bobbed in his lips like a fishing lure. "That's what I keep telling the man. But he don't wanna listen. Tells me keep diggin' holes till I find a spot's clear." Removing his hat, he wiped his forehead and gestured his bald head toward the cleared ground behind him. It was dotted with holes. "So that's what I been doin'. Diggin' holes and bustin' shovels—for eight-fifty an hour."

"What are the holes for?"

"Place to put a foundation for a house. So we gotta be able to go down pretty far and without spending the money for blasting. I don' find a spot here, I'm 'posed to start going along those rows of corn. But you didn't hear that from me. Guy rents this field from the original owner's got growin' rights till season's end. And he don't like me bein' here as it is. Sends his sons to check up on me. Guess he thinks I'm crazy digging these holes, but, hey, Mr. Marjani's got the cash, I do what he says."

"Marjani wants to build a house here? You mean a clubhouse."

"Clubhouse? Hell no. This a little itsy-bitsy thing. Fifteen by twenty, those're my perimeter wall dimensions. Fifteen by twenty anywheres back here, just not too close to the road. Can't be near the road. Probably end up down by the water."

"Where's water?"

The man waved his straw hat due south. "Waaaaay down there's a feeder circles through the trees on a neighbor property and runs to Hurricane Bay. She'd been fillin' up with silt last few years, but Mr. Marjani ran a big-ass cut through her. Opened up a canal 'bout big enough for a small boat. Did it one cloudy night—hadda be kind of secret plowing up wetlands."

"So where's the golf course going to go?"

"Golf course?" The man squinted, clearly puzzled. "Don't know nothin' 'bout no golf course. But I don't suspect it would be here."

"Why not?"

"Golf courses got trees, don't they?"

"You could plant those."

The man tapped the broken shovel handle into his hole and smiled cowboy-knowing. "*Lahmstone*. Run about fifteen, twenty feet deep. Big swirls of it *allll* 'round here. Far and wide as the eye can see. Not bad for corn—shallow roots. Or you could quarry her. But trees?" He shook his head. "They just ain't gonna work here."

34

"HERBIE CALL?" DALLAS ASKED.

Susan was seated behind the front desk, catching up on Ocean Tides' bookkeeping. "Not yet."

Dallas checked the clock—four-thirty—wondering what time Pamela Meyers got home from work. "Any other messages?"

Susan looked at him with a degree of accusation.

"What?"

"If you want to know if she called, why don't you just ask. I'm not allergic to her name."

"I was just asking if—"

"Dallas. You *never* ask who called, because that might remind me to tell you someone did call, like the accountant"—Susan hefted the cash ledger—"trying to figure out these scribbles you put in here as tax deductions."

"Those're legitimate expenses."

"So if you want to know if she called, just ask. Say, Susan, did Vicky Sterrett call?" She waited.

Dallas sighed, caught again. "Susan, did Vicky Sterrett call?"

"No."

He tried not to be disappointed. As much as he was beginning to sense—maybe had known all along—that Vicky's return to his life would end badly, he wanted a few more sips of nectar before it fermented to a frothy mess. Or so he told himself now. Go for it, it's the beach, live for today. So how come when he was actually with her, he couldn't always seem to remember that?

"You going to ride some waves?" Susan asked when he headed for the door.

"I'm gonna lay down awhile. I feel like I've been up all day." He stopped short of the office that connected to his room. "Nothing else new from Rup or on Harvey Crenshaw or—" He stopped himself, jealous again.

"Roland Gunderson?" Susan guessed correctly. "I'm just going to see if I can track his wife down. As a surprise. Roland doesn't have any idea where she might be. I know it's a long shot, but maybe that's good. Maybe it's been long enough for her to forget whatever drove her away in the first place."

Dallas wasn't sure that was a good idea. Like seeing Vicky again. "It's never the same," he said and left it at that.

In his room, he rummaged through the CDs he'd been paid as a fee for losing the obscene record store case, and found one he hadn't played yet. Earl Klugh on guitar, *Heartstring*. What he and Vicky used to listen to in her apartment downtown—on a vinyl LP in those low-tech days.

Hopeless case, Dallas chided himself, popping the silver disc in the portable player, slipping on the headset, lying down. Hopeless, hopeless, hopeless . . .

Gradually he drifted off into a pleasant half-sleep, then went out like a light, slipping into a REM state where his subconscious wound back the years, and the confines of time and space abated. . . .

Dreaming about law school, in Vicky's apartment the first night he'd seen the *real* her . . .

Just like a movie . . .

Vicky excusing herself . . . coming back ten minutes later . . . in the Victoria Secrets teddy . . . frilly, sheer, unbelievable . . .

Surprising *and* seducing the hell out of him . . . showing and giving all he could ever ask with a passion he could have never guessed . . .

The sort of beginning to which there was never an end, only interruptions. Years would go by and then she'd be back again, an unannounced surprise . . . in a suite at Coconut Malerie's. . . .

Strolling into the bedroom . . . shadow undressing for him . . .

"Dallas. Dallas!" Susan jostled his shoulder.

He opened his eyes. Where the hell was he? It was dark until Susan turned on the lamp.

Home. Dallas recognized it now. His mouth was dry from snoring. He sat up and half strangled himself with the headset wires. He took off the cushy earphones and saw that the portable CD player's batteries had run dead. His brain was fuzzy. "What time is it?"

"Eight-fifteen."

"Eight?"

"I checked on you a couple of times; you really zonked. Dreaming about something good, though," Susan teased with a wink. "If you know what I mean."

He didn't.

"Let's just say—in those shorts—the physical state of your arousal was obvious."

Dallas laughed behind his smile. "I get it. You should've jumped right in."

"Mmmm."

He managed to get his legs over the side of the bed. Next step: standing. He *had* been sleeping hard, and felt its residual effects like a hangover.

"Herbie's called a couple of times," Susan reported, going through Dallas's closet for something for him to change into.

Dallas's pulse got a slight kick-start at the mention of the case. "And?"

"Pamela Meyers came home around six. Alone. Holding a carryout bag from JR's."

"Yum. Ribs."

"She's been inside since. The windows all have curtains or shades drawn so Herbie can't see what she's doing."

"That's okay. I just want to know a few basics about her, nothing too personal."

Susan found a long-sleeved black T-shirt and tossed it to Dallas with a pair of worn jeans.

Black clothing wasn't a good sign. It meant he was going to be hiding somewhere in the dark. "I take it I'm going out."

"It might be nothing, but Herbie's been checking in every half hour. No changes so far. Pamela Meyers has been home. But Herbie missed his call at eight. I wanted a few minutes, then called *him*. No answer. Which means either the battery's gone dead or, for some reason, Herbie's turned off the phone."

"For this I'm wearing black?"

". . . just me, dear, and my conifer friends . . ." Dallas sang his "Lonesome Pines" tune, finding his way in the dark.

Porch lights from neighboring homes and a rising full moon gave the night just enough shades of gray for him to see.

All was now quiet in this part of Ocean Pines, the day-care-on-the-fly house was shut down for the night, and everyone else was settled inside to be hypnotized by bad TV like real Americans.

". . . So lonely, me here with my evergreens. Just waiting, so forsaken without you."

Dallas hummed the bars he hadn't worked up lyrics for yet, walking into the partially constructed house where Herbie was supposed to be.

The smell of fresh lumber sweetened the naturally woodsy setting.

"Herbie?" Dallas's stage whisper and footsteps echoed faintly between the concrete first floor and framed upper level. The studded walls remained open. "Hey, Herbie?"

No answer.

Probably asleep, Dallas thought, going up the stairs. Rectangles of glowing moon shone through holes left in the roof for skylights. In one block of light, Dallas saw the portable cellular phone, but no Herbie. And the phone had been turned off.

"Herbie?" A little concerned now. "Herbie?"

Outside, running footsteps slapped down the street. Hard breathing. Coming closer. Dallas stepped quickly and quietly beside a front window and peeked out.

Herbie sprinted into the house, hair flailing behind him like a wind sock . . . Sunny Surplus Jack Percells beating hard up the steps.

"What the hell?"

"Whooaa!" Herbie jumped back with shock and clutched his chest. Saw Dallas. "Oh, jeez! Don't do that!"

"What the hell's going on?"

"I was just going to call you." He started back outside. "Come on. We got something."

"What?"

Herbie was already on the lawn, making Dallas do a quick sprint to catch up. They kept to the dark side of the street, running on grass to quiet their footfall the closer they got to Pamela Meyers's.

Dallas breathed heavily.

Herbie spoke without breaking stride. "About forty minutes ago, some guy walked by Meyers's house, gave it a good long look, then came back where I was. When he came inside, I got upstairs and hoped for the best. He stayed on the first floor and walked around, mostly by the front windows. Like he was waiting for something."

Dallas started to ask why Herbie hadn't called with this, but realized the answer to his own question: the house was so open, the intruder on the first floor would have heard the beep-beep dialing of the cellular phone had Herbie so much as tried to tap out code. It was also why Herbie had turned the phone off: so an incoming call wouldn't ring.

Herbie slowed and motioned for Dallas to do likewise as they reached Pamela Meyers's street. Concealed by the substantial breadth of a Douglas fir, Herbie took a breath. "When this guy left the house I was in, he went right back to Meyers's. I followed him.

Saw him creeping around that hedge toward the back." Herbie pointed to a trimmed row of arborvitae that created a natural fence between the Meyers and "day-care" houses. "He had something under his arm—I couldn't tell what. Something sort of grayish white. About this big." Herbie's hands shaped a square of air about the size of a first-base bag.

"What's this guy look like?"

"I didn't get a good look at his face, but he had a real short buzz haircut. Not quite six foot tall. Stocky, though. Strong. White. He's got on a black sweatshirt with short sleeves."

Dallas had a flashback: the man he'd chased at Crenshaw's funeral, the one who'd taken shots at Mack Trial.

"How about a gun?"

"Didn't see one, but maybe tucked in his belt, his shirttail was out. Or in the thing he was carrying."

"Did you see him after the hedge?"

Herbie shook his head and took another deep breath. "He might still be there."

"Okay . . ." Dallas played out options in his head.

Meyers's house looked quiet, but with the curtains closed and no outside lights save a pole lamp at the driveway's end, it was difficult to see. Herbie's suspect could be anywhere.

The last prowler Dallas had chased off had been with his patented naked kamikaze. He doubted the less secluded Ocean Pines area would appreciate that.

"All right." Dallas watched the hedge for movement, saw none. "Here's what we do. You hang right here, watch the front of the house. I'm goin' around back."

Herbie nodded.

Just as Dallas stepped out from behind the big fir tree, a car door thumped shut, the sound coming from the direction of Meyers's place. The 4Runner was pulled around the far side of the house, but Dallas couldn't see much more of it than the grille.

Dallas withdrew behind the tree.

Another car door shut. Engine turned over. The 4Runner's headlights came on. It moved down the driveway, crunching stones beneath its wheels. As the vehicle reached the street, a quick glimpse of light off the pole lamp passed across the driver's window. Just enough to show Dallas something he really didn't want to see. Pamela Meyers wasn't at the wheel. It was a man with short, short hair. A fleshy face. Pronounced horsey mouth. Even meaner eyes than his pictures. Jumbi Berrell.

$\triangledown$

35

"P<small>AMELA</small>!" D<small>ALLAS WAS</small> inside her house. "Pamela Meyers!"

No answer.

Dallas searched hurriedly, room to room; there wasn't that much floor space to cover: kitchen, living room, two bedrooms, and one bath downstairs; small master bedroom suite above. A modest place. Coordinated though mediocre furnishings showed some age. A few pieces of discount art hung haphazardly on otherwise bare walls. A full range of low-end appliances. Very little clutter or accumulation of personal effects. Dallas guessed this was a furnished rental.

"Pamela!" Calling her name a final time even though he'd been through every part of the house.

No one was home.

The back door didn't show any sign of forced entry. So either she kept it unlocked or let Berrell in. Either way, Berrell had been inside, Dallas was certain of that.

Adjacent to the eat-in kitchen was the living room. Where a struggle had taken place. Not much of a struggle, though. One cherry curio table had been knocked over. A collection of ceramic dolls bought from magazine mail-order ads was scattered across beige carpet. Two figurines were crushed into the floor covering's worn fibers as though stepped on.

Near one of the dolls was an amorphous stain about the size of a misshapen silver dollar: fresh blood, as though the miniature ballerina had been murdered.

There was also a small moss green leaf. Dallas rubbed it between his fingers. Slippery, cool, and wet. Seaweed?

Outside, Herbie honked the horn.

Dallas sprinted out, jumped in, and they were off.

Assuming Berrell was leaving Ocean Pines, there was only one logical route for him to take. The direction Herbie was driving now—driving fast while doing some quick calculations, estimating Berrell's speed and his head start to get an idea just how fast the screaming VW would have to go to catch up before Berrell reached the main highway.

Herbie shouted over the engine and warm air rushing through opened windows. "Better hit the hyperspeed button." He flicked an imaginary switch and pushed the accelerator to the floor.

Dallas looked behind his seat. "Where's the portable phone?"

"Back at the house."

"What!"

"No time. We'll be lucky to catch up as it is."

Herbie laid on the horn when a big Buick started backing out of a driveway. The Buick slammed on its brakes, hit its horn. A banker with three Tom Collinses in him got out and shook his fist. "Crazy damned kids!"

Dallas stuck his head out the window and waved. "Thank you."

Two minutes later, scanning the empty road ahead, Herbie muttered, "Damn, damn, damn."

They'd reached the highway. Signs pointing north toward Dover, south to Snow Hill and Berlin (Maryland, not Germany). Light, but steady, traffic. Shopping centers. No Toyota 4Runner.

Herbie lifted his hands from the wheel, said, "Pick it."

Dallas's instincts told him *left*, but he said, "Right."

Herbie turned and gunned it.

"No, wait. Left." Always go with your first instinct. "Go back that way. *Back that way!*"

"Oh, you mean my *other* right," Herbie replied sarcastically. He swerved across the grass median. No drivers bothered laying on their horn, but you could almost read their lips: *Goddamned kids! I'll be glad when summer's over.*

Three miles later, Herbie's lips formed a different word: "Bingo."

Dallas saw.

Mocking a military radio voice, Herbie cupped his hand to his mouth. "*Fsssst.*" Imitating static. "Target Four-Runner located dead ahead. Advise how to proceed." He turned to Dallas and, in regular voice, asked, "How do we proceed, Cap'n?"

"Maintain pace and pursue."

"Maintain pace and pursue," Herbie relayed to his imaginary engineer. "*Fsssst*. Maintain pace and pursue. Roger," the control room confirmed. Herbie drummed the steering wheel. "Any guesses where we're going?"

Dallas didn't answer. The question hung in the air as they remained ten to twenty car lengths behind the 4Runner.

Two-lane highway narrowed to a single lane. Still very little traffic. At Route 50, a busier road, Berrell turned east, a course that would take him across the downtown bridge back into Ocean City if he stayed on it. But before that point, Berrell turned south, and Dallas offered a hunch. "We're going to Hurricane Bay and Pete Marjani."

"Wrong," Herbie said, applying the brakes. He switched off the VW's lights.

The 4Runner didn't turn onto Big Drive. It proceeded past the palm-treed entrance to Hurricane Bay Country Club.

"Son of a bitch," Dallas swore, watching red taillights continue toward the darkness that was Roland Gunderson's property.

"So now what?" Hand resting on the wheel, Herbie's pointer finger aimed ahead. "I follow him down there we're gonna get spotted."

"Pull up a little further. No headlights."

Herbie cranked the Beetle into first and eased forward. Incidental light from the country club got them close to the mouth of Gunderson's long driveway.

From there, it was moonlight or next to nothing—Dallas recalling Gunderson's statement about not having electricity, a white lie that conveniently overlooked how he powered his refrigerator.

Across the field, the still waters of Hurricane Bay shimmered silver-black along the horizon. Towering oaks appeared as lace silhouettes pasted against a midnight blue sky.

Gunderson's little abode was hidden somewhere out there in the dark, approximately, Dallas guessed, where a lantern shone a burning yellow dot. Another lantern was down by the pier where Gunderson tied his fishing skiff.

Herbie said, "Where's the jeep?"

Dallas sat forward. "Good question." Where *was* the damned 4Runner?

They looked at the darkness, said "There" in unison when red brake lights came on like staring demonic eyes. The lights glowed for a three count, about halfway down the driveway, moving forward slowly, then went off, then came on again a few seconds later.

"He's driving without his lights," Dallas observed. "What the hell's going on?"

"Sneak attack?" Herbie suggested. "Maybe Berrell's out rounding up his enemies."

"What enemies? *Crenshaw* was the one who had him put away, not Gunderson."

"Okay, so he's kidnapping and/or maiming and/or killing all his best friends. Who knows?"

"And we're not gonna know sitting here." Dallas got out of the car. Urged, "Come on, come on," when Herbie wasn't too keen on following.

"How about you go and I'll call the police?"

"Not a bad idea."

Herbie breathed a sigh of relief and shifted into reverse.

Dallas started down the half-mile driveway thinking that Susan was something, knowing to dress him in black.

36

THE 4RUNNER STOPPED ABOUT fifty feet from Gunderson's tilted front porch. The engine was turned off. Driver's door shoved open. Jumbi Berrell stepped out and circled the rear of the vehicle, heading for the tiny house.

From three hundred yards away, Dallas lost Berrell to the darkness, but heard him on the dark porch. The heel of hard shoes or boots hit wood planks. A firm series of raps on the door.

Dallas, who'd been alternately running, pausing, and fast-walking down the driveway—as though playing the old red-light green-light game as a kid—slowed his approach to a stealthy crawl. Staying as low to the ground as possible without going on all fours. Needing to make certain wherever Berrell went, his line of sight to Dallas would keep tall trees and darkness at Dallas's back, thereby blending Dallas into his surroundings.

The problem was the glow off the country club. Floodlights from Hurricane Bay brightened an areola of black sky to pale gray. If Dallas inadvertently stepped across that background, his chances of being seen increased dramatically.

Plus, Berrell's eyes—like Dallas's—would be growing increasingly accustomed to the dark. Quick motions were the easiest to spot.

Dallas eased within 150 yards. Staying low. Reminding himself the closer he got, the more telling the sound of his steps became. Also, Berrell might have someone else with him besides Pamela Meyers. Until Dallas saw inside the 4Runner, he wouldn't know for sure.

A hundred yards away, Berrell stalked impatiently across Gunderson's porch. His steps were hard and determined. Posture aggressive, head bearing forward atop broad shoulders. Emitting an aura of anger and violence. The sort of man smarter men stayed away from.

Dallas crouched alongside the driveway in soft grass, testing each step before shifting his weight to his front foot. Constantly alternating his glance from the 4Runner to Berrell, moving twenty-five yards closer.

Berrell pounded his fist on Gunderson's door.

Dallas used the loud rapping to cover any sound he might make and took the next twenty-five yards faster than the last. He stopped when he could hear Berrell breathing. The escaped con snorted through congested nostrils like a bull hunting the matador who'd tried to skewer him.

Berrell punched the door so hard the windows rattled. Taking his frustration out on the house, as though it was the door's fault Gunderson wasn't there.

Berrell stepped off the porch and headed in Dallas's direction.

Dallas immediately looked down to hide his face; he put his hands behind his legs, covering skin that might reflect light. He listened with pinched-back ears.

Not far in front of him, Berrell came to a stop. Why, Dallas didn't know. He kept his head down. Couldn't risk moving now, not even to look up.

Standing in place, Berrell's weight shifted from leg to leg, cracking tiny pebbles under his shoes. As though he was looking for something.

Dallas hoped not for him.

Berrell took a few steps, feet scuffing dry dirt. Dallas could smell the dust he'd kicked up. But Berrell was walking away.

Slowly, Dallas lifted his head.

Berrell tracked past the 4Runner and headed toward the water. A long, dark walk across uneven field to where a lantern glowed rich yellow on Gunderson's pier. A lantern just like the one Berrell noticed much closer by, about forty feet left of Gunderson's house, perched atop a post.

Berrell paused. Every passing moment seemed to aggravate him further. He was here for some purpose, and that it wasn't happening crawled under his skin like a burrowing reptile.

At least the lantern would light his way across the field, a trek Berrell apparently hadn't planned to make. He went for it, was reaching for the lantern, when he suddenly, inexplicably, fell.

Grunting with surprise, arms flailing for balance, Berrell dropped not to the ground, but *through* it. Clean out of sight. Into a hole, the bottom of which he smacked pretty quickly. Making a bizarre sound upon contact. Not just a thud, but a squishy echo. Somewhat like stepping into mud, but more precise.

Berrell emitted a harsh, painful groan that, almost at once, turned to a gurgle, then stopped.

Dallas waited.

The night was suddenly very still. Random puffs of warm breeze ruffled distant trees. Marsh frogs' melodic chirps echoed from the bay. A lonely heron cried as she took flight over starlit waters.

Dallas stared at the hole Berrell had fallen into. A hole that hadn't been there before Berrell's weight landed on top of it. A trap hole.

Dallas crept forward on all fours, palms and shoes skimming pebbly dirt. He glanced quickly inside the 4Runner. Front seats empty. Backseats folded down.

A long shape in the trunk was wrapped in something white, a sheet perhaps. Bare feet protruded at one end of the "package": a body that showed no signs of life.

Dallas moved quickly to the trap hole, hunched forward as though running beneath a wire fence. He took a fast peek in and pulled back in case an angry Jumbi Berrell had a gun aimed at whoever came along to claim him.

The lantern was high enough off the ground to shine into the hole, probably by design. Jumbi Berrell was in there all right. In there good.

Dallas took a longer, better look. It was safe. The hole resembled a deep wishing well gone dry. Eight-foot-diameter concrete pipe had been turned on end and sunk well below the marshy water table.

Berrell looked small at the bottom of the pit, facedown, neck cocked slightly to the side, impaled by a series of twelve-inch spikes driven through two-by-fours and laid across the pit floor like a fatal asterisk.

Dallas repressed the urge to vomit. He pivoted away and clutched his stomach. He staggered to the 4Runner, afraid of what he'd find inside that sheet.

He opened the rear door. An interior light switched on with what seemed like blinding brightness. The scent of lavender perfume or body lotion flicked his nostrils.

Dallas gingerly pulled away the canvas sailcloth that wrapped the body of—as he suspected—Pamela Meyers.

She was on her side. Wearing a short bathrobe, the skirt of which had twisted and risen to her waist, exposing white panties. Her ankles and wrists were bound with lengths of damp seaweed. A dishcloth was stuffed into her mouth. A large contusion, about an inch into her hairline, was the source of blood matted in her wet hair.

She looked to have been surprised after taking a shower. But she *was* alive. Her chest moved with the faint echo of breaths drawn through her nose. When Dallas removed the rag from her mouth, she gasped sharply as though gaining consciousness, but did not.

Something made Dallas think he knew her. Suddenly, his memory was snagged as though hitting a trip rope. This was the woman who'd argued with Mack Trial in the restaurant.

Dallas no sooner realized that than he was distracted by the lantern down by the pier. It was walking toward him.

$\triangledown$

37

"**O**H, MY GOD. OH, MY GOD. Oh, my God." Roland Gunderson stared into the trap hole with horror. "Oh, my God. Oh, my God." Repeating that over and over, unable to pull himself from the gruesome sight of Jumbi Berrell's corpse riddled with blood-smeared spikes until Dallas urged him away.

Trembling, Gunderson looked up at Dallas. Face lit by reflections of the 4Runner headlights Dallas had switched on, Gunderson appeared frail and frightened, no longer the sturdy figure he had previously shown.

"I . . . I put it there for deer," Gunderson stammered. "Not people." He pointed a shaky arm, words running together in fast explanation. "There's a salt lick they come over to and . . . and they fall in and . . . I know it's illegal, but I don't eat much meat otherwise . . . I'm not the shot I once was . . . and . . . oh, my God . . . oh, my God."

Afraid Gunderson might go into shock, Dallas walked him to the porch. When the older man's gait became wobbly, Dallas held him upright.

Gunderson grasped the railing for support. "Just let me sit—let me sit here a minute." He uneasily lowered himself to the top porch step. "Oh, my God . . . I hope I don't have a heart attack. I've always been afraid of living alone. That no one would be here."

Dallas kept his arm around the old man. "Are you having any pains?"

"I'm—I'm not feeling anything."

Holding him steady, Dallas felt Gunderson's wrist; his pulse beat hard, but evenly, not that rapid at all. Strong old bird.

The ambulance arrived before the police. Two paramedics went to work on the unconscious Pamela Meyers. They were young, efficient, and justified in their suspicions as to what had happened. The circumstances were questionable; even at the beach, bathrobed women with head injuries didn't turn up too often in the back of jeeps.

Dallas's assurances he'd already called the police relieved the two men somewhat. Then again, Dallas didn't tell them about the trap hole into which Jumbi Berrell had spent his last breaths.

Chief Dawson settled into his herculean-durable office chair. The girth of his torso and resting elbows concealed that the chair had arms. Dawson's face was moist with perspiration; damned air-conditioning in the interrogation room never kept it as cool as he liked. He'd been in there the past hour with Roland Gunderson.

Susan had been there, too, part questioner and part counselor to Gunderson, treading a fine line of conflicting interests.

"So," Dawson said to Dallas, "whaddayou think?"

Dallas wished he knew what he thought. He'd been turning possibilities over in his head for two hours now, ever since the ambulance hustled Pamela Meyers off to Peninsula General. "I keep coming up with Mack Trial—he's a common denominator—but I'm not sure how he fits in. He writes letters to the parole board on Jumbi Berrell's behalf, but then a guy who maybe was, maybe wasn't Berrell tries to shoot Trial at Crenshaw's funeral. Trial is also being sued by his former clients now represented by Crenshaw. And last night I saw Trial arguing with Pamela Meyers—though, actually, I guess, she was screaming at him."

"Of the three people you connect to Trial, two are dead."

"I think Pamela Meyers was meant to get it tonight, though, not Berrell. That seaweed tied around her ankles and wrists?"

"Yeah?"

"Berrell tosses her in the water alive, weighed down with something, fish eventually nibble away the seaweed, and if she washes ashore in a few months with a gash on her head, it looks suspicious, but who knows? Could be she donked her noodle and fell off a boat. Could have been accidental."

"Just like Crenshaw being hit by a car."

"Right. Similar MO."

"So where's Gunderson fit in? He says he didn't know Berrell, but from what you described seeing tonight, it sure seems like Berrell knew him."

"I thought that at first, too, but I never heard Berrell call Gunderson's name. You knock on someone's door and they don't answer, you usually call out to them. Especially in a setting like this. Big open field. Pitch black. Maybe Gunderson's outside roaming around. You'd call his name, right?"

Dawson rocked easily in his chair. The creek of upholstery springs and ailing air-conditioner compressor filled moments of silence. "So where was Berrell gonna go with that lantern?"

"There was another lantern down by the pier. Maybe he thought Gunderson was there and was going looking for him."

"But Gunderson says he doesn't know Berrell."

"But Berrell's looking for him, so he looks down by the pier."

"So then Berrell's not trying to sneak up on Gunderson. First he bangs on the door, then he's gonna carry a light across an open field?"

Dallas saw the inconsistency. "Yeah, Berrell did turn down Gunderson's driveway with his headlights off. I don't know. Maybe he didn't expect Gunderson to be there. Maybe he was expecting someone else."

"Mack Trial?"

Dallas shrugged. "Maybe Trial was supposed to take care of Gunderson, Berrell does Meyers, and they toss them both in Hurricane Bay."

"You got anything besides some letter to a parole board that links Berrell and Trial?"

"Pamela Meyers."

"Besides her, because she also connects to Crenshaw and Pete Marjani? Works for them both."

"Yeah."

"So you got anything else to put them together?"

"No."

Dawson rocked his chair. "Berrell did have a gun. We found it hauling his body out of that hole. My guess is he bought it or stole it off one of the guards at the detention center."

"How's that?"

"Got rubber bullets in it. Like they use in riot situations."

"Or maybe he was going hunting for rubber duckies." Dallas set his sneakered feet on Dawson's desk and stared at the air conditioner. Both men thinking for a while until Dallas said, "Mmph."

"What?"

"Deer," Dallas said, "aren't attracted to light. Gunderson says that he had that trap hole put in to get deer. That he lured them to it with a salt lick. But the lantern was right there. Deer would stay away from the light. But someone wanting a way to see across a dark field . . . *they'd* want the lantern. Instead of getting the light, they go in the hole."

"I asked him that. Says the lantern's to keep *him* from falling in the hole. Says he puts the lantern to show where the trap is while he's outside. Tonight he was down at his boat. Says he likes to lay there, let the water sway the boat, and watch the stars. Says he and his wife used to do that all the time."

Dallas dropped his feet to the floor. So much for that theory. "So what the hell was Berrell doing there?"

"Ask that goofball medical examiner after he does the autopsy. See if Berrell's conscience left any Post-it notes attached to his soul."

Dallas smiled. "That was almost funny, Rup."

Dawson having been referring to Sam Paul, the county ME, whose autopsies occasionally delved into the occult, Sam thinking a corpse's eyes were like mini-VCRs, recording information that Sam could somehow play back through his own spiritual antenna. Dawson rarely paid heed to Sam Paul's suspicions even though he'd been dead on the money more than once.

"You charging Gunderson for Berrell's death."

Dawson watched his hands rub the chair arms a few strokes. "Way I see it, Gunderson's done us a favor. Escaped prisoner gets what he deserves." Dawson's sense of practicality was one reason he'd never go any further than heading Ocean City's police force, which was fine with Dawson, because this was all the further he wanted to go. "Of course, your pal Brent Bannister's likely to see it an entirely different way. Likely you'll get a *supenni* to testify before the grand jury. See if they should indict for murder, maybe just manslaughter if Bannister's not feeling full of himself. That's not my decision to make. I'll just get Gunderson to fill in the hole, that's about it." Dawson tilted as far to the side as his size and chair would allow. He looked down the hall leading from his office. "Susan's still in there with Gunderson. Maybe she's gettin' something out of him."

"By the way . . ." Dallas paused, wondering how to phrase this. ". . . You got some kid locked up for skipping out on a restaurant tab. Cheeseburger and fries."

Dawson nodded. "I told that asshole Morris not to lock up anybody for that anymore, but the goddamned kid won't tell us his name, so I can't rightly tell Morris to cut him loose. Especially not when the restaurant owner happens to be the mayor's goddamned neighbor and I'd catch it for dropping the case."

"Well, maybe the kid's got a reason to keep quiet."

"He got priors? Outstanding warrants?"

"It's not because of that."

"What, then?"

"I can't tell you."

Dawson scowled, about to say something when his intercom buzzed. He didn't pick up the phone, but shouted "What?" down the hall.

"Call from Peninsula General," came the hollered reply.

"Yeah?"

"You got Dallas Henry in there?"

Dawson shouted back, "Yeah."

"Somebody wants to talk to him."

"Who?"

"Pamela Meyers."

Dawson glared at Dallas. "You said you didn't know her."

"I swear to God." For once, he hadn't been lying to the police.

$\triangledown$

38

ONE OF THE PARAMEDICS who'd brought Pamela Meyers to Peninsula General stood guard outside the screened cubicle in which she was resting. He looked strong, standing chest out, arms folded, legs straight, watching Chief Dawson, Dallas, and Susan cross the emergency room.

It was quiet, which Dallas was glad to see. He didn't need anyone getting a twelve-inch needle in their eye or bleeding all over the place. The little Jumbi Berrell kabob he'd witnessed earlier had been quite enough, thank you.

The paramedic said, "Everything okay, Chief?"

"No problem, Mike. How you doing? Pretty calm in here for a change."

"Couple other calls came in, but med center handled them in town." He nodded toward Dallas. "This the guy she's been asking for?"

"Uh-huh," Dawson replied. "Disappointing, ain't it?"

Dallas said, "Thanks, Rup."

Mike gestured to the movable screen behind him. "She started asking for him as soon as she came to. She said she had to talk to him right away. Only she wouldn't say who he was—that's why I hung around. Sometimes with spouse abuse, the first person they want to talk to is who beat them up. I figure some loser comes here to take another pop at her, he's gonna go through me first. And he ain't gettin' through me."

"It's okay, Mike," Dawson assured. "That's not the case here."

The paramedic didn't seem too eager to leave his self-appointed post, but he had that "problem": becoming too attached to his patients.

Behind the screen, a woman's voice said, "Is that him?" Her tone was a mix of insistence and apprehension.

"She all right to talk?" Dawson asked.

Mike nodded. "Been doing real well. Got a couple stitches—but a real good job on them—shouldn't be more than a tiny scar. They'll cut her loose in an hour or so." Mike wheeled aside a partition wall.

Dawson went in first.

Pamela Meyers sat up abruptly. "I didn't ask for the police. I don't want to file any charges. I'm not talking to the police about—"

Mike moved to her bedside. "Miss Meyers, this is Chief—"

"Where's Dallas Henry? I want Dallas Henry!" Angry, as though they were trying to trick her.

Dawson grabbed Dallas's arm and jerked him into the cubicle. Whispered, "What the hell's goin' on?"

From the corner of his mouth, Dallas replied, "I don't know."

"Like hell."

"Where's Dallas Henry!" Pamela Meyers demanded.

"He's right here," Mike said, concerned she didn't recognize the man she'd asked to see. Maybe her condition was worse than Doc Majowski thought.

"Oh." She calmed somewhat. Her hair was pulled straight back, a section of it shaved where a patch covered her stitches. She focused on Dallas.

Dallas gave a quick wave. "Hi."

Pamela Meyers looked like someone who'd just met her blind date—and clearly had been given the wrong impression. "You're Dallas Henry?"

"Yup."

Mike asked if she was feeling all right. Headaches? Dizziness?

She ignored him, asked Dallas, "Do you have any identification?"

"Sure." Dallas reached into his pocket, then looked at Susan. "You forgot to put my wallet in these pants."

Dawson mumbled, "Oh, for God's sake."

Dallas turned apologetically to Pamela Meyers. "I can go get it if—"

She held up her hand, taking charge. A woman used to making decisions for herself. "You're the right one."

Insisting on privacy, Pamela Meyers and Dallas moved from the ER to a closed-door office. Windowless, cramped quarters likely of a minion assistant to the assistant of someone not that important. Slapped-on paint, worn carpet, and fluorescent lights that hummed like a nest of angry hornets.

She told Dallas she wanted to hire him as her attorney and immediately invoked the lawyer-client privilege. Assured their communications would remain in strict confidence, she said:

"The judge told me you were a little loose. In a good way."

"Crenshaw talked about me?"

Pamela Meyers nodded. "He said you could be trusted. That if there was a time he couldn't be there to help me, I should call you. You're the only person he ever said that about. He liked you."

"He had a funny way of showing it."

"That was his nature. The yelling and screaming. He was a very lonely man. The fact few people remained close with him once he took the bench upset him a great deal. Even his son abandoned him for a time."

"Harvey's not exactly your endearing personality."

"Harvey took his parents' divorce hard. He was very young and, thanks to his mother's brainwashing, he blamed it all on his father. . . ."

Dallas wondered why she wasn't asking who hit her on the head, how she'd ended up in the hospital. Often the unasked questions were more telling than the spoken ones.

". . . Harvey had a lot of drug and alcohol problems. His mother never did *anything* about it. She figured if Harvey suffered, it was the judge's fault. It was the price the judge paid for leaving her. The fact remains, she was as much a cause of the problem as he was."

Pamela Meyers spoke clearly and with authority. Dallas could picture her working for someone like Pete Marjani—or Raymond Crenshaw. She had an organizational brain that would function efficiently under the stress of an overly demanding boss.

She shifted uncomfortably in the wheelchair Mike insisted she use, not at all self-conscious about her appearance, the ill-fitting surgical bottoms the hospital had given her to wear under her robe; the gauze bandage taped to a bruised lump high on her forehead; the sallow tone of her complexion under fluorescent lights.

"I always tried to tell the judge Harvey wasn't his fault, but"— she shook her head sadly—"he never once believed me. Harvey did manage to straighten himself out for a little while. Or should I say Sandra straightened him out. Sandra was Harvey's wife. They met in college. When she got Harvey interested in law school, the judge was ecstatic. He had to do a little dirty work to get Harvey admitted, but once Harvey was in, he did okay." Pamela Meyers sounded surprised even now relating that fact.

"Harvey and Sandra were married during his final year, but when Harvey started looking for a job things started coming apart again. People misunderstood the judge so badly, no one but the lowliest firms wanted anything to do with Harvey. . . ."

Dallas figured that was a nice way of saying everyone hated

Crenshaw's guts and his son got hated by default.

"... And Harvey had assumed his father would get him into some big downtown firm. When that didn't happen, Harvey went off the deep end. He blamed his father for lying to him. He got back into the booze heavily. His marriage to Sandra collapsed. He left the state and went to Pennsylvania. He was part of a few different firms, but the same result every time. The drinking became obvious and they'd let him go.

"The only time Harvey called the judge was for money. And the judge . . ." She shook her head sadly. ". . . well, he couldn't say no. Each check he wrote he was sure would be the last, the final stake Harvey was going to need to turn himself around. . . . It never was." Pamela Meyers spoke with such emotion, Dallas guessed the answer to his next question before he asked it.

"What was your relationship with the judge?"

"My relationship . . . ? That's a very good question, Mr. Henry."

"Nobody calls me mister."

"Yes, well . . . Dallas, then." She looked at him with plain bookkeeper's eyes. A pleasant, though uninspiring woman; someone who blended into a room, who people could meet three or four times in their life and always think it was the first. Like a hand without fingerprints, her personality didn't leave a distinguishing mark on whatever she touched.

"My relationship with the judge . . . ? I suppose a lawyer trying to make me look bad would call me his mistress—although that's not what it was."

"Girlfriend, maybe."

"Friend, mostly. Companion now and again. Girlfriend just for a time. I can't explain the attraction—I stopped trying years ago—but I *was* drawn to him. Perhaps his being a judge was aphrodisiac. They say power does that. But as abusive as he was on the bench, he never said a cross word to me. Never. He was always kind and gentle."

Her eyes lifted to a blank wall, watching it as though her past were being replayed there. "When it started, we were both working in the court system. I was with the state's attorney's office, enforcing child support delinquencies. The judge was on the bench. We started with lunch, but I think from very early on, it was clear we both wanted more. It took over a year for the 'more' to happen. . . ." She smiled faintly. "And it lasted two years after that, but then—I don't know—all of a sudden it just didn't seem right. I don't know why, and I've tried to figure it out a thousand times. Something just changed between us. We continued to see one another, but it became strictly platonic. The judge never pressured me otherwise." In a way, she was bragging about him.

"You know," she continued, "the amusing part was that no one ever suspected us of having an affair. *Never* once. They saw us together, but never uttered a word. I suppose they figured only beautiful girls had affairs, and then only with dashing men. And the judge and I certainly didn't fit that bill.

"After a time, I left the state's attorney's office to finish college full-time. I'd been going at night for six years. I had some money and finished my degree in three semesters—in accounting. I went to work with a small CPA firm in the county. Over the last five years, the company grew and my salary increased commensurately. I saved my money. Lived very frugally and made some good investments. And then . . ." She took a deep breath. ". . . I decided to right an old wrong."

Dallas waited for her to continue. He had at least a dozen questions, but often found the best answers came from letting the story be told willingly, wanderingly.

She paused before continuing. "Here I am again." She looked away. "Back at that point of no return."

"I don't understand."

"When I wondered how best to do this—righting this wrong—I came down here and saw the judge. It was the first time we'd been together since he'd retired. What I had to tell him was difficult, because it referred to what had been going on while he and I had our affair. That I hadn't told him then made me a liar."

She hesitated . . . took a breath . . . got on with it. "While I was in the state's attorney's office—you have to understand, I came from a poor background. My father died when I was very young and I saw my mother work hard for a lot of years just so we could get along. And we didn't get along that well. When she got sick—this wonderful woman who had always talked about traveling and seeing things, but never did—and I saw her time running out . . ."

Dallas waited. Confessions were painful.

Pamela lowered her head, then abruptly raised it again. ". . . One day . . . at work . . . I had a phone conversation with a man. He owed about eight thousand dollars in back child support. He was supposed to pay four hundred dollars a month, but rarely did. This one day, I don't know why, feeling extra aggressive I guess, I got on him—really rode him—to send not just what he owed for that month, but to make a double payment. He did.

"I was shocked when it came in: money orders for eight hundred dollars. Now . . . I knew his wife was only expecting to get four hundred. I also knew the man and his wife didn't speak to one another—most of the cases I had for enforcement were like that. So his wife wouldn't have any idea he'd sent in a double payment. And each money order was blank on the pay-to line—which wasn't unusual, lots of people left it blank, because it was rather long to write out: State's Attorney's Office, Child Support Division.

"So here I am with these signed money orders, made out to no one, that I know won't be receipted back to the payor like a canceled check, and that no one is expecting to receive. I put his regular payment in the enforcement account and processed it to his wife. The extra four hundred I took home.

"But I didn't cash it right away," she added quickly. "I agonized about it for weeks, truly *agonized* . . . but, ultimately, I kept the money. It was a terrible decision—there is no justification. I know the people the money was supposed to go to were as much in need, if not more so, than my mother. But I didn't know *them*. I never saw *their* pain. They were just anonymous files. My mother was dying every night in front of me. And four hundred dollars was more than I made in two weeks.

"After that one time, I waited to get caught. I barely slept. But no one ever said anything. So I started looking for opportunities to take money. I started actively calling delinquent accounts, worked overtime without pay and without lunch. I became ruthless. Anytime I could convince a husband to make a double payment and it came in money orders, I'd keep half. I justified it two ways, that it was like a commission for getting men who rarely made any payment to make a double payment, and that one day—after my mother died—I'd find a way to get the money back into the system."

"How long did this go on?"

"Three years."

"You never got caught?"

"The auditing system was a joke. You know state government. It's set up as a license to steal. There were a few close calls. Sometimes ex-husbands and wives did talk. But husbands were always lying about even making a single payment, so a double payment sounded dubious to start off with. But if either of them called in to check, I'd blame someone 'new in the office' for making a clerical error and send the money. And since I was the only person working on those accounts, that was all I had to worry about. As far as the rest of the office was concerned, I was as likely to embezzle money as I was to have an affair. An unmarried woman who wore inexpensive clothes and lived with her sick mother."

"How much money are we talking about?"

"About forty thousand dollars."

Dallas tried not to show his shock.

"That was *my* share."

"Your share?"

"Toward the end, there were two of us."

$\triangledown$

39

"H<small>E WAS IN CHARGE</small> of prosecuting delinquent accounts that fell way behind. It was the lowest job in the office for a prosecutor and he resented it. He thought he should have been trying murder cases and here he was going after 'baddy daddies'—that's what he called them. There was one case where the husband being charged claimed he'd sent in more money than we'd credited him for. But Mack Trial never came to me about it *before* the case was set for hearing. If he had, I could have covered my tracks. But . . ." Pamela Meyers shrugged. "Well, some things never change."

"If Trial had prepared for court, he'd have seen where defense counsel subpoenaed American Express records and had copies of cleared money orders his client had sent to our office. The endorsements on these money orders were always very simple. Whether put in the enforcement account or my own, I merely signed them For Deposit Only, never in my own name. But that only protected me from the obvious. The defendant's lawyer pointed out to Trial that certain money orders—in an amount equal to what his client hadn't been credited for—had been deposited in a different bank than the money orders he *had* been given credit for. The lawyer didn't suspect anything other than poor bookkeeping. He assumed we'd sent payment to the wrong person and credited some other deadbeat husband for what his client had paid.

"I don't know what Trial thought, or if he thought anything. He came to me during a court recess and asked if I could explain it." Pamela squeezed her fist. "I panicked. My worst fears were being realized. I got cold and started trembling. All I could see was jail. Trial thought I was getting sick. He was going to get a doctor, but I stopped him. And—I don't know why, *believe me*, I don't know why—but I told him. Maybe it was my guilt overflowing. For whatever reason, it all came spewing out.

"He was as shocked as you looked a few moments ago. He sat down and put his hands on his face. For a moment, I felt as though he was sharing my agony, that he'd seen my mistake for what it was and was in pain with me. After a few minutes, he looked up.

So determined. He said he was going to cover it on the case he had in court and we'd talk later.

"I was so grateful at first, but it didn't take long—no more than a few hours—before I started hating him for finding out. Because it was all going to end, and I knew I was going to pay the price. Trial would have to tell our boss. He'd have to. But he didn't.

"That night, Trial had me meet him in the parking garage of the old Towson Plaza—back before they turned it into a big mall—anyway, I met him and that's when he told me what we were going to do. That I was going to show him how I'd been getting the money out and we were going to do it together."

She made a vacant gesture. "What choice did I have? None. So we became a team—me and Mack Trial—only he improved on it. He took collection calls himself, threatening husbands with prosecution. He even tracked some of these guys down in person. He had a cousin who was an investigator with the IRS who got us *all kinds* of information on these guys. It was incredible. The money started rolling in.

"All of a sudden—and maybe because someone else knew—it was dirty money to me. I told Mack it had always been my plan to pay the money back. He said that was fine. He just wanted enough to start his own law office and once he'd made it, he'd pay back his share and I'd pay back mine."

She shook her head. "Only when I approached him a year and a half ago, he said there was no way he was repaying a cent. That we'd committed the perfect crime. The statute of limitations had almost passed. I pressed him, but he wouldn't change his mind. He finally stopped answering my calls. That was when I went to Judge Crenshaw and told him about it."

"What did he say?"

"I was so ashamed . . . but the judge seemed to dismiss what I'd done. I guess after so many years on the bench, hearing so much crime, he'd become hardened to it. He told me he'd make the son of a bitch pay back the money."

"Mack Trial?"

"Yes."

"Ms. Meyers—"

"Pam."

"Mack Trial may be the reason you're in the hospital right now."

"I assumed so." She nodded, matter-of-fact. "I should have been prepared for him trying to threaten me. After the judge's death, I tried contacting Trial on my own. He didn't return my calls, so I found him. I made a real scene, telling him I was going to get a new lawyer to replace the judge if Mack didn't pay attention to me."

"Pam, I don't think you're taking what happened tonight very seriously. The man who attacked you was an escaped felon who *tried* to kill Crenshaw years ago—who may have been successful at it a few days ago."

She turned her head a notch to the side. "*Was?*"

Dallas wasn't sure of her question.

"You said he *was* an escaped convict. Not *is*."

"He's dead."

"How did—?"

"That doesn't matter." She was missing the point. "The fact is, you were tied up and taken to Roland Gunderson's farm. From the looks of it, you were going to be dumped in the bay and left to drown."

This revelation clearly disoriented her. Apparently, she thought she'd been found unconscious at home. Her already blanched skin tone paled further. Her hands gripped the wheelchair rails.

"Are you all right?"

She shut her eyes and swallowed heavily.

"Should I get the doctor?"

"No. Give me a minute." She opened her eyes as though to clear them and, although slightly short of breath, said, "I didn't see the man who hit me. Just a flash from the corner of my eye . . ." Her voice couldn't shake a sudden quiver of nerves. "I assumed he—Trial—had just been trying to scare me. I don't scare easily. B-but, I didn't think he would try to have me . . . have me killed."

"Pam, you should talk to the police . . . about what you told me."

She seemed stunned by the suggestion. "That's impossible. I'd have to tell them what *I'd* done."

"You'd have to do that anyway, right?" Dallas suggested softly. "Repaying stolen money is pretty much equal to a confession."

"No. I—I thought of it more as making a—a donation or a gift—something like that—to the police department. Or a child or family-in-need charity."

"What if I could work out a deal for you? I don't know exactly how. But no admission of guilt, just a repayment of monies, and—"

She shook her head, working to regain her composure and will. "As much as I regret what I did—and I know this is selfish—but I, I just want to return the money. I *don't* want the humiliation of a criminal proceeding—even if I deserve it. Because Mack Trial is right about one thing: *No one suspects a crime has been committed*. No one ever missed the money."

Dallas was at a loss. "So what can I possibly do to represent you?"

"Make a deal for me with Trial. Tell him you're taking over Crenshaw's malpractice cases and you'll settle them reasonably. Cut your percentage of the fee if you have to."

"What's that got to do with—?"

She cut him off by chopping the air with her hand as though cleaving meat. "When the judge went to Trial to demand he repay the money we stole, Trial told the judge he was 'up to his ass in debt.' He was opening all these new offices, buying TV time, and business wasn't as good as he'd hoped. The judge pushed him—he was very good at that. After about a month, Trial had an idea.

"He told the judge he was being sued by two former clients for malpractice, and that the cases were legitimate. He suggested the judge get these clients to leave their present attorneys, sign on with the judge, and Trial would get his insurance company to settle quickly and quietly. Trial would even help the judge make his case. He didn't want any bad publicity. One malpractice case would kill a year's worth of advertising. Trial also gave the judge the names of three or four other clients who had potential malpractice actions against him; people who'd never realized they'd been damaged by his bad legal advice. The judge got them all."

Dallas had wondered how Crenshaw had located all those clients. Susan had suggested Crenshaw might have had someone inside Trial's office, never suspecting it was Trial himself.

"The idea," Pam explained, "was for Trial's malpractice carrier to pay off these claims and the judge—since Trial was helping him win these cases—would split his fee with Trial."

"He's sharing fees with Trial on cases he's bringing *against* Trial?"

Pam nodded. She had her nerve back and recounted details with clarity. "But the judge wouldn't ever actually hand any money back to Trial. He'd use it to repay what Trial stole with me."

"That's nuts."

"But it was working. Half the cases were very close to settlement. Everything was going well until *Harvey* paid the judge a visit. He needed money. As always." Pam's attitude was suddenly much less accepting than during earlier references to Crenshaw's son. "He was deeper in debt than ever. His credit cards were overextended. *Two* car loans. I think he even had a boat. And was about to lose it all.

"The judge was as willing to give Harvey money as always, but he was running out of cash himself. He'd never accumulated any savings. All that went to Harvey. And his pension would have been all right, but he had a mortgage on his cabin, because when he'd sold his house in Baltimore before retiring down here, he'd given most of the equity to Harvey to cover some other problem. It was a vicious spiral. Harvey kept taking more and more, while the judge was making less and less.

"After Harvey's visit, the judge decided to get the money Harvey needed in Trial's malpractice cases. He doubled his demand in the three cases about to settle and tripled it on the others. Mack Trial went berserk. The judge said he didn't care, that if he had to take Trial down, he was going to do it."

"Crazy," Dallas muttered. "Absolutely crazy."

"I begged the judge not to do it. I said it wasn't worth it. I even offered to give him some of the money I'd saved. He wouldn't hear of it. He told me he'd get the money the way he'd always gotten it, by working hard. He decided to take other cases, not just against Trial. That he was going back into full-time practice. I even got a case for him."

Dallas shook his head: what seemingly intelligent people got themselves into. Un-absolutely-believable.

"My boss," Pamela Meyers said, "had been having a terrible time trying to buy a piece of property. I happened to mention it to the judge and when he heard what it was about, he said he'd take the case. He said he could make Roland Gunderson do anything he wanted. He said he'd taught Gunderson that lesson when their law firm split up."

"Your boss is Pete Marjani."

"That's right." She seemed surprised he knew that.

"Go on—"

"Anyway, Gunderson wouldn't sell. He *was* putting up a fight."

"Did Gunderson and Crenshaw meet about this?"

"The judge never told me details. Only that he was making progress and Pete shouldn't worry. He'd be getting that land. I think he would have, too," she announced, bragging about Crenshaw again. "The judge was very determined. Plus, he had a huge contingency fee riding on the deal: five percent ownership in Hurricane Bay. Marjani signed a fee contract specifying it. That was the only document I ever saw on that case. Whatever paperwork the judge was doing, he must have handled himself."

While Pamela Meyers was reviewing the "head sheet" with Doc Majowski, being advised of what symptoms she should be aware of now that she was being released, Chief Dawson pulled Dallas aside.

"Well . . . ?" He gestured toward the administrator's office Dallas had been using as an ad hoc conference room. "What was that about?"

"She's hired me as her attorney, Rup. I can't talk about it."

Dawson's meaty jaw turned to granite. "Swell. That's what Susan just told me about her and Gunderson."

$\triangledown$

40

DALLAS FOUND SUSAN OUTSIDE the hospital gift shop, which was closed.

Through a darkened smoked-glass wall, she read the headline on a stack of *USA Today*s tied and bundled on the floor.

At the beach, you tended to forget there was a rest of the world out there, waging the same wars, problems, and prejudices that had been going on in one form or another since the beginning of time. Which, Dallas often suspected, was why there was a beach.

"So." He gently grasped Susan's arms from behind and rested his chin on her shoulder. "Are we going to have a conflict of interest, you and I?" He watched their reflection in the glass.

"I don't think I can keep looking into Crenshaw's death, Dallas. I'm sorry." She was sincere about that.

"Because you're representing Gunderson?"

She nodded.

"Makes it sound like he did it."

"He's told me certain things that would help the investigation, but asked me not to divulge them. So I really don't have a choice."

"Funny. Pamela Meyers just hired me and I've got the same problem. Rup"—Dallas shook his head against Susan's shoulder—"is not happy." He wrapped his arms around Susan's waist.

In the unoccupied hospital corridor, lights low with inactivity, Susan leaned back against him.

He kissed her neck.

She offered a pleasant, humming smile, turned to him, and for the most delicious moment, their mouths met. "Be good," she urged, withdrawing her kiss with a gentle push of tongue that Dallas knew would be the highlight of his summer.

Pamela Meyers was released from Peninsula General an hour later. Against her wishes, Dallas put her in the Ocean Tides' lone vacant room. In that sense, he accomplished the one goal he'd set out for himself: get the motel filled by the weekend so any lawyers coming in for the bar convention finale couldn't stay there.

Pamela Meyers wasn't keen on the arrangement. She'd wanted

to go home. "I'll be fine," she'd told Dallas. "You talk to Trial in the morning, get the deal ironed out with him, and it'll be over." The longer she was conscious, the more bossy she became.

Dallas was beginning to prefer her knocked out. He said if she wanted him to represent her—which he wasn't looking forward to now that he knew what she wanted him to do—she was staying close by. At least for tonight.

In case Jumbi Berrell wasn't the only person looking to do her harm, Dallas staked a guard by her door: OC's champion of fleeing and eluding, the perennially unshaven Bobby—with a case of beer.

"Nobody goes in, she doesn't go out, okay?"

"Gotcha," Bobby belched.

"And check on her every hour or so—"

"I got no watch."

"Check on her every six-pack and make sure she's feeling okay. Any nausea, headaches, neck pains, call the hospital."

Pffssst. Bobby opened a can of Schlitz. "Gotcha."

That done, Dallas drove north, knowing full well he should call first. It was the polite thing to do, especially at two in the morning, but maybe he didn't call for a reason he didn't want to admit.

In Coconut Malerie's, he went up the open lobby staircase two steps at a time, passing the spot where Vicky had lost her skirt the other night. He knew before he got to her door that he had it pegged.

He stood outside and listened. Vicky wasn't a timid soul in bed, never had been. She let her pleasure be known, as though part of the turn-on was letting other people hear her rapt in the throes. In this case—tonight—rapt by someone else's throes, not Dallas's.

He stayed there a few terrible minutes, so the impression left in his brain would be indelible. So that an hour from now—ten years from now—he'd never mistake what he'd heard as anything other than Vicky having sex. So the next time they met, she couldn't brush this off, lie to him like saying he hadn't seen her getting into Jack Whiting's car, heading off for a weekend with Jack when she was supposed to be visiting her parents.

Dallas was calm for a while, then he was sad, then angry. He drove home along Ocean Highway with the 280's custom ragtop peeled down. Elbow bent against the open window, head resting on his hand. The paragon of emotional hypocrites. In love with Susan, willingly seduced by Vicky, all against his better judgment, of which, he decided that very moment, he had none.

To make matters worse, he had just taken on a client who was an embezzler and a liar, who knew a man she'd once loved and still appeared to care for had been run over by a car, and she was more concerned about getting away with an old crime than worrying about who committed this one.

Back at the Ocean Tides, he sat on the roof. Down on the beach, the waves were up, pounding the shore. White water appeared like silver froth under the moonlight.

Late-night stragglers prowled the boardwalk. Teenage boys on the hustle, looking for beer and sex. Teenage girls trying to look interested when most were more scared than anything else. Sex education on the sand, all that wasted breath in school about alcohol abuse and safe sex blown off by inherent curiosity and a daredevil grasp for pleasure. It *was* a miracle anyone lived past the age of nineteen.

Dallas stretched his legs, leaned back, and watched the stars. He was always here, it seemed. On the roof, where time didn't really stop, but slowed long enough for him to feel it. Watching the stars dance between thin clouds . . . Watching the stars . . . Watching the stars . . .

And then he knew.

41

As THE NIGHT SKY FADED into pastel shades of daybreak, the sun pushed warm coral light above the horizon. The ocean glowed liquid gold. Joggers and beachcombers laid footprints in smooth sand. Families rode bicycles, wheels thumping rhythmically across slats of boardwalk. Sea gulls renewed their scavenger hunt for food.

Dallas only saw the sunrise when he didn't make it to bed.

He was stiff from spending the night on the roof, his back and neck tight until self-chiropractic cracked his spine with relief. He secured his lounge chair and climbed down the roof hatch.

On the second floor, Bobby was sprawled across the balcony outside Pamela Meyers's room, outlined by crushed beer cans like homicide detectives drew chalk silhouettes around dead bodies. He snored peacefully.

Dallas passed the volleyball girls' room, heard quiet, awakening chatter inside. That would be Jill and Meghan, the cheerful early risers. There were also some moans. Which would be Laura, Laurie, and Lisa.

In his own room, Dallas showered, shaved, and put on decent shorts, a wrinkled golf shirt, and broken-in deck shoes—no socks. His wet hair dried on the ride to the Sheraton. He got there just before seven-thirty, parked in a spot near the door marked VIP GUESTS ONLY, and went into the lobby. Nodded to a sleepy-eyed bellhop. Plunked a quarter in the pay phone.

Susan answered on the fifth ring, irritated; if this was a salesman, she was going to do him bodily harm.

Dallas said, "Don't complain. I gave you a few extra minutes of sleep."

"Dallas?" A real switch: him waking her for a change.

"Get your 'client' and meet me in the war room by nine-thirty. Okay?"

"What's going on?"

"A meeting of interested parties."

"Dallas . . . ?" Susan didn't like it when he planned things without her input. But what choice was there? Last night's ethical obligations to new clients positioned them as adversaries.

"Nine-thirty, okay?"

"I'll call Gunderson."

"Thanks." Dallas hung up and went to the front desk; asked for Mack Trial's room number.

As the elevator door opened to the ninth floor, Dallas came face-to-face with a familiar face. Mack Trial's makeup girl, the dinner companion Trial ignored the other night in Waves.

Like the shoemaker's kids who go barefoot, she hadn't taken advantage of her own expertise this morning. Her face was blotchy, a patch of acne left uncovered on her chin. The remains of eyeliner were smeared into the corners of puffy eyes. Her coarse hair was knotted beyond immediate repair.

She snorted disgust at seeing Dallas. One of those *sheesh, men!* reactions. Fed up with the gender as a whole. Haphazardly packed weekend bag slung over her shoulder, she got in the elevator.

Dallas stayed with her. "Rough night?"

The doors closed and they started going up. Miss Clairol wanted down. She muttered, "Shit." Repeatedly jabbed the Lobby button as though she could change their direction. Two floors later, she turned hands on hips toward Dallas. "Yeah, it was a lousy night. Lousy *life*."

"Maybe you should work on your choice of dinner dates." Wrong thing to say.

"Yeah, right, stud. Like you'd be an improvement." So nasty even her T-shirt and cuffed shorts looked mean.

"I didn't say that."

"No, but you're thinking it. Every line's a come-on. You guys are all alike." Near the fifteenth floor, she pushed the button for sixteen. When the doors opened, she stomped out.

"Here," Dallas offered, holding the door, "you take this one. I'll walk down."

She stopped with her back to him.

Dallas said, "Is Trial awake?"

She didn't answer at first, then did an abrupt about-face and got back into the elevator, not looking at Dallas, who stepped out into the carpeted hall.

The door started to shut. She pushed a button to keep it open and threw a room key at Dallas, which he caught. "He's passed out. Last night, when he couldn't—you know, *couldn't!*—because he was a wound-out ball of nerves. He started drinking. All night, he keeps drinking, like *that's* going to help. So what am I? His mother and his whore?"

"Quick piece of advice?" Dallas proposed.

She didn't want to hear it, but didn't allow the door to close, either. "What?"

"Take it from a lawyer: stay away from lawyers."

"Now you tell me."

The door slid shut. Dallas walked down to Trial's floor.

"Get up, you bagworm!" Dallas was generally more congenial, but something about the sight of Lenny Sawgrass aka Mack Trial sprawled half off the bed, knees on the floor, clinging to the mattress from the waist up, made Dallas plant his foot across the back of Trial's red bikini briefs and give a little push-kick.

Trial rolled over like a beanbag. Slid the rest of the way off the bed, dragging covers with him. His butt landed with a thud; his head bounced against the boxspring and listed toward the padded headboard, hair plugs sticking up like paintbrushes at attention.

Call me. Mack Trial. I've got thirty offices across the state. And remember, it feels great to litigate. Dallas could hear the TV spot in his head like a deranged mantra. The price for watching too much late-night TV.

Dallas went into the bathroom and filled an ice bucket with water. "Surf's up!" He sloshed a cold, wet greeting across Trial's bald chest.

"Whoa-wow-whadehellsgoinon!" Trial jerked to life. His neck worked hard at balancing his head atop his shoulders, but lost the battle. Trial slumped back into oblivion.

The room smelled horrible. A sour mix of hair spray, cheap cologne, and liquor. Dallas slid open the balcony door. He dragged Trial outside and propped him against the railing. Tied him there in his red briefs with a length of sheet. Put a pair of sunglasses on him. Strung Trial's left hand in the air like he was the pope blessing the parking lot.

Back inside, Dallas tore a few pages off a blank legal pad and wrote out in big letters: CALL ME. MACK TRIAL. I'VE GOT THIRTY OFFICES STATEWIDE. He Scotch-taped this sign to the balcony, then left Trial a more personal note for when he came to.

Call me. Dallas Henry. I've got one office and I think you better haul your embezzling ass down there.

42

MACK TRIAL DIDN'T KNOCK. He busted into the Ocean Tides' war room like a narc squad point man on a crack house raid. Face swirling with outrage, slamming the door into the wall, he had Dallas's note balled up in his hand.

"What the hell's the idea leaving me out on the balcony. . . ." Trial saw Roland Gunderson on the sofa next to Susan and lost his train of thought. He started over, with emphasis. "What the *hell's* . . ." He saw Pamela Meyers sitting, arms crossed, looking very unhappy with this entire proceeding. Trial did a double take and forgot what he'd started to say.

Mack Trial Infuriation Take 3. *"What the hell . . ."* Trial worked hard to keep up his affront in the face of diminishing odds. ". . . *is going on* . . ." His voice faded off. ". . . here?" He stopped at the bed nearest the rest of the group. "Shit's bells."

Dallas said, "Your fly's down, Mack."

Wind sucked from aggressive sails, Trial plopped on a corner of the bed and closed his eyes when a wave of hangover nausea wobbled him.

Dallas crossed the room and locked the front door. The oceanfront curtains were already closed, blocking out light. Given everyone's disposition, it was impossible to believe it was a bright and sunny day outside, even as the sound of children playing on the beach echoed through the sliding-glass door.

"I won't bother with introductions." Dallas leaned against a paneled wall, hands in his shorts pockets. "So . . ." He scanned his guests. ". . . who wants to go first?"

Susan whispered to Roland Gunderson, who nodded and kept his gaze fixed on his own knees as though something was crawling up his leg.

Pamela Meyers fanned herself with a ragged copy of the since-defunct *Bodyboarding* magazine she'd picked off the floor. She seemed to be boiling under her skin, no doubt mentally dictating a letter she was going to send the legal ethics committee to report Dallas for violating the lawyer-client privilege. She wore a faded denim shirt and sweatshorts—not her personal taste, but about all

Dallas had come up with from the lost and found that fit her. The gauze patch on her head needed freshening up.

Mack Trial looked mainly at Gunderson and tried to make it seem like he wasn't when Dallas turned toward him.

"Okay," Dallas offered, "I'll start." He made himself comfortable on the floor, legs stretched out. "What I never could figure out was why Raymond Crenshaw wouldn't say who or why he thought someone might try to kill him. And why he called me at three in the morning and not the police.

"*Now* I get it. Crenshaw was involved in something illegal. Hardly the sort of thing he could admit to the police. He tells them person X is looking to kill him, the police start wondering why, start asking questions, and Crenshaw's game is blown.

"He couldn't tell me, either. Or Vicky Sterrett, who redrafted his will. Because, as lawyers, we'd be legally required to report any knowledge of an *ongoing*—not completed—criminal enterprise." Dallas glanced at Pamela Meyers. "*That's* an exception to the lawyer-client privilege.

"At the same time, however, Crenshaw doesn't want his suspicions to go unknown if he does end up dead, so he leaves me a clue. A box I'm not supposed to open *until* he's dead. A box with a golf ball inside." Dallas checked if any of his guests registered surprise that he *did* know what was in that box.

"Now, I wonder," Dallas continued, "why the riddle? Why a golf ball? Probably, in case I opened the box while Crenshaw was still alive. I find a golf ball, Crenshaw can make some joke about it, that he was tricking me all along.

"But there's a man's name imprinted on the ball. So is this who Crenshaw was afraid of? Good possibility, right? Only that name— that lead—doesn't pan out. But it does point me in the right direction. At least sort of. Crenshaw probably never realized how intricate the plot against him had become.

"Anyway—the golf ball. As well as having a name on it, it *also* has a logo. Hurricane Bay. A golf club that needs land for a new eighteen holes. The obvious choice is Roland Gunderson's farm. Beautiful spot right next door, right on the water. Great natural habitat. A blend of open land and forest. Property Marjani went to a lot of trouble to get out of the federal wetlands program and now he can't have it. Not at any price. But what can Marjani do?

"If you won't sell," Dallas said directly to Gunderson, "you won't sell. But Marjani's already telling his members Tropical Storm is being built on your property. He's got a big architectural drawing posted in the clubhouse. Marjani's a desperate man. He'll try anything to get the land. He even bought another piece of property and, from the looks of it, was going to build you a duplicate house on the sheer futile hope he could toss in some cash and convince you to trade. That if you had somewhere else to go and wouldn't have to look for a new place—wouldn't have to interrupt your reclusive life—you might bite. Marjani was *that* kind of desperate . . . but not murder desperate.

"Some years ago, Marjani was involved in a pyramid scheme and got sued. One angry link in his entire operation brought Marjani's consumer rip-off tumbling down. If Marjani was going to kill someone, it would have been that guy. But Marjani didn't. He took his lumps and went on. Got into the development and building business down here, and did well."

Mack Trial, who still hadn't pulled up his zipper, listened with some relief that he hadn't been mentioned so far. He was, however, concerned about the R-Kive boxes stashed in a corner marked RCC CASE FILES.

"But Hurricane Bay," Dallas said, "was not the starting point. It was the end. The beginning was when a former acquaintance of Crenshaw's came to him with a problem."

Pamela Meyers stopped fanning her face.

Mack Trial took a here-it-comes breath.

"You two"—Dallas pointed between them—"had a nice little scheme going. Embezzling funds from the state's attorney's office. You made a pact to one day pay back the money. You," he directed to Trial, "would use what you stole to get a private law practice off the ground. And you," turning his head toward Pamela Meyers, "were going to care for your sick mother. Although from the amount you took, I figure you decided to throw in a few niceties for yourself. Sorry," he said in response to Meyers's accusing stare, "but I learned early on the sick mother line's usually a lie.

"So . . ." Dallas rolled onto his side, propped his head on his hand, and couldn't avoid noticing that, at this angle, he could see a lot of Susan's legs in that skirt. Quite distracting. ". . . where was I?"

"I think you said 'sick mother,' " Pamela Meyers spat, meaning the term as an insult.

"Right. So, Crenshaw, on behalf of Miss Meyers, goes to Mr. TV Lawyer and tells you to pay up. But you're broke."

"Up to his ass in debt," Pamela Meyers chimed in spitefully.

"Broke—but," Dallas said sarcastically, "you had a *great* plan. You'll give Crenshaw the names of former clients who could sue you for malpractice. Crenshaw collects from your insurance company, to whom you confess liability, and half of Crenshaw's fee goes to pay back money you stole."

Roland Gunderson blurted, "You've got to be kidding?" Looking directly at Trial.

Susan quickly admonished Gunderson with a hand gesture. On the advice of counsel, Gunderson lowered his head again, but was shaking it.

"Now," Dallas resumed, "asinine as the plan was, it might have worked except Crenshaw's son appears whining for money, and suddenly Crenshaw needs more cash. So Crenshaw ups his demands in the malpractice cases and Mr. TV Lawyer Boy goes nuts.

"About this time, Miss Meyers, who is moonlighting as Crenshaw's secretary, happens to mention her day-job boss, Pete Marjani, is hot to buy a piece of land from—none other than—Roland Gunderson, Crenshaw's former law partner.

"*Mmmmmm*, wish I could've been there to see the look on Marjani's face when the judge who destroyed his pyramid scheme years ago shows up to suggest a new alliance. But how could Marjani turn Crenshaw away? Crenshaw's likely in a near feeding frenzy from the smell of fresh blood. Telling Marjani how he squeezed Gunderson half a lifetime ago when they split their partnership, and how he's sure he can do it again. Marjani *had* to be interested, especially when Crenshaw was so sure he'd be successful he took the job on a contingency basis.

"Why, though"—Dallas idly rotated his foot, cracked his ankle—"is Crenshaw so sure he can pull this off? Why would he think he could get an edge on Gunderson *again* twenty years *after* he's screwed Gunderson on another deal? They're not friends, they're enemies. Mr. Gunderson is an intelligent man. All he has to say is no, he's not selling.

"Unless . . ." Dallas faced Gunderson. "Unless Crenshaw has something to hold over your head, something that was just as valuable to him twenty years ago as it is now. Something that forced you out of the partnership. *That* was the only way Crenshaw could have—I think you said, 'kicked you while you were down.' Partnerships are assumed to be fifty-fifty unless there's a written agreement to the contrary. The only way one partner walks away empty-handed is because he doesn't want to pursue the matter. Doesn't pursue because of something outside the partnership. Something one partner knows about the other partner *to use against him.*"

Gunderson's head bowed closer to his stomach, as though he

was beginning a slow process of reverse evolution, going into a protective fetal ball.

"It always bothered me about your wife," Dallas said. "How much you missed her. It was *too* good, *too* endearing. At first I thought it was to impress Susan. That you wanted your onetime phone relationship to turn into more. But that wasn't it. You were selling me as much as you were selling her.

"You said your wife was a small-town girl who'd never lived anywhere but where she was born until she got involved with you. Yet when she left you, you had no idea where she went? Where would she go? You never suggested she'd run off with another man. And it seems to me, her family's displeasure over her relationship with you notwithstanding, she would have gone back to them. Or certainly over twenty years, someone would have heard *something* from her. Or *you* could have looked for her instead of building a replica of her parents' house in what was then the middle of nowhere—some supposedly magic lure designed to bring her back."

Dallas shook his head. "It was the timing of it. Your partnership with Crenshaw breaking off soon after your wife leaves. Crenshaw knew what happened to your wife, didn't he? And what he knew is just as harmful now as twenty years ago. Which is also why you *didn't* sell your property to Pete Marjani. Why you took a stand this time and ran the last. Because this time, even if you went along with Crenshaw's demands that you sell, you could have been found out. Which is why one murder had to cover up another."

Susan stood aggressively, gold pen pointing at Dallas like a saber. "This conference is over. I knew we shouldn't have—"

"Sus, hang on a second." Dallas sat up. "This isn't an inquisition. There's no cops here. No tape recorders. The curtains and doors are closed. In about half an hour, it's going to start getting hot in here because the AC's busted."

Susan remained adamant. "We're leaving."

"Ask your client if he'd like to stay. I think he might."

"Roland . . . ?"

Gunderson didn't move.

"We can walk out of here and—"

Hand a bit unsteady, Gunderson reached for Susan's wrist, held it firmly, and urged her to retake her seat beside him.

Mack Trial looked like a man at a funeral, possibly his own.

"When we were at your house," Dallas told Gunderson, "the first day, you said I wasn't the only person who thought Crenshaw was crazy. But I never said anything to you about that. I told that to

Crenshaw himself . . . at three in the morning when he'd called me to his house. The only way for you to know that was to have been outside Crenshaw's house, listening through an opened window.

"The person prowling around Crenshaw's knew his way in those woods. I chased someone from the house and they got through the trees real well in the dark. I also stumbled over a tripwire, which I'd assumed the judge set to trap whoever he thought was stalking him. But it was you that strung that rope—just like you set the bales of hay inside your garage and the trap hole Jumbi Berrell fell into. I imagine a few other booby traps were set in those woods. Figured maybe Crenshaw'd stumble or hurt himself enough so you could finish him off in a way that looked like an accident.

"But before that could happen, I came along. You heard Cren shaw and me talking, and figured there was a chance I could spoil your plan, especially once Crenshaw gave me that box. You didn't know what was in it, if you could have been implicated somehow, so you had to act fast, you had to get back the box. You already had bent masonry nails picked up from Marjani's construction projects—Marjani had security guards who saw you vandalizing his job sites. Maybe those nails were originally to go under Crenshaw's tires, so if you chased him out of the house in the middle of the night, he might get a flat somewhere isolated and you could kill him there.

"But in this case, the nails got set in *my* tires, so I'd be stopped along the road. Maybe you'd offer me a ride, maybe run me over, but when I left the box in the car, that was all you needed. The idea of killing me may have crossed your mind, but doing me *and* Crenshaw would definitely be suspicious. Crenshaw alone might pass as an accident, especially with all the kids racing cars back there, but both of us . . . ? That was too risky for you. So you settled for just taking the box.

"Now I'm not sure why you moved my car. I guess to make it look like joyriders set the whole thing up; that their plan was to use Fix-A-Flat if I left the car, but I figure the Fix-A-Flat was really intended in case you chased Crenshaw out in his car. That you could kill him wherever he broke down, then move his car if it suited you.

"Of course, it almost goes without saying, you didn't do all this alone. You needed an accomplice." Dallas looked at Trial, who looked away. "*Two* of you had to follow me from Crenshaw's. One to drive my car and the other to drive your car. That's where Jumbi Berrell comes in.

"You," Dallas accused Trial, "had gotten very chummy with Berrell. Writing letters to the parole board to get him released, visiting him in prison. Now"—Dallas waggled his finger between Trial and Gunderson—"I don't know how you two ever connected to begin with, but my guess is when Crenshaw went bonkers on the malpractice cases, you"—indicating Trial—"tried to figure out how you could possibly control Crenshaw. Probably started looking for something in Crenshaw's past you could use against him. You remember Jumbi Berrell and wonder if he still has enough vengeance in him to try again what he missed doing a few years ago: killing Crenshaw.

"Somewhere else along the line, you stumble across the judge's old law partner who doesn't have any helpful wedge for you to pry the judge off your back, but he does have his own problem with Crenshaw. And thus a plan is hatched.

"By the way," Dallas added, congratulating Trial, "using Jumbi Berrell to fake an assassination attempt against you was a real clever way to get free publicity. But there's no way a man who's just been shot at has the presence of mind immediately after the fact—even an attention junkie like you—to film the aftermath and send it to network news. And you parading around in restaurants with your makeup girl a few days later, and neither one of you too concerned your prospective killer is at large? Very Hollywood, Mack. Very Hollywood. Although it *was* a good idea to have Berrell use rubber bullets in case he 'missed' and hit you."

Gunderson, apparently learning this little sidebar only now, again shook his head in disbelief.

Dallas shifted positions on the floor. "So here you were, two lawyers with your backs to the wall, in partnership with a felon. Volatile mix. No wonder you had to kill Berrell. It must've been eating you both alive worrying he might be caught. Or talk." Unable to get comfortable, Dallas sat up. He considered Gunderson. "Although having Berrell stashed in your garage probably helped keep him on a leash. I figure the bales of hay set to drop on whoever walked in the garage was for that purpose. I doubt anyone would come all the way out to your property to steal some used tools, but maybe I'm wrong about that.

"I am sure, though, that Berrell had been to your property before. Enough times to be able to negotiate your driveway with his headlights off. When he had Miss Meyers tied up in the Four-Runner, he turned off his headlights in case someone might happen to see him heading to your house. He knew you'd be there. But got irritated as hell when you didn't answer the door. He doesn't yell for you because voices carry across open land. You've got no real close neighbors, but maybe someone's strolling the golf course at night with their dog, so better safe than sorry.

"Berrell sees the lantern down by the pier. Figures that's where you are and is going to go get you. Only it's dark and he can't make his way. He doesn't want to drive the Four-Runner across the field, because he can't use the headlights and without headlights, he might sink into the marsh if he makes a wrong turn—and how would you explain Pamela Meyers's jeep axle-deep in your field? So Berrell goes for the lantern. A lantern he has to walk across a trap hole to get. And in he goes. Gets impaled by spikes—which I also assume you stole from one of Marjani's construction projects. I saw one of Marjani's crew using them to join landscaping ties.

"So, Berrell falls in. He's dead. Crenshaw's dead. Pamela here—well, I'm not sure if Berrell was supposed to have killed her before he got to your place or not, but probably not. Cops stop him on the way for some reason, he can always claim he was taking her to the hospital. Maybe says he wrapped her in a sheet to keep her warm. Which leaves you to dump Berrell in the bay, maybe put Pam in with him, and the job's done.

"You see," Dallas told Gunderson, "that trap hole deal was a little fishy from the get-go. If I hadn't been there, you could have filled in the hole, buried Berrell, and washed your hands. You did a pretty good recovery with the deer bit, and that the lantern would keep away deer was to keep you from falling in the hole, but you've lived there almost twenty years. You'd know your way around blindfolded. And that you were down by the pier while Berrell was at your house? That you were laying in your boat, watching the stars like you used to do with your wife . . . ? That was a problem. Because you had another lantern down there with you. A lantern that was *up on a piling of your pier*. If you were in the boat, you'd've been well below the lantern and the light it gave off would interrupt your view of the stars. You weren't gazing at constellations. You were waiting for Jumbi Berrell to fall in that trap hole and die."

After a few moments, Roland Gunderson patted Susan's knee like a father and stood. His hands went deep into the pockets of trousers permanently stained by the oils of fish he'd caught and filleted years ago. When Susan stood beside him, thinking he was preparing to leave, he shook his head and she retook her seat.

Mack Trial said, "Don't—" but cut himself short. Silence you could talk your way out of later; words were like bullets—once fired, you couldn't get them back.

Gunderson managed to draw himself together. He spoke like a judge who, after careful deliberation, was about to hand down a verdict he knew would be unpopular. "Raymond wasn't supposed to die. The . . ." He searched carefully for the correct word. " . . . *concept* was that the very presence of Jumbi Berrell would scare Raymond into backing off. That if we *showed* Berrell . . . like some countries display nuclear weapons—a show of force—actual violence wouldn't be necessary.

"Mack made contact with Berrell in prison to see if he'd be interested. He was. Berrell knew Crenshaw had been writing letters to someone on the parole board and as long as those letters kept coming, Berrell wasn't getting out. Funny"—Gunderson smiled ironically—"but one of Raymond's last friends was somewhere he could use him . . . on that parole board. . . .

"Anyway . . . Mack made arrangements for Berrell to be placed on work release, so he could get out of prison without breaking out. Berrell was more than willing to come down here, figuring hiding for the rest of his life would be better than spending eleven more years in jail."

Gunderson paused gravely, then continued with quiet emphasis. "*But it wasn't supposed to happen the way it did.*" He took a breath. "Unfortunately . . . the night we sabotaged your car, I was driving it back to Raymond's when a deer bolted in front of me. It happened very quickly. I braked, but still hit it. A sizable buck—it dropped to the road. I got out to see if it was dead, but it was merely dazed. It got to its feet and ran off. That slight delay, however, allowed Berrell to get back to Raymond's street ahead of me.

"By the time I got there Raymond was dead. Berrell said he'd come running out of the trees right into the road. Like he was being chased. Apparently we'd been doing a good job of scaring him. His imagination was getting the worst of him. Berrell said Raymond froze in the lights."

Gunderson shook his head. "Berrell *didn't say* that he hit Raymond with the car on purpose . . . but I think he did. He had that look afterwards, like he'd just eaten a satisfying meal. He wasn't shook up at all. But after what he'd been through in prison, that's not surprising. They always come out better criminals than they go in.

"It seemed," Gunderson continued, "that would be that. Raymond was dead. We had the box he'd given you. Berrell was supposed to be on his way to Florida. I had a spare car in the garage all ready to go. Only she"—nodding to Pamela Meyers—"started making noise. Mack assured me he could handle her, but she was very persistent. It became clear we had to do something, especially when she threatened to get a new lawyer to take over for Raymond.

"Berrell had been hanging around to make sure the entire matter was cleared up. No one seemed to be looking for him that hard. The police didn't have anything on Crenshaw's death. They never even spoke to me about it, so when Berrell found out about her"—again indicating Pamela Meyers—"he said we couldn't take any chances. He said, she had to go."

Pam stiffened from this revelation.

"We talked," Gunderson admitted. "Mack and I. Actually, this all got started—this business with Raymond—by my going to him. I'd heard through old acquaintances in Baltimore about Raymond going back into practice. That he had cases against Mack he was trying to milk. Mack and I met one day. I don't know what I expected to come of it . . . but something did." Gunderson looked apologetically at Susan, who now saw him with betrayed eyes. Whatever he'd told her last night to get her to represent him, it hadn't been this.

"Anyway," Gunderson said, "when Mack and I spoke after his run-in with Pamela in a restaurant, and talked about how convinced Berrell was that she had to be killed, Mack and I decided Berrell was the real problem. We told him to do what he had to do, but to bring her to my house and we'd take her out in the boat and dump her.

"What Berrell didn't know was that I was already out at the boat. That he'd have to walk out there to get me. I'd told him ahead of time to keep his headlights off so no one would see him, and he accepted that. Still, I wasn't sure he'd use the lantern, but risked that if he saw me with one down by the pier, he'd get the hint. Either way . . . I had my shotgun at the boat." Gunderson's mouth formed a pained smile. "I must admit, I'm glad he fell in the hole."

Susan fought through disbelief and, after a moment, asked an obvious question, one Dallas had purposely skipped. "When Crenshaw tried to blackmail you into selling your farm, if what he had on you was so damaging, why didn't you sell?"

Dallas said, "Because you don't dry flowers in the shade."

Susan turned to him quizzically.

"There were always fresh-cut flowers *under* the house. I thought they were drying there, but you don't dry flowers in the shade. What you do with flowers . . . you put them over a grave."

43

"LIMESTONE! DUCK FARTS! I don't want to hear it!" Pete Marjani's face was so tomato red it looked as though seeds might pop out his ears. "You keep digging, goddammit! Don't tell me about limestone!"

Marjani slammed down his office phone, still wearing the golf shirt and yellow slacks he'd hacked through eleven holes in this morning. "I'm surrounded by gloom-sayers. Goddamned do-noth-ings!" Shouting this to no one in particular because all his employ-ees were lying low. "No wonder nothing ever gets done around here! Too many goddamned people telling me it *can't* be done. Duck *farts!*" His fist pounded his desk, jumping a globe lamp a good two inches above a cowhide writing blotter.

Dallas's arrival didn't brighten the mood of the executive suite.

"Whaddayou want I'm not gonna give you!"

"I got a deal for you, Pete."

"Yeah, I bet! You and every other duck fart hustler's got his webbed feet stuck in a goin'-nowhere marsh!"

"I think you're gonna like this."

Marjani scowled doubtfully.

Dallas nodded to the only window wall that was covered by lowered blinds. "Why don't you open those, Pete. . . . Go ahead."

Marjani crossed his arms. "Why?"

"Because that's the deal."

A twinkle of disbelief danced like fairy dust over the big man's eyes. He turned as though revolving on a slow-moving pedestal and pulled up the blinds as though unveiling a new sports car at the auto show.

There it was: Roland Gunderson's land. Glorious trees, sweet fields, and gorgeous wetlands lingering in visual poetry with Hur-ricane Bay. But best of all, no limestone.

Marjani actually gasped at the vista that had been so long denied him.

"The deal," Dallas advised, "is nonnegotiable and no questions can be asked. *No questions.* Violate any term or condition and it's off."

Marjani braced himself. The fantasy ended that quickly; he was ready for a financial screwing.

Dallas laid out the terms: "You build a decent house on the land where you've got that poor guy digging holes. Then swap it for Gunderson's farm. You throw in another hundred grand, in trust, that pays Gunderson interest until his death, remainder to a charity called MINOA. Plus, another four hundred grand directly to MINOA."

"What's MINOA?—not that I'm asking." Marjani didn't want to ruin the deal; Dallas did say no questions. "I just want to know if it's a legitimate write-off. A real charity."

"It will be in a few months, which is when you'll write the check. It's a good cause. Mothers In Need Of Assistance. The idea is to help mothers whose divorced or estranged husbands are welshing on their child support."

"Yeah, fine." Such social problems were beyond Marjani's comprehension. "Can I get some good publicity out of this? Like a Pete Marjani bequest or something?"

"Publicize it however you want, just make sure the check's good."

"It'll be good. . . ." Marjani's expression turned conspiratorial. "Mothers in need . . . maybe this'll shut up the members' wives always complaining I don't give a shit about women. Let 'em take a shot at me now." He puffed out his chest. "Hah. Mr. Charity." He scribbled a note on the cowhide memo pad that matched his desk blotter. "Get me a hat with 'Mr. Charity' printed on it. Have a Mr. Duck Farts Charity golf tournament, raise some more money for this Minnie Mouse thing."

"MINOA."

"Fine." Marjani was beaming. Pen at ready, he said, "What else?"

"Gunderson's existing house?"

"Yeah?"

"You can't knock it down."

"What! That eyesore lean-to!"

"You can't move it, or disturb the land around or under it. Ever. That's going in the deed. You violate that covenant, the land goes to MINOA."

"How the hell'm I supposed to have a first-class golf course with a run-down shanty shack smack dab in the middle of it!"

"If you don't want the deal—"

Marjani waved his left hand, the one less tan than the other from wearing a golf glove. "I didn't say that. I'm just . . . I'm not asking a question, either . . . I'm just . . . I'm just thinking out loud. That's all."

Dallas nodded.

Marjani hesitated. "Is it a question if I ask if it's all right for me to fix the place up a little? You know, put some new wood siding on it, paint it, fix the porch . . . something like that?" Marjani paused hopefully. "Maybe use it as a snack bar on the course."

"As long as you don't so much as scratch the land under the house or for a ten-foot perimeter around it."

Marjani was burning a hole in his thinking cap. "How about you let me sink some pilings outside that perimeter you just described—*way* outside." Marjani pushed air with his hand as though shoving it across the horizon. "And I put a complete wooden walkway—like a floor—all over that couple hundred square feet under and around the house. *All over it.*" His hand smoothed an invisible flat plane over his desk as though icing a massive cake. "It'll be like a big party deck. And that way, you know for sure the land underneath doesn't get touched."

"I've got to be there when you dig."

"You got it." Marjani nodded. "What else?"

"That's it. Oh, and you also get a release from Judge Crenshaw's estate about his five percent ownership in Hurricane Bay."

Marjani was clearly, pleasantly stunned. He spread his hands. "Hell, that's duck fart simple. You got a deal. Tell you what." He picked up his phone, punched an intercom button. "I'll even throw in a little something for you. How about a free lifetime membership to Hurricane Bay. Even give you the VIP treatment, free hundred bucks a month to use around here as you like."

"That's a nice offer, but I can't do it, Pete. That would make it look like I'm working for you. And I'm not."

"Hell, it's not payment for anything. It's a gift." Marjani hit the intercom button again, boomed, "Jack, where the hell are you?"

Dallas thought, well, if it's a gift . . . "Maybe a Christmas present." What the hell.

"You got it." Marjani hit the intercom again, and when there was no reply, he stormed to the head of the stairs. "Jack, god-dammit! Where are you!" He started down the steps. "Get me some goddamned lawyers on the phone. We gotta draw up papers. We're building a duck fartin' new golf course!"

"What is this place?" Mack Trial wasn't too hot on this part of the deal Dallas had hammered out in the war room. But he'd looked for every conceivable route of escape and realized maybe he was better off going along with Dallas's plan. It would be a little painful, but, as Dallas pointed out, Trial deserved more than a little pain for the crap he'd been pulling.

Dallas entered Big Sales Bar, a run-down wood building not too far from the old icehouse. The kind of tavern that hadn't yet been—nor would it ever be—dressed up with hanging ferns, brass rails, and party favors. People went to Big Sales to get drunk and made no attempt to camouflage their alcoholism behind sips of expensive cognac or fancy wine.

The clientele was equal male to female; blue-collar vacationers who stayed in lesser-priced motels at the lower end of town and fished the Route 50 bridge. Their conversation was ribald, politics ultraconservative, music oldies rock and roll. A beer and a shot cost a buck. A price that sometimes lured in eager-to-be-drunk preppy college kids, who usually got beat up.

Somehow, Harvey Crenshaw was surviving, although just barely. He was slumped over a table in a corner booth. A slow-turning ceiling fan caused a desperate fog of cigarette smoke to collect in Harvey's corner, making it look as though it was going to rain tar and nicotine any minute now.

"Oh, God," Mack Trial moaned, "the smell."

It was rugged. Spilled beer, whiskey breath, and doorless bathrooms that relied on melting ice for flushing.

Dallas exchanged hellos with a few regulars glued to barstools. When Desales Jones, gravel-voiced bouffant real-estate-sales leader, bought this place five years ago, half the bar's patrons had been listed on the bulk sales transfer as fixtures.

Trial was aghast Dallas knew not only this place but the people in it. Trial was very ethnocentric when it came to socializing. He abandoned prejudice only in business, where he'd squeeze a fee regardless of race, creed, or color.

At Harvey's booth, Dallas said, "This's him."

"God . . ." Trial moaned. "I'd lift his head up, but I'm not sure what it's laying in."

"But look, he's got on a good dress shirt. Just waiting to go to work."

"Swell."

Dallas jostled Harvey's arm. "Hey. Harvey! Come on, Harvey, wake up." Dallas propped Judge Crenshaw's son into the corner. Of the wet spots on the table and Harvey's chin, he said, "See, it's only drool."

Trial looked nauseated.

"Harvey. *Harvey!*"

"Disgusting," Trial spat.

"And exactly what you looked like about six hours ago." Dallas slapped Harvey's face. "Come on, boy."

"How'm I going to explain this to my malpractice carrier? I got enough trouble with them as it is."

"You tell them you've hired a fine legal mind—that as soon as you pay for him to go through an alcohol rehabilitation program, he's going to be a real winner for you."

"Sure . . ."

"Harvey, pal, buddy, compadre . . ." Dallas shook him harder. "Come on . . . any day now . . . here we go."

Harvey, as swift as ice melting in a refrigerator, rolled into consciousness. His eyes wandered off in different directions. "Dad . . . ?"

"Sorry, kid. Dad's dead. And he died broke."

"*Daaaad!* I came over to see you, Dad. . . ." Looking at Mack Trial, sounding like a little boy.

"Aw," Dallas said, "you remind him of his father."

"Great."

"Dad . . ." Harvey grabbed for Trial's sleeve. "I was right on time just like you said . . . but you weren't there . . . nobody was home. I found your gun out by the street . . . I picked it up for you. . . ." Harvey waited for a compliment that never came. "Dad . . . *Daaaad!* Please don't be dead."

"More bad news." Dallas broke it to him gently. "You're going to have to get a job."

"Noo-noo-nooooooo!" Harvey howled like an old hound.

Dallas said to Trial, "He's all yours."

"You're not leaving. You can't be leaving. Don't leave me here with him!" Trial became frantic as Dallas headed for the exit. "What'm I supposed to do now? How'm I supposed to get him, out of—*at least help me carry him, for God's sake!*"

"Am I going to like this deal?" Three chins resting on his chest, Rupert Dawson moved his eyes toward the top of deep sockets like a fishing bobber coming to the surface.

"Probably not." Dallas sat forward in the chair he'd occupied many times in the past, always mindful to keep the chief's desk between them in case things got hairy.

"Is Bannister going to like the deal?"

Dallas shrugged.

"Better let him in, then. We'll find out." Dawson motioned for Dallas to open the door.

Brent Bannister puffed in like a sack of hot air, not caring for being left out in the hall. He stood against Dawson's desk, fleshy fingertips resting on dull wood. His other hand held something against the cocked hip of too-tight khaki pants. "Did you," he demanded of Dallas, "put this on my car?" A Maryland vanity tag: IMNASS.

"Sit down, Brent," Dawson instructed.

Bannister slapped the fake license plate on the desk. "Someone assaulted my vehicle."

"Wasn't me," Dallas said. "Must've been one of your many other admirers."

"Sit down, Brent."

Bannister finally did so. The cuffs of his super-yuppie trousers rose halfway to his knee, exposing plain brown socks and white leg.

"Okay . . ." Dawson gestured with both hands as though inviting Dallas closer for a fistfight. "Let's hear it."

"All right. Here's the deal: Roland Gunderson is prepared to enter a guilty plea to manslaughter in the death of Jumbi Berrell . . ."

Dawson's eyes formed questioning slits.

". . . under the following binding—get that Brent, *binding*—plea agreement: five-year suspended sentence, three years unsupervised probation, five-hundred-dollar fine, and he performs two thousand hours of community service. . . . That's it."

"Susan approve this?" Dawson asked. "Last I heard, *she* was representing Gunderson."

"Susan approves. But we'll have it all in writing by the time it comes to trial."

Bannister was shaking his head. "I'm waiting," he whined, "to hear about what plea *you're* going to enter for running down Judge Crenshaw."

"Give it up, Brent. You've got no witnesses. You're not going to find any witnesses. And, although this has never mattered to you in any other criminal case you've handled, you've charged the wrong guy."

"Self-serving statement."

Dawson rocked his squeaky chair and ran a hand across his short-bristled hair. "You can live with this, can't you, Brent." Not really posing that as a question. "You wouldn't have any case at all if Dallas hadn't been at Gunderson's. And while Berrell's death was clearly an accident, you've still got wanton disregard for human life, which gives you manslaughter."

"Susan has some case cites if you forget where the bar library is," Dallas offered.

"I know the goddamned law."

"Good," Dawson declared, "then I think we got a wrap, Brent. Give Dallas a grand jury date, get your indictment."

"Afternoon session, if you please. You know me and mornings."

Bannister wanted to confront Dawson, but didn't dare. His question came out mouse meek. "I take it you're closing your investigation into Judge Crenshaw's death."

"It'll go inactive," Dawson advised, playing diplomat. "But, some witness crawls up out of the woods . . ."

Bannister mutterd something unintelligible and turned for the door. "I have work at the office."

Dallas said, "See ya."

Dawson nodded. "Don't forget your vanity tag."

"It's not my tag!" Bannister and his too-short pants snapped out of the room.

When he was gone, Dawson motioned for Dallas to shut the door again. Said, "Seems to me you're leaving out a lot of details."

"I have to, Rup. I tell you the whole deal, you'd have to act on it."

Dawson gave a quick snort that expanded his chest and bumped his resting chins. "Then I'll ask you this: Can I *live* with what you've got arranged?"

"It's close."

Dawson considered the sunny day outside through his smeary window. After a few moments, he turned back to Dallas. "Hope I don't see you the rest of the summer, then."

"Aw, come on, Rup, it's only July. . . . Besides, I can't go quite yet—I need a little favor."

Dallas knocked on the door to Gina and South's room. Gina opened it and stared in disbelief. Cutback stood beside Dallas. She wrapped her arms around him hard, whispered, "Thank God you're back . . . you're all right . . . thank God."

Dallas turned to leave only to have the back of his shirt grabbed. Gina reached out for him, her brown eyes not looking quite so hard. "Thank you."

"Anytime."

44

"I T'S A NEW GAME. *Whole* new game."

Ten o'clock that night, following a six-hour nap, Dallas was on the beach at the volleyball net. Six on six.

"Team Real Men Belch" included Dallas, shirtless Chad wearing a string of peace beads resurrected from a time-warp hippie, C.J. with his hat on backwards, South practicing his vertical leap, Cutback looking damned glad not to be on his way home to an insane father, and Jas making a rare out-of-room appearance.

"Team Betty" was the three Ls and an M; a smiling and occasionally laughing Gina; and Wendy, who, like Jas, was making a rare out-of-room appearance.

"New game," Chad said. "New rules."

"New rules," C.J. cheered. "New rules, watch out. New rules."

"What," Dallas asked, "are the rules?"

"There are no rules," Chad advised. "That's why it's called suicide volleyball. You can hit the net. You can carry the ball. You can hit the ball as many times as you want so long as it never touches the ground. You can reach under the net and trip, kick, grab, or fondle an opponent."

C.J. pumped his arm. "Fondle opponents. Yesss!"

"Works both ways!" Team Betty laughed, making plans of their own.

"Everything," Chad said, "and anything goes."

Dallas figured that only made sense. This was the beach. Rules were in a permanent state of suspension here. If beach folks weren't so lazy, they'd probably secede from the Union.

It was where a man like Roland Gunderson came twenty years ago, a nervous drive across the Eastern Shore with his wife's body in the trunk of his car. His law partner Raymond Crenshaw seated beside him.

Gunderson had argued with his wife about an affair he was having. Physically struggled with her when she tried to leave the house. The level of violence accelerated quickly, uncontrollably. Both of them were scratched and bruised before she fell down a length of stairs, so Gunderson knew there was no way he could avoid being implicated in her death when her neck was snapped by the fall.

Gunderson had needed someone to talk to, someone to help him, and turned to the man he trusted most. Raymond Crenshaw. It was Crenshaw's idea to bury Penny's body. Take her to land Gunderson had just bought outside Ocean City. Undeveloped wilderness. No one would see them. No one would ever know.

They buried Gunderson's wife in a homemade pine box in a shallow grave. Only three feet down before they hit water. Crenshaw, interrupting the otherwise solemn drive back to Baltimore, said, "Well, that's that."

But it wasn't. Gunderson was devastated by guilt. A week later, he considered going to the police, but was too afraid. He'd seen the inside of jails and knew he couldn't survive it for a single day. He contemplated suicide, but was even more frightened of death than jail. Extreme remorse sapped his concentration. His law career plummeted.

Crenshaw worked frantically to cover his partner's increasingly frequent errors. Finally, Crenshaw was exhausted. He told Gunderson their partnership was over. And Crenshaw was taking it all.

When Gunderson tried to salvage reasonable equity out of the practice he'd worked so hard to build, Crenshaw threatened to expose him to the police. Gunderson's story about his wife leaving him—while suspicious to friends—had never caused anyone to think Gunderson might have killed her. But they'd believe the body Crenshaw would lead them to.

At first Gunderson thought it was a bluff, that Crenshaw wouldn't reveal a crime in which he'd been an accessory after the fact. But back then, Crenshaw had friends all over the state's attorney's office; they'd look out for him and put Gunderson on death row.

So Gunderson surrendered his interest in the partnership. Moved to the land where he'd buried his wife and dedicated his guilt to her memory to ease his pain. Building a house like she'd been raised in. Growing her favorite flowers and placing them over her grave. Guarding her final resting place—and the evidence of his crime—when offered substantial dollars for the land.

There was no way he could sell. Bones would be dug up. Questions would be asked.

So when Raymond Crenshaw recently appeared on Gunderson's crooked front porch and told his ex-partner he *had* to sell, what could Gunderson do but cover up an old crime with a new one? Try to scare Crenshaw away with Jumbi Berrell, only a misdemeanor turned into a felony, and then another felony, and then another.

And now, it was over. Or at least resolved. Gunderson's two thousand hours of community service would be performed for Mothers In Need Of Assistance, the charity Dallas had thought of and named (he thought MINOA sounded exotic, almost Hawaiian). Susan would put the legal paperwork in motion and oversee expenditures; Pamela Meyers would administer the fund (under the close scrutiny of trustworthy accountants, her claims of redemption notwithstanding).

The charity would likely allow Pamela Meyers to go back through old state's attorney's files in an attempt to repay the monies she'd stolen, so that those who should have been paid then would be paid now, with interest.

Pete Marjani's money would help MINOA a lot.

So would Mack Trial's letter of intent for his law firms to donate $150,000 and perform two thousand hours of free legal service to enforce child support payments from deadbeat spouses. Mack Trial might even assign his newest "associate-for-life," Harvey Crenshaw, to help that cause.

It wasn't the way Rupert Dawson would have settled the entire episode, certainly not how Brent Bannister would have done it. Because the legal system was being circumvented. The "great and noble cause of justice" wouldn't turn its slovenly, outdated wheels through hundreds of thousands of hours and millions of taxpayer dollars to investigate Pamela Meyers and Mack Trial's embezzlement or to identify the body under Roland Gunderson's house.

Mack Trial would keep practicing law and it was a damned shame about that; Dallas's only consolation was that anyone stupid enough to pick a lawyer from a TV commercial deserved to get screwed. And maybe Roland Gunderson was buying his way out of a horrendous crime—but at what price to him compared to what benefit to the rest of society?

Yeah, Dallas could live with the deal. Even if it wasn't going by the rules. After all, this was the beach. There were no rules at the beach . . .

. . . especially not in suicide volleyball, where Laura served and before C.J. could jump to attempt a block, Lisa yanked down his shorts.

"Cute, Lisa. Real cute." C.J. hiked back up his trunks. "You're asking for it now."

Beside Chad in the back row, Dallas said, "I think I'm gonna like this game."